**Typewriter Pub**, an imprint of Blvnp Incorporated
A Nevada Corporation
1887 Whitney Mesa DR #2002
Henderson, NV 89014
www.typewriterpub.com/info@typewriterpub.com

ISBN: 978-1-68030-988-1

## DISCLAIMER
This book is a work of fiction. The characters, incidents, and dialogue are drawn from the author's imagination and are not to be construed as real. While references might be made to actual historical events or existing locations, the names, characters, places, and incidents are either products of the author's imagination or are used fictitiously, and any resemblance to actual persons living or dead, business establishments, events or locales is entirely coincidental.

# LIFE SUCKS IF YOU'RE MARRIED TO A BILLIONAIRE

KRYSTEL GRACE

*To all the LGBTQIA+ people everywhere—you're my inspiration.*
*Shine as bright as you want!*

**Trigger Warning:**
The following story contains profanities and depictions of physical violence.
Reader discretion is advised.

# CHAPTER ONE
## Life Sucks

I woke up with a massive headache.

*Damn, it hurts.* My body felt like lead, and my ears were ringing. *Shit, did I drink last night? How come I don't remember a thing?*

Then, I heard the sound of sheets ruffling. I slowly turned my head to see what or who caused the noise when suddenly . . .

*Oomph!* I was pushed deeper into the bed and felt a body on top of mine. *Ugh, not again.*

"Jace Langlois! Get the fuck off me, you idiot!" I shouted at my husband.

Much to my distaste, Jace simply ignored me and snuggled even closer.

*God, I hate this man.*

"Get! Off!" I said.

*I don't know why I still refer to him as my husband. I hate him. I hate being married to him. I hate having to admit being married, let alone married to him.*

We have been married for almost a year now, but I still find it difficult to like him. I wish I weren't married, but I am, all because of an added stipulation in my deceased parents' will that I only learned when I turned twenty-one.

\*      \*      \*

*On my twenty-first birthday*

    *The lawyer, a Mr. Lowes, said, "Mr. Forest, here is a letter your parents wanted you to read on your twenty-first birthday. After you've read it, I will proceed with handling their last will and testament."*

    *I stared at him. He was not the lawyer who administered my parents' will last time. I took the document and began reading. Almost immediately, I felt boredom creeping in. The first few paragraphs were filled with the usual "I love yous," "I'm sorrys," and "Wish you a happy life," alongside legal jargon that flew over my head. Despite this, I couldn't bring myself to cry. I had long since come to terms with their deaths. I persisted in reading until I reached a part that completely caught me off guard.*

        *"Lastly, Kei, our dear son, we led you to believe that the inheritance you received upon our death was the entirety of it. We love you immensely, but we simply couldn't afford to give you all of it right away. We apologize, but for reasons we cannot disclose, it was essential to withhold the remaining portion until today, your twenty-first birthday.*

        *However, this cannot be fulfilled unless you adhere to our simple condition. Now, don't be upset about this, our dear son. It's all for your own good."*

    *I scoffed. I may be young, but I knew that when people preface their speeches with "Don't be upset" or "Don't get me wrong," it usually causes upset or worry.*

        *You must marry the only son of our longtime friends and business partners—the Langlois. You've probably heard us talk about them, but you were never interested in our business ventures. You are too young to be involved in business, and your interests lie elsewhere.*

*With the most important condition being met—both of you being single and emotionally unattached—we hope you will honor our final wish.*

*That being said, he is the right man for you to spend the rest of your life with. Do not worry; this man will find you, and when he does, please let him take your hand in marriage.*

*We understand your preferences and are aware of his, although, as of this writing, he remains, so to speak, "in the closet." Your father and I hope that you won't need to hide who you are. We hope you are happy with yourself.*

*We hope you are happy. We love you.*

*Love,*

*Mom & Dad.*

I was dumbfounded as their words sank in. This left me confused. I thought I had already received my inheritance, but it was held in trust until I turned twenty-five. Consequently, I only received a monthly allowance and a separate budget for my household expenses, including tuition payments covered by the trust fund.

Speaking of the trust fund, aren't the Langlois my trustees? I thought to myself.

While I received updates and reports about my trust fund, as well as birthday cards and gifts every year, I had only met them a couple of times—during the funeral and the guardianship hearing. But I really had not idea who the fuck they were, and when I turned eighteen, that guardianship ended. Ans most importantly, I had no idea what the fuck was going on.

This was entirely new and fantastical, so I didn't believe it. So much didn't add up. All lingering doubts vanished when a man named Jace Langlois came in the middle of my art history survey class at university and proposed to me on the spot.

*I was extremely embarrassed when it happened, with all the people in the vast room witnessing that unforgettable moment. I ran away that day, afraid, disgusted, and resentful.*

*Nevertheless, after a few weeks of burying my head in the sand and a couple of "conversations" with Jace Langlois, I accepted his hand in marriage, just as my parents expected.*

*After all, I had no choice; my inheritance was on the line.*

\* \* \*

Ever since I began fulfilling the stipulations of that will, my life had gradually unraveled in real time. What made it worse was that my parents weren't exactly adept at picking other people's life partners. So, while I greatly appreciated what they left me, there was still the issue I detested from the very depths of my soul . . .

"Hey!" Jace snapped. "You've gone back to sleep! Make me breakfast. Pronto," he ordered.

I gritted my teeth, restraining myself from cursing him out, finding solace in thoughts of my inheritance, which I would receive in full in due course.

This man was incredibly bossy, insisting that I wait on him despite having household staff to cook and clean for him. He seemed to believe he had me wrapped around his fucking finger because he gave up his damn bachelordom for me—or perhaps because he thought he was several times wealthier than me.

Hell, he could even surpass Bill Gates if he weren't such a lazy ass. The Langlois family is incredibly wealthy, with numerous huge companies spanning across Europe and America. They are currently planning further expansion into Asia, including China and Japan.

Despite all that, he is uncouth. How could I even begin to like this guy when he had the attitude of a bull in a china shop?

A very, very evil bull.

"So get the fuck off me, asshole," I grumbled.

6

He finally pulled away, though not before he messed up my bed hair. *Ugh, I hate it when he did that.* It had been a habit of his ever since we got married, ever since I was forced to share his bed or forfeit.

After showering and dressing, I headed straight to the kitchen—a massive, and I mean massive, modern one where the chef wasn't allowed to set foot when I was home, and I was ordered to cook by my overlord, which seemed to be always the case now.

I supposed I should feel lucky to have a wealthy husband. I continued live as I always have—in the lap of comfort and now in luxury. Ironically, he treated me like I was some lowlife servant at the very bottom of the food chain. His attitude was what angered me almost every second of the day.

As usual, I cooked his favorite: an omelet with caviar. How he could eat that disgusting food, I could never tell. He wouldn't eat anything without caviar, so as his husband, I was obligated to cook several dishes that included it for him.

I still had a headache, but it was slowly fading away. Thank goodness.

"Where's my coffee?" Jace asked.

*Huh, so the devil finally came to eat.*

I flipped the omelet and adjusted the heat to a minimum, not bothering to acknowledge his demand. I knew my routine by now.

"You know, you look exactly like a caring housewife right now."

I scowled. "Shut the fuck up."

"That damn mouth of yours again. It doesn't suit you."

"You're one to talk," I said.

I turned on the coffee machine, allowed it to warm up, and let it grind the coffee beans. Everything had been prepared by the staff—the machine cleaned, fresh filtered water in the tank, the proper amount of fresh beans in the grinder, portafilter in place, and his beloved coffee mug at the ready inside the cup warmer. All I had to do was press the on button, wait for the coffee to grind, tamp the grounds to the proper firmness, attach the portafilter to the group head, and wait for it to extract.

If I did not love coffee, I would have found this seeming ritual tedious, especially when I had gotten used to brewing my coffee with a drip coffee maker and even resorted to drinking instant coffee when I was extremely busy.

I took the omelet from the pan and placed it carefully onto a plate. I was just about to put caviar on the side when he grabbed my hand, startling me.

"W-what now?" I asked.

He stared at me intensely, then looked away as he slowly let go of my hand. *What's with him?*

Suddenly, the atmosphere of the room turned quiet. It was so eerily silent that you could practically hear a needle drop. I turned away from him to make our coffees—double espresso for him and latté for me.

Jace usually didn't stay quiet like this. Normally, he would go on and on about his work and business and whatnot, but today seemed to be different for him. My instincts picked up on this at once, and I decided to be careful around him today, lest I struck a nerve. Maybe he was just in a bad mood or something.

"You're going out with me tonight, so you better be ready at six. Exactly six," he announced, maintaining his distance as he sat at his usual place at the dining table.

*The fuck?*

"What? But I have art class tonight!" I exclaimed.

Jace glared at me, and I returned his glare. *Who does he think he is, ordering me around and controlling my life?* Even though he was my husband, it didn't give him the right to my actions or disregard my feelings. His airs of superiority only fueled my growing resentment.

"Cancel it," he said casually, dismissing my art class as if it held no importance.

I stood my ground. "No, you are not the boss of me, Jace Langlois."

Slowly, he walked over to me. I flinched as his tall frame loomed over mine.

"Oh yes, I can be, Kei Langlois," he slowly said, his tone menacing and dangerous.

I put on a neutral expression to convey that I wasn't intimidated by him. I knew his personality well. While people assumed he was the noblest and greatest guy around, the reality was quite the opposite. Jace Langlois was simply the worst kind of guy in the whole planet. He always got what he wanted, by whatever means necessary. That was just who he was.

"Now, are we clear?"

I had no choice but to nod.

He smiled triumphantly and settled back into his seat as if nothing had happened.

I sighed, served him his coffee, finished making my own, and then went to eat my breakfast.

This had been my life since I married him, and I hated it. I didn't blame my parents though. I was just going to face this without any qualms . . .

I sighed. *Hate and without any qualms are contradictory.*

# CHAPTER TWO
## Do You Believe Me Now?

My art history class just ended, and I was on my way to the entrance of the School of Arts and Architecture building to wait for Jace to come pick me up. I already told my digital media professor that I couldn't make it tonight, and he said that it was okay. I had hoped that he would say no, giving me an excuse to avoid Jace's plans for the evening, but life's a bitch, so this happened.

"Kei!" a female voice shouted from behind.

I turned around to see my only three friends at the university. I greeted them all with a wave and a smile.

"Hey, what's up?" I said.

"Kei, will you go shopping with me? Please? These two jerks don't want to go with me," Summer said.

She was the only girl in our little circle of friends, and the two "jerks" she referred to were actually her brothers, Autumn and Winter.

I laughed inwardly and continue walking. I still couldn't get over the fact that they have names based on seasons. Hurray for that! Plus, they're triplets. Amazing!

"Shut your mouth, Summer," Autumn said as they walked with me. If you weren't such a shopaholic, we would've come with you."

Autumn was the oldest triplet. He might act a bit too wild and free sometimes, but he was a good listener.

"Yeah, what he said," Winter mumbled.

Winter was what most people would peg as a person with a huge big brother complex. It was obvious that he loved Autumn and was never shy with showing his affection. Because of this, most people would immediately interpret their relationship as "too close for comfort," but that certainly wasn't the case at all. It was simply "excessive brotherly love," or whatever Summer liked to call it.

Among the three of them, Summer was the most independent triplet. While she loved her brothers, she wasn't as close to them because she was the only girl.

"I hate to say this, but I can't go with you," I told Summer.

She pouted. "Eh, why not?"

*Should I tell them? I guess I better get it over with.*

"Um, yeah. Jace is taking me out tonight."

The three of them went silent. I fidgeted, waiting for them to go all crazy on me.

*Three . . . two . . . one . . .*

"Holy shit!"

*As expected.*

Ever since I told them I was going to marry Jace Langlois, the three of them had been acting insane. Their main refrain was that I wasn't the type to do something like that out of the blue. Moreover, they assumed I wasn't the type to commit. After all, I hadn't been in a relationship with anyone until Jace came into my life.

Nevertheless, even after I had already told them that I was marrying *the* Jace Langlois, they still didn't believe me, despite knowing exactly who my husband was. I mean, who wouldn't? The man was like the second richest man after Bill Gates—*that's how wealthy he is.*

"I knew about the gossip floating around about a man making a spectacle of proposing during art class, but there's never really any evidence of that. There are a few videos, blurry or out of angle, or— But . . . I don't know, Kei," Summer said.

11

"I still refuse to believe that you're married to Mr. Langlois, at least, not until I see the two of you together," Autumn said.

Winter nodded, clearly agreeing with his older brother.

"Why should I prove anything to you? It's not like it's a big deal," I muttered.

I glanced at my watch and then at the driveway. He should be here any minute.

Summer scowled. "Not a big deal? It is a huge deal, Kei! We're talking about the richest man on the entire planet!"

I rolled my eyes. Now she was just exaggerating. Technically, he's the second richest, but all technicalities aside . . .

"Guys, stop it. If you don't want to believe me, then don't. I don't really care anyway. It's not like it's something to celebrate or get excited about—or like I haven't told you about this for over a—"

I stopped abruptly as Jace's car suddenly pulled up in front of us, followed closely by his bodyguards' black Jeep. My jaw dropped.

*Honestly, could this guy make a more dramatic entrance?*

The door swung open, and Jace casually stepped out his sleek silver Porsche, removing his sunglasses. His eyes locked on mine, seemingly oblivious to any inconvenience he might be causing other cars and completely ignoring my friends.

I glanced at them out of the corner of my eye and noticed their expressions. They were speechless, clearly in awe of him. If I hadn't been so annoyed with my husband's entrance, I would have snapped a photo of their surprised faces.

If only I dared to whip out my mobile phone . . .

"Y-you're . . . J-Jace . . . Mr. Jace Langlois?" Summer said.

Jace shifted his focus on her and flashed a devastatingly charming smile. He certainly knew how to put on a public persona. Too bad he was the most two-faced man I had ever met in my entire life.

"Call me Jace, *mademoiselle*.[1] And may I know your name?"

12

Summer blushed. "S-S-Summer."

*Well, no need for formal introductions, then.* Meanwhile, Winter and Autumn finally recovered from their temporary coma.

They glared at my husband, and Autumn asked sternly, "Is it true that Kei married you?"

He tried to act tough, not that it was of any use; after all, nothing fazes Jace Langlois. Jace chuckled and glanced around. People were starting to notice, and I just hoped no one recognized him.

"If being legally declared as husbands to each other is married, then yes. Yes, we are married."

Winter's eyes widened in disbelief. Summer was still blushing, and unable to tear her gaze away from Jace, who seemed to have already forgotten her existence. Autumn, perhaps still in shock, accidentally choked on his own spit and was pounding on the chest, while his younger brother looked at him in concern.

I sighed. *This clearly isn't going well. It's all Jace's fault. Why did he have to come and pick me up?*

"Kei, we'll be late. Let's go. *Au revoir, mademoiselle*[2]," Jace said, dismissing the boys and preparing to leave as he got into his car.

"Y-yeah . . . uhm, I'll see you tomorrow, guys," I said awkwardly.

Just as I was about to follow him to the vehicle, Summer grabbed my arm. *Oh no. Here we go again.*

"Kei."

"Yes?" I asked, already knowing that this was not going to be good.

"Can I have his number?"

"W-what?" I asked as I actually choked on my spit in disbelief while Autumn snickered.

---

[1] Miss.
[2] Goodbye, Miss.

13

"Oh, come on! You didn't tell me he's even more handsome in person! I always just see him in magazines and on social media," Summer shrieked like an excited fangirl.

I covered her mouth, feeling something moist and sticky on my palm. *Ew, lipstick.*

"Shhh! He'll hear you!"

Autumn smacked me hard on the back. "You are one lucky man, Kei."

I stepped away from them. "Do you believe me now?"

They nodded.

"Kei! Hurry up!" Jace shouted from his car.

I said goodbye to my friends and hurried to Jace's car. The car ride was silent until Jace asked, "You haven't told your friends about us?"

I shifted uncomfortably. *Is he mad?*

"I did. Several times. They hadn't believed me. I suppose they do now," I explained.

He hummed.

I stole a glance at him. *What was he thinking?* I couldn't tell from his expression whether he was mad or something else.

*Still, why would he be mad anyway?* Our marriage didn't need to be announced in public. After all, the reason we had a low-key marriage was to maintain our privacy.

I let out a sigh. I sincerely hoped the triplets wouldn't spread the news around university, or I would really get in trouble.

# CHAPTER THREE
## Burgers, Fries, and Rings

"Fast food? What's gotten into you? You hate these places," I said.

Jace unexpectedly drove us to McDonald's, loosening his tie the moment we arrived. He shot me an icy glare.

"Shut up. I'm just curious about their wacky menu."

It was clear that he was nervous, and I can see why.

*Had he ever been to a fast-food restaurant before? Tried their burgers and fries? Probably not.*

Jace Langlois grew up with the finest foods, and he still did. Just your typical twenty-eight-year-old brat.

We entered, and I immediately guided us to a booth. I wondered whether his bodyguards would follow us inside and what their reactions would be to this unexpected scenario.

"Uhuh, stay here. I'll order for us. What do you want?"

Without waiting for his reply, I turned to go to the counter, but he abruptly stood up and grabbed my sleeve hard, almost causing me fall.

"Hey! What the hell? Let go, you asshole. You're acting like a baby!" I scolded him in a hiss.

"Where do you think you're going? Don't think I'm gonna to let you escape," he growled.

My jaw nearly dropped at this. *Was he serious?*

"I'm not going anywhere, idiot! I was just gonna order our food," I explained.

He scowled. "Then let the waiters do their jobs!"

I smacked my forehead in disbelief. He was practically embarrassing himself in front of all these people without even realizing it.

"You're impossible," I said with a sigh. "You see that line of people there? That's the first step to getting your food."

He scoffed and let me go.

When I brought our food back, I noticed his guard in the line, blending in with the midweek crowd of students, university staff, and locals. After I put down our tray of food, I didn't spare another second before digging into my cheeseburger. While chewing, I glanced at Jace to see how he was doing.

"Eat up. That burger isn't going to bite you back or anything," I said after I swallowed.

He glared at me before looking at his burger. I made sure to order us the same meal so he wouldn't freak out.

His eyes narrowed. "Are you sure this is safe to eat?"

I was tempted to flick a few of my fries over to him in exasperation, but I held it in.

*Why did he even bother taking us to a fast-food place if he didn't trust its sanitary practices?*

"Just eat it already," I said, exasperated.

He took a deep breath and picked up the burger. After a brief hesitation, he took a small bite and shut his eyes as he chewed.

"So how is it, your majesty?" I couldn't help but snicker as I asked.

He was still chewing, as though to savor the taste. Finally, he swallowed and, in a slightly surprised tone, replied, "It's . . . it's actually good."

I nodded. "I guess. I mean it's okay." My lips curled into a small smile at this. I suppose I got so used to eating McDonald's that the taste doesn't surprise me anymore. "Geez, I can't believe it's your first time eating a hamburger at McDonald's."

He didn't reply and instead took another bite, this time bigger than the last. He even had a few fries along with his meal without complaining.

I couldn't help but watch him as he continued to eat. This man. *The* Jace Langlois really was my husband . . .

"These fries are surprisingly good for a fast food," Jace suddenly exclaimed loudly, pulling me away from my thoughts.

My eyes widened and in response, I covered his mouth with a hand.

"Shhh! Be quiet, there are people around!"

I was aware that the moment we entered the restaurant, he had already attracted attention—tall, handsome, well-dressed, and possibly familiar-looking. I didn't want to draw any more.

"Mmmph! Ummmph shumm!"

Slowly, I retracted my hand and leaned back against my seat. *This was gonna be a long night.*

"What? I was just giving my opinion?" he said, this time in a quieter tone.

I was just about to answer when a man approached our table. He was holding a tray with fries and a large Coke. He was wearing a navy blue shirt and a pair of black jeans. He looked strangely familiar.

"Kei? Kei Forest?" the guy asked.

My eyes widened as I recognized him.

"Ryan Roberts?"

He nodded enthusiastically. I laughed and stood up to hug him in greeting.

"Woah! You've gotten taller!" he said with a laugh.

I pulled away and pouted playfully. "Why wouldn't I?"

Ryan didn't answer and instead chuckled as he messed up my hair while I grinned like an idiot.

*God, I missed this guy.*

17

Ryan Roberts became my close friend when I was a freshman in high school. During that time, he helped me cope with the loss of both my parents and never left my side. Despite the difficulty of not having parents, Ryan always managed to cheer me up when I needed it most. He was my like my personal savior. When we got older, he even asked me to be his boyfriend, but I rejected him. I was young and naive, and I wasn't ready for a relationship. We lost contact once we went to different universities.

"I missed you, man!" he exclaimed, and I couldn't help but smile at this. He was still the same, and as hyper as ever.

"I missed you too."

"Hey do you wanna go out sometime? You know, to catch up on things?" he offered.

I contemplated this. *Hmmm, I don't have morning classes tomorrow.* It would be great to catch up, and I wouldn't have to spend any more time with my devil of a husband.

"Yeah, su—"

"*Désolé*[3]," Jace said, grabbing my left hand.

Speaking of the devil, I was immediately cut off by Mr. Satan himself.

"But he's already married," Jace added with a smile.

I was taken by surprise and about to scold him for it, but noticed his intimidating gaze was fixed on Ryan. I looked at him in alarm.

*What the hell is he doing?*

Ryan stared at me, shocked. "Really? Since when? And to whom?"

I stammered, unable to form a coherent response. I was still in shock.

*He is so gonna fucking get it.*

---

[3] Sorry.

Jace smiled knowingly. As if to answer Ryan's questions, he immediately clasped our hands together, revealing our matching wedding rings.

To say that I almost died would be the understatement. I wished the ground would open up and swallow me whole right then and there.

Ryan was left speechless. Another minute passed before he finally put two and two together. With a squeal of realization, he pointed a finger at Jace.

"You're Jace Langlois!" he shouted.

"Ryan!" I warned.

*Too late. We were in a public place, surrounded by many people. This could only mean . . . This situation was gonna get bad. Really, really bad.*

"*Oui*[4]. You are correct. I am Jace Langlois. And this is Kei Forest . . ." He grabbed me by the waist and stared down at Ryan. "My husband."

The few murmurs quickly gained momentum until, in my mind, the entire restaurant became a frenzy. Some customers began taking pictures and videos, while others looked at Jace and me in utter shock and disbelief.

Eventually, Ryan joined the crowd. I mean, why wouldn't he? He took a picture of Jace, then of me and Jace, and then of the three of us. Jace was like a celebrity and probably had more fans than Justin Bieber. Everything seemed to have a life of its own.

Grinning as if he had won a huge prize, Ryan said, "Mr. Langlois! Um . . . What a small world . . . I was—"

Jace ignored him but whispered in my ear, "Now that we're officially married and public, this will be all over the news tomorrow."

I clenched my fists and gritted my teeth. I couldn't believe this was happening. I just wanted to dig a deep hole and stay there forever.

---

[4] Yes.

19

*Why was Jace doing this all of a sudden? Was he doing this on purpose?*

I grimaced when I remembered the triplets and our earlier encounter.

*Well, Jace certainly beat them to announcing our marriage first.*

# CHAPTER FOUR
## Like a Celebrity

"Ow! Fucking son of a—" I cursed out loud as I looked at my bleeding thumb.

*Shit, it hurts.*

I was making breakfast when I accidentally cut myself while cutting tomatoes. It was partly my fault because my mind kept drifting back to yesterday's incident at McDonald's.

*Curse that stupid, idiotic, overbearing, jerk, dumb asshole . . . That Jace Langlois!*

Why did he do that yesterday? Was he making fun of me? That son of the devil really had the nerve to announce our marriage in public without my consent.

"Good morning. Where's my coffee?" Jace asked as he walked in.

I glanced at him and noticed that he wasn't wearing his usual business suit and tie. Today, he had on casual clothes—a sky blue long-sleeved polo shirt and black jeans. As much as I hated to admit it, he looked goddamn hot in those clothes.

"Hey! Are you deaf or what?"

I snapped out from my daze and glared at him as I slammed his mug of coffee on the island counter.

"The hell? You're gonna break it!" Jace snarled.

"I don't care," I said calmly.

He frowned. "What's with you?"

The frustration, anger, and humiliation from yesterday's events finally boiled over, and my nerves snapped.

"What's with me? What's with me! Are you fucking kidding me right now? You know damn well what you did yesterday, you piece of shit! Now explain to me why you did that!"

I panted after my tirade ended. There, I let it all out. Now let's see if he would try to worm his way out of this one. If he does, I'll make sure he regrets it.

Jace gaped at me, seemingly shocked by my outburst before quickly recovering and clearing his throat. Then, he smirked.

If this was a cartoon, I could imagine steam rising out of my ears. *How dare he smirk at me!* I took a deep breath.

"Why are you smirking?" I asked, making sure to keep my composure.

He grabbed his coffee mug and stared into it, seemingly without a care in the world.

"I just wanted to show the world how adorable my husband is. Besides, it's about time the world knows about us."

I gritted my teeth at this.

"By the way, your finger is bleeding. How clumsy of you," he said nonchalantly as he took a sip of his coffee.

*Yeah, he's definitely going to hell.*

\*     \*     \*

I gripped the seat belt tightly as I looked outside. Much to my chagrin, several students were already milling around the school grounds, their attention drawn to Jace's silver Porsche. He insisted on driving me to school, claiming it was his duty as my husband and something he should have done already. What I would do to take public transport again or occasionally be driven by his chauffeur, who was following us in the massive black Jeep with his bodyguard.

Jace switched off the engine and stepped out. As he walked around to my side to open the car door, I beat him to it. Instead of blushing at his "romantic" gesture, I gave him a death glare.

"Now, now. Don't be like that. It ruins your face," he whispered in my ear.

To an onlooker, it might seemed like Jace was kissing my cheek, but it was far from it.

I pushed his face away. "And whose fault is that?"

He shrugged. "I dunno. Could be anyone."

"You fu—" His action cut me off as he forcefully pulled me toward him, grabbing my waist.

I put my hands on his chest to push him away, but he had a firm grip. His weekly gym routine wasn't for nothing, after all.

"Let go of me, you asshole! People are watching!" I half-whispered and half-yelled at him.

He smirked. "Let them watch."

I glanced around in hesitation. *Well, stick a knife in my chest already. They're all looking at me. I hate this unwanted attention!*

Jace flashed me his most insincere yet charming smile before he finally released me.

I adjusted my bag and turned my back on him.

"Go away already!" I grumbled.

I glanced at the ground. *Shit, this is so embarrassing.* I was just about to walk away when Jace suddenly grabbed my shoulder and kissed my cheek.

"See you tonight, Kei."

He then got into his car and drove away, escaping the prying eyes of the students around me.

Thanks to Jace Langlois, my once peaceful college life was now in shambles. I swear I blushed so hard that my face could melt the Antarctic.

As I went up the stairs of the arts and architecture building, I looked up and saw Summer, Autumn, and Winter heading toward me.

"Kei! What happened? Are you okay?" Summer asked with concern.

"Man, you should have heard what people inside are saying!" Autumn said.

"Why is your face so red?" Winter mumbled.

I blinked, then repeatedly slapped my face.

Autumn winced. "Oooh, that's gotta hurt."

I looked at the triplets in confusion. "Why? What's the ruckus?"

They exchanged looks before they sheepishly cast their eyes on me.

"Well, almost all the students inside are talking about you . . ." Winter looked like he was afraid of my reaction.

"Particularly about your marriage to the one and only Jace Langlois, the CEO of Langlois Inc. and the number one benefactor of our school," Summer said.

My jaw dropped. *Jace is a benefactor of our school? How come I didn't know that until now?*

"Damn, bro. You're like a celebrity!" Autumn clapped my back.

I stayed quiet. I still couldn't fully grasp what was happening. I didn't want to be the sole focus of the daily school gossip. Worse, I bet the paparazzi were now swarming all over the place.

Autumn was right. I was already treated like a celebrity simply because I was associated with money, regardless of my talents or skills. And it was not what I wanted or had dreamed of.

# CHAPTER FIVE
## Caught in the Rain

I had never hated my life so much that I almost considered jumping out of my art theory and criticism classroom window. I just wanted this day to end right now.

I was not suicidal, but even the most stoic individual would consider escaping danger.

After the triplets filled me in on the gossip swirling around the school, we entered the lobby and were immediately swarmed by fellow students. Many fired question after question:

*"When did you get married?"*

*"How did you meet him?"*

*"Where did you spend your honeymoon?"*

*"Are you planning to have kids?"*

*"What did you give Mr. Langlois to get him to marry someone like you?"*

That question rubbed me the wrong way, and I struggled to suppress my anger. *What the fuck do they mean someone like me? Poor? Ugly? What the fuck!?*

"Whoa, man. Looks like a press interview situation here," Autumn teased, trying to lighten the onslaught of questions.

Eventually, he managed to end what he called my "mini-press interview," and we navigated through the crowd with ease.

I hated it. Being the center of attention was the worst. All I wanted was to be left alone in peace. *Was that too much to ask?*

*   *   *

Several days later, after doing some research in the library, I went searching for my favorite book in the literature section.

"Shit! Where is it?" I hissed to no one in particular.

The online catalog said it was available, but after checking every shelf in the area, I gave up my search.

*Someone probably hid it. Yeah, that's it.*

I looked around. Our college library was deserted at this time of the day, just the way I like it. Truth be told, the library was one of my favorite places on campus, now serving as the perfect hideaway from nosy people. I relished its quiet and serene atmosphere. It had also become a sanctuary from the house I shared with Jace. Lately, I had been "escaping" early and staying late here. I told him I had projects and essays to submit, leaving him to endure meals cooked by his chef. Despite university legends about ghosts and evil spirits haunting the library, I dismissed such stories. After all, I had never believed in ghosts, not even as a child.

I grabbed a random book and settled into a seat near the windows. Making myself comfortable, I flipped through the pages before I stared at the front cover: Rebecca's Tale.

I had never read this one before. The cover illustration was slightly dark and gloomy, featuring an ominous-looking cliff.

*Was this some kind of horror story?*

I shrugged and decided to read it anyway. I lost track of time, and when I paused to rest my eyes, it was already dark outside. Glancing at my watch, I realized it was fifteen minutes to six.

"Well, shit," I muttered, suddenly feeling faint from hunger.

I placed the book on the book truck and hurried out. Just as I cleared the electronic door scanner, I was halted by lightning and thunder. With cautious steps, I ventured a few paces before a sudden downpour of heavy rain drenched the surroundings, the skies growing darker by the minute.

*Now what? How am I supposed to get home in this state?* I didn't have an umbrella with me, and I certainly didn't want to step outside and get my clothes soaked from the rain. My mind scrambled for ideas to get home when an idea popped into my head. *Like really!*

"My cell phone . . . ," I mumbled, fishing it out of my pocket and noticing the battery was low.

*Damn it!* There were so many missed calls and text notifications. I rummaged through my bag for my charger, but alas, it wasn't there. I must have left it at home. I glanced at my watch: 6:15 PM already. As I looked outside again, it was clear that the rain showed no signs of stopping any time soon.

Glancing at the library door, I contemplated going back inside and waiting out the rain, or maybe using my laptop to message the triplets.

*Honk! Honk!*

I practically jumped in the air when I heard the sudden honk of a car. Squinting my eyes, I looked toward the source of the sound. It was a black Porsche. *Jace!*

He honked again when he came to a full stop. Then the car door opened and out came Jace with an umbrella. He ran toward me.

"Idiot! Why didn't you answer my calls?" he scolded.

I scowled. "I was busy!"

Jace sighed exasperatedly, and grabbed me by the shoulders. "I only brought one umbrella, so we have no other choice but to share."

I nodded and walked back to the car with him, feeling grateful despite everything else.

He opened the door for me before heading to the driver's side. As he drove off, his menacing-looking Jeep of his bodyguards followed closely behind.

"Next time, call me if you're coming home late," he said.

I glanced at him out of the corner of my eye. "Okay."

Usually, I would call Harry—his household manager, chauffeur, chef, butler, or whatever capacity he was serving Jace. Or I would take a taxi when something like this happened. Harry was likely driving that black Jeep right now.

"How did you know I was in the library anyway?"

"When you didn't answer, I asked Lucy where you usually hang out."

*Was Jace worrying about me?* I shook my head. That was impossible. This man wasn't the type to get concerned easily. Whatever his reason, it wasn't out of the goodness of his heart. He probably just picked me up for the same reason he drove me to school, or maybe he didn't want the burden of dealing with the media if something happened to me, like if I went missing. That would certainly be a press nightmare.

I blinked. *Was I really just a burden to him?*

Which reminded me, all this time, we never treated each other as spouses or even acted like a newly married couple. Our marriage was purely for convenience: I married him to secure my inheritance, and he married me, supposedly to please his parents—if that were true. He never told me his real reason.

*What was the real purpose of our marriage? Once I fulfill all the will's stipulations and receive my entire inheritance, does that mean I can leave Jace?*

"Uh . . . Jace? Can I ask you something?" I asked hesitantly.

He glanced at me briefly before returning his focus to the road. "You already did."

I gritted my teeth. *Never mind.*

"What do you want to ask? If this is about you finally wanting to have sex with me, then shoot. We'll do it tonight once we get home," he teased.

I punched his thigh.

"Ow! You little . . ."

Smirking, I looked out the car window. While he mentioned sex jokingly, it still thrilled me. Green trees and tall buildings passed by in a blur. I should ask Jace next time.

28

*Next time . . .*

# CHAPTER SIX
## Personal Maid

It was Saturday, and I still hadn't told Jace what was bugging me every night ever since that rainy day when he picked me up from the university library.

All I knew was that the stipulations required me to receive the rest of my inheritance over the course of five years—money here, estate there, and so on. However, it would all be forfeited if I were not married to Jace and living in the same house.

But what happened after? I had been feeling like shit, with heavy bags under my eyes. Lately, I have been feeling anxious and nervous, though I hadn't planned on telling him about it. Also, he didn't seem to notice how awful I looked because of his work. His paperwork from his office has been filling up the house, and when I asked him about it, he got pissed and locked himself in his study. Jerk.

At the moment, I was cooking sausages coated with caviar, as usual.

*Ew.* How could someone eat this disgusting piece of . . . of . . . whatever. It will always baffle me.

When the sausages were cooked, I poured the hot espresso in Jace's mug and placed them together on a silver tray. With hesitant steps, I walked to his study and knocked softly. There was no answer. I knocked again, but still no response.

Growing annoyed, I kicked the door.

"Hey! Open the goddamn door! My hands are full!" I shouted.

The door opened a few seconds later, reavealing an angry-looking Jace, who growled, "What?"

I raised an eyebrow. "No need to get your panties in a bunch, idiot. I brought your breakfast assuming you didn't want to leave your paperwork behind."

He looked at me strangely before he pushed the door wider.

I entered the room and looked around. Honestly, this was only my second time in his study. The first time was right after we got married, when we talked with a lawyer about my inheritance. I didn't exactly know the reason, but Jace didn't want anyone to enter his study, and I mean no one. Not even me, his husband.

Jace pointed to his desk. "Just put it there."

I blinked. "Put what there?"

He scowled impatiently. "*Le petit déjeuner*.[5] Don't act stupid and just leave! *Je suis fatigué*[6] . . ."

I stayed quiet and let him rant in French. At least now I was starting to understand what he was saying. Initially, I didn't really care, but after a while, I began to feel at a disadvantage, so I secretly enrolled in French classes.

As he ranted on, I thought about our marriage. I decided I wouldn't mention it to him until he was calm and didn't have any work to do. *Yeah, I should do that.* Besides, I knew he was just acting this way because he was swamped, and his temper was through the roof as a result.

I heard Jace took a deep breath before he flopped down on his chair. He closed his eyes and rubbed his temples.

"So . . . anything else? Can I go now?" I asked as I slowly took a few steps backward.

He put his elbows on the desk and leaned on them.

---

[5] Breakfast.
[6] I am tired.

I had to admit, no matter how much I hated this man, I still had an unhealthy attraction to him. His hair was a sexy mess, and his clothes, likely yesterday's, were crumpled. It was criminal how good-looking he was, even when he was stressed to the bone.

Jace sighed. "Yeah."

I was about to open the door when I heard a loud thud. I turned around and gasped.

Jace had fainted.

\*     \*     \*

After Harry and I carried Jace to the bedroom and placed him in our king-size bed, I carefully placed a wet cloth on his forehead. Jace had fainted due to overwork and fatigue. Besides nearly working himself to death, he hadn't touched any of the meals I had prepared for him this week—not even a single bite.

I knew he hardly ate because Lucy, my parents' housekeeper who decided to stay and care for me after they died, told me. She not only told me things but also had strong opinions about how Jace was treating me. By now, she was more a friend than an employee. While Harry took care of Jace, Lucy took care of me. She had been with my parents long before I was born, and it was likely my parents' will stipulated that she remain my caretaker until I came of age. When I did come of age, I found I couldn't bear to let her go. She also had no family of her own, so . . .

*Speaking of family, Jace is my family now, for better or for worse . . . until inheritance do us part . . .*

I knew Jace worked hard; millionaires and billionaires wouldn't retain their wealth if they slacked off. But what shocked me most was the sheer amount of paperwork on his desk, mostly from his office. It made me wonder if something was wrong with his company. He clearly hadn't rested enough since he started bringing home more work.

I called his secretary and discreetly asked if there were any issues in the company that required Jace's immediate attention. When she assured me that everything was running smoothly, I politely requested that she refrain from giving Jace any new tasks until he felt better. She promptly notified the legal counsel, and they agreed that Jace would only be contacted in case of an emergency.

I sat on the side of the bed and observed Jace's sleeping form. He looked so innocent and angelic while asleep. Too bad he turned into a merciless devil when awake.

I sighed. I was unexpectedly finding this difficult. How should I explain to him that I wanted to sleep in my own room and, eventually, end our marriage? The will's stipulation only required that we live in the same house, not necessarily sleep in the same bed. Despite what everyone said we should do, it is still *our* marriage. I knew he wouldn't understand at first and would demand an explanation, something I had been struggling to come up with.

*Wait! Why would he get mad?* He wasn't in love with me. And I certainly wasn't in love with him.

The feelings between us were mutual. Our wedding was purely for convenience and our own benefit. As much as I was embarrassed to admit it, our marriage still hadn't been consummated.

I. Am. A. Virgin.

"Kei?"

I snapped back from my stupor and turned to face Jace. His face was covered in sweat, and his breathing was slow and deep. Leaning back, I picked up a glass of water from the bedside table and handed it to him carefully.

He slowly sat up and leaned his back against the headboard. Taking the glass from me, he drank quick gulps of water.

"How long have I been out?" he asked hoarsely, and goddamn did he sound sexy.

I glanced at the small digital clock on the bedside table. "For about five hours."

"Fuck."

He abruptly kicked the duvet away from him and got out the bed. Stretching briefly, he revealed those oh-so-sexy toned muscles beneath his white shirt.

"Where are you going? You're supposed to rest for the day," I said, standing up.

He ran his fingers through his bed hair. "Work."

I grinned smugly. "Well, doctor's orders—let the brain rest and plenty of sleep. In case you're wondering why your left arm is sore, the doctor gave you intravenous nutrition or something. Plus, I called your secretary and told her to stop giving you more paperwork. So you'll have to thank me for that."

He froze for a second before he recovered. "And why would I thank you?" he said, rolling his shirt sleeve to check his arm.

My jaw dropped. "Seriously?"

He turned to face me and gave me a smirk.

"You ungrateful douchebag!" I yelled.

*I couldn't believe this man! After everything I had done for him, he couldn't even thank me? He really was the devil.*

"Oh, by the way. I'm hungry. Cook me something."

I clenched my fists so hard that my knuckles turned white. The fact that he was asking me to cook something for him after not eating the meals I made pissed me off. On the other hand . . .

"What do you want?" I gritted my teeth.

He paused as if thinking about it before shrugging. "*Les rognons de veau.*[7]"

My eyes widened, and my shoulders slumped in horror. Of all the foods, why must it be that horrid stuff?

"Are you insane? That's veal kidney, stupid! I hate those!" I exclaimed.

I may not be fluent in French, but I knew what that word meant.

---

[7] Veal kidneys.

"Why are you reacting like that? You're not the one who's gonna eat it," he said casually.

I was speechless. He did have a point. *But still* . . .

"I'm the one who's cooking it! Obviously, I'm gonna smell it and have to handle it, and it's really disgusting as fuck!"

He went to the door and opened it wide. Before stepping outside, he said something that I would make him regret ever saying it.

"You're my personal maid for today until I get better."

# CHAPTER SEVEN
## Runaway

My head hurt.

My neck hurt.

My back hurt.

My arms hurt.

Basically, my whole body hurt.

Who was to blame for this? None other than Jace Langlois.

He certainly took his word seriously when he assigned me as his "personal maid" until he got better.

To make his statement possible, he dismissed all the staff in the house for the week, including the indispensable Harry and my Lucy. No explanations were given; he simply instructed them to return the following Monday and assured them not to worry about their salaries. While Harry and Lucy who were reluctant, the rest of the staff were quite happy. Technically, it was an eight-day vacation for them, but it felt like slavery to me.

After I cooked him the horrid veal kidney, he gave me a long list of what to do as his personal maid.

For the rest of that day, he made me rearrange all his clothes in his wardrobe and polish his shoes. To mess with me further, he purposely ruined his neatly-folded ties and socks, which Harry always kept pristine.

The following day, Sunday, instead of resting or doing school work, I cleaned all eight bedrooms and their en suite bathrooms, plus a couple of powder rooms at the living room and kitchen. I vacuumed every speck of dust from every nook and cranny—starting from the largest bookshelves to the smallest crevices between hundreds of art and picture frames throughout the mansion. I even scrubbed an already shiny kitchen.

One would think that with three full-time staff, not counting Harry and Lucy, everything would be spick and span. However, that was not the case. Some housekeeping tasks were left undone or done carelessly, possibly due to a couple of staff members being let go before I arrived here.

Afterward, I took care of the garden—watering all the plants and flowers, which took about an hour. There wasn't much to do in the grounds; they were kept show-worthy and picture-perfect by the gardener even in early spring. I cleared out all the useless junk kept in the garden storage, which, upon second thought, might not have been useless to the gardener. Nevertheless, doing so somehow eased the anger simmering in my brain.

It took me the entire day to finish all his damn chores. I didn't even eat lunch or have any snacks, though I did have breakfast—I consider it the most important meal of the day, especially since the asshole demanded his food. After all that hard work, my whole body ached. Sweat clung to me, and my hair was a tangled mess. I kept sneezing from all the dust, and my eyes were watering.

*Fuck this shit.* I was on the verge of killing myself to prevent any more of this stupid torture.

"Servant! Prepare dinner!" Jace yelled from the front door.
I stood up from the dirt, facing him with exhaustion and frustration written across my face. He wore his signature smirk that I hated and loved so much. I gave Jace the middle finger before I walked away. *Screw dinner! I'm leaving this hell hole!*

"Hey! Where are you going?"

"Far! Far, far away from you!" I yelled over my shoulder, picking up speed toward the main gate of his estate.

Thankfully, there was no guard—probably given the week off too, which was quite risky for the idiot—and thank God for electronic locks.

*Lucky.*

I glanced back, relieved to see no sign of Jace following. At least he knew when to stop, for now. I closed the gate behind me, and I bolted. I ran as fast as I could, not caring where I was heading as long as I wouldn't see even a glimpse of that fucking asshole anymore.

I couldn't take it anymore. Jace was just evil, pure evil, caring only for himself and oblivious to the pain he caused. I hated men like him. If it weren't for people like Jace, I wouldn't be so jaded.

Jace's mansion was located a few miles away from the main road. The estate was surrounded by hundreds of trees that obscured the gate. Beyond it stretched a wide pathway leading to the main road.

I slowed my pace to a walk for the rest of the way to the exit, glancing over my shoulder every so often to check for any sign of Jace or his bodyguards.

*So far, so good.* I stopped when I finally caught a glimpse of the main road.

"What am I doing?" I asked myself.

*Why am I running away? Was it because I was tired of Jace's antics?*

Running away like this felt like I was escaping from my problems. The fact that I was tempted to do so reminded me of what my parents always told me—that fleeing from difficult situations was a cowardly move.

My legs wobbled, and I crumpled to the ground. To make matters worse, clouds above opened up, and rain started to pour. In the distance, I could hear thunder roaring. It was as if the weather was scolding me for what I was about to do.

The guilt gnawed at me, consuming my thoughts. I was such a coward. If my parents were still alive, they would surely lecture me for a whole day on taking responsibility and all that.

"Kei!"

I snapped my focus to the source of the familiar voice, my vision blurred by the relentless rain.

"Kei! Where are you?"

I abruptly stood. *It can't be . . .*

"Kei!"

Slowly, I turned around.

Lo and behold, the voice belonged to Jace himself. He stood there, gazing down at me, sheltering us both under an umbrella held in one hand while reaching out to me with the other.

"Kei! Are you crazy? Why did you run away? *Je suis inquiétée!*" he yelled.

"W-what are . . . you doing here?"

He sighed exasperatedly. "I came to look for you!"

I scowled. "Yeah, right."

My scowl deepened as a black-clad man, whom I recognized as one of his bodyguards, walked past us to stand a few feet away, while another dark silhoutte loomed a few yards behind Jace.

"You came to look for me so you could torture me with more chores. Well, news flash! I'm not coming back to your prison, asshole! I'm leaving!"

I got up and started to walk away from him, but much to my dismay, he followed. Every so often, he tried to shield me with his umbrella, but I managed to dodge every attempt.

Eventually, I grew tired of this game and stopped in my tracks. Slowly, I turned to face him angrily.

"Will you stop following me?" I hissed.

He rolled his eyes. "Stop being so immature and come back home."

---

[8] I am worried.

He grabbed my wrist, but I slapped his hand away, which shocked him.

*Screw it. I couldn't do this. Not anymore . . .*

"No, I'm leaving, Jace! I won't let you drag me down with your awful personality!"

"You're acting like a child!" he retorted.

I jabbed my finger into his chest. "No, you're the one who's acting like a child! I hate you so goddamn much, and I will never ever tolerate being with you! In fact . . ."

I took off the wedding band from my ring finger and threw it at him. He didn't catch it, and the ring fell onto the sidewalk, amidst puddles.

"There's your fucking ring, jackass! I'm leaving! And this time, for good!"

I turned around and continued walking, hoping for a taxi. It didn't take long before a cab stopped in front of me. I opened the door and hopped inside.

I didn't spare another glance at Jace and just looked straight ahead.

"Where to?" the driver asked monotonously.

I crossed my arms. There was only one place I could go where Jace wouldn't find me.

Hopefully, he could never find me.

# CHAPTER EIGHT
## What Are Friends For?

The rain continued to pour heavily as I arrived at my destination. The sky was nothing but thick gray clouds, with not a bird in sight.

I exited the taxi and banged the door closed, immediately feeling guilty. *Fuck it!* My mood had soured again as the taxi driver gave me grief about electronic payment. I hurried to the five-story apartment building right in front of me. The sliding glass doors automatically opened, and I rushed inside to avoid getting any wetter from the damned rain.

The interior resembled more of a luxurious hotel than an apartment building, with high beige ceilings adorned by a fair-sized silver chandelier. In one section of the lobby, several seating areas were arranged, along with a reception counter near the entrance.

I approached the lady behind the counter, and she glanced at my bedraggled state with slightly raised eyebrows.

"Good evening, sir. Welcome to Silverline Apartments. How may I help you?" the lady greeted with a smile.

I adjusted my jacket. "Uh, yeah. The Winstons, please. They're expecting me."

The lady shifted to her computer monitor and rapidly typed on the keyboard before she turned back to me with a smile. I had to hand it to her, she sure knew how to stay perky in this depressing weather.

"Ah, yes! The Winstons are in. Can I have your name please?"

I was just about to tell her my name when I just remembered that I was now carrying Jace's last name, Langlois. My hesitation earned a curious look from the receptionist.

"Sir, is something wrong?"

I sighed, knowing I had no other choice but to tell her my full name. Speaking it out loud left a bitter taste in my mouth. Memories of what transpired at his place lingered fresh in my mind. My emotions were a jumbled mess. The depressing weather outside worsened my already foul mood.

"Sir? Sir!"

I snapped back from my thoughts and saw the concern eyes of the lady.

I cleared my throat."Sorry. Kei Forest . . . Langlois," I said without meeting her eyes.

"Could you spell your name for me," she asked, professional and polite.

I did a double take and raised an eyebrow in confusion. That was weird. She didn't react as I expected her to. Most people who heard the Langlois name usually reacted in awe and excitement which annoyed me.

After I gave her the spelling, she nodded and said, "Right. You're on their list. May I see some identification please?"

*Fuck it! I was not actually planning to leave the house today.*

"Um . . . I left my wallet at home . . ." Thinking fast, I said, "I have photos with the triplets, if that's alright?"

She smiled kindly and nodded, and I showed her photos of me with the triplets.

"That's alright, sir. Just following protocols. They did say they are expecting you. Thank you all the same! They're on the third floor, apartment number eight. Enjoy your visit, Mr. Langlois," she said and smiled again.

She had probably seen me on TV or, most likely, on social media due the latest frenzy; that was why she was not strict with the ID.

"Thank you," I said.

I couldn't help but return the smile before I headed straight for the elevators. Inside, I pressed for level three and leaned against the mirrored wall. After a few seconds, the bell dinged, and the doors opened.

Stepping out, I looked around, turned left, and walked toward the door labeled 308.

"Coming!" a voice from the other side yelled immediately after I knocked.

The door opened, revealing Summer in an oversized dark blue sweater and white joggers. Her hair was tied in a messy bun, and her face was free of makeup.

Her eyes widened when she saw me. "Kei! What happened? You're soaking wet!" she asked as she gestured for me to enter and closed the door behind us.

She led me to a cozy living room. I instantly flopped down on the three-seater couch.

*Man, I felt like I was dying—all these mixed emotions and spiraling thoughts about Jace, terrible body pains from all the housework I had done, wet from the rain, and now cold from . . . the AC? This early in spring?*

"Hey, get away from the couch, moron! You're soaking wet!" she scolded.

I didn't listen to her and just closed my eyes instead. I really, really wanted to sleep already. I heard some shuffling and then *bang!*

"Jesus Christ! Kei, what are you doing here?" Autumn's surprised voice echoed in the room.

I slowly opened my eyes again but looked up at the ceiling. "I texted you I was coming."

"Yes, but why?

"No reason."

43

Autumn scoffed in disbelief while Winter just stood in the corner, their faces sporting similar shocked expressions.

You're here in the middle of a storm, soaking wet!" Autumn said.

"There's no storm."

Suddenly, a towel landed on my face.

"No reason, my ass. What— Did something happen at your place? Your husband's company didn't go bankrupt, did it?" Autumn asked.

"Autumn, stop being an idiot for once in your pathetic life. It's obvious Kei had a fight with Mr. Langlois. Am I right, Kei?" Summer said as she adjusted her position to get comfortable on the beanbag she had taken.

I sighed in defeat, and before I knew it, I was blurting out all the events that occurred between Jace and me throughout yesterday and today. The triplets kept quiet and just listened attentively. Well, except for Autumn who threw curse words every time I mentioned Jace.

After I was finished, I waited for the three of them to say something. Whatever they would have to say, somehow, I felt some sense of relief.

"First of all, why did you choose to hide here?" Summer asked. "We know you have an empty, big, beautiful house . . ."

"Yeah, what if he actually finds you? Your husband is rich as fuck. He can hire hundreds of investigators to search for you. Even the SWAT team! Whoa, that is cool! I've always wanted to be an FBI secret agent or something!" Autumn exclaimed excitedly.

Winter just shook his head at his brother. Meanwhile, Summer had other ideas. She stood up and slapped Autumn on the cheek, to which he howled in response.

Watching them bicker like little kids actually eased my mood a bit and made me forget Jace for a second. Alas, it didn't last long.

"Autumn, shut up. You're missing the whole point," Summer scolded him.

I fiddled with my fingers. "I know what I'm doing, guys. That's why I came here and not to my house. He'll never find me. He doesn't even know I have friends of my own. He's too stupid to notice that."

Summer and Autumn fell silent. We remained silent before Winter shyly raised his hand. We looked at him in surprise. Maybe he had something to say.

"Um, have you forgotten? Mr. Langlois came to pick you up at school saw us. And remember, he's also the main sponsor of the school, so doesn't that give him the advantage and connections to find you?" Winter pointed out.

Summer's jaw dropped at this revelation. Winter rarely spoke up, but his observation struck a chord. Despite the seriousness of the situation, Autumn couldn't help but smile slightly at his brother's ingenuity.

I grimaced. It seemed I definitely overlooked some facts and underestimated Jace. How could I forget that Jace usually picks me up, and the fact that he already met the triples before? That meant he certainly had way more chances of finding my whereabouts.

*Shit.*

I could feel the panic rise in my chest once more and was about to run away again when I felt two pairs of hands on my shoulders. Looking up, I saw Summer and Autumn, both of whom gave me reassuring smiles, while Winter sat down next to me.

"Hey, don't worry about a thing. We'll handle this," Summer said reassuringly.

Autumn gave me a clap on the back. "Yeah, man. We're the Winstons. No one can scare us!"

I grinned at his goofiness. "Thanks, guys."

"What are friends for?" Winter said.

"Now, would you be so kind as to give me something to change into? My clothes are clammy."

# CHAPTER NINE
## Glass Marble

Sluggishly, I used my right foot to pick up the TV remote from the table. After several attempts, I gave up and just stared at the ceiling of the triplets' apartment.

Today was Monday, and I was all alone with nothing to do. The triplets went to university early this morning because they had classes. As for me, my first class had already started twenty minutes ago, but I didn't care. I was too lazy and tired to even go. I also wasn't ready to face nosy students who had nothing better to do than disturb other people's privacy.

Summer was reluctant to leave me alone. Fortunately, thanks to Autumn's speech about the consequences of failing classes and potentially becoming homeless, Summer finally gave in and went with them, but not before giving me her own speech that would make any mother proud.

*"Make sure to lock the door, Kei."*

*"Don't answer any phone calls."*

*"If there's a knock on the door and you're not expecting anyone, Kei, don't ever open it."*

*"Kei, are you gonna be okay all by yourself?"*

*"Make sure to call 911 if there's an emergency. Better yet, just call me!"*

I nodded to them all without bothering to listen. I felt terrible at first but it got annoying real fast.

46

My stomach rumbled. I sighed and practically crawled my way to the kitchen. I couldn't help but groan and grimace in disappointment when I opened the fridge—inside was only a jar of pickles and expired milk. It was then that I remembered the triplets only ever ate fast food never bothered to buy any groceries.

I slammed the fridge shut and padded back to the living room. I contemplated ordering myself a box of pizza but decided against it. I wasn't really in the mood for pizza today.

I thought about buying clothes, but I was too apathetic to leave the apartment. I also considered going back to Jace's house to get my school things, but I was wary about possibly meeting him there.

So many thoughts crossed my mind, including visiting the house where I had lived after leaving my parents' house following their deaths and before my marriage. It was a couple of blocks from the university campus and not far from here.

Concerned about my well-being and aware that I had some money, Lucy suggested we find an apartment within the city, away from our house in the suburbs that I was barely in anymore. It had become unbearable to return to without either of my parents. It took us a while to make the final leap, but when I was accepted into the university, I hardly looked back. I had never returned there.

I knew Lucy went home there after Jace forced them to take a vacation, so maybe I should go home too. *But not today . . .*

*     *     *

Today was the second day I missed school, which made me feel unsettled. *If I lost both school and my marriage at the same time, where would that leave me?*

So I risked going back to the house to get my school things—especially my art portfolio, risking meeting Jace, but of course it was empty. His business was far too important to be set aside, even for his health. Well, he had probably recovered by now.

As I was exiting the gate of the estate to wait for the car I had booked, a courier service stopped in front of the gate.

The driver rolled down his window and called out to me, "Excuse me, I have a package for this address. Could you help me?"

I shrugged and pulled the gate closed, engaging the automatic locking mechanism. When I turned around, the courier was walking toward me, holding a box.

"Delivery for a Mr. Kei Forest," he said.

I paled at what he said.

*For me? Why? How had he . . . Who could . . .*

"Sir? Do you live in that house?" The delivery man's voice snapped me back from my anxious stupor.

"Yes. Yes, I'm Kei Forest."

"Alright, can I see some ID, sir?"

I did not bother replying; my mind was busy wondering where the package from or who it could be from. Instead, I showed him my ID.

"Thank you. Please sign here."

I blinked and shakily signed my name on the electronic clipboard he was holding. He then handed me the small box, said thank you, and left.

"W-what is this . . . ?" I said, shaking the box.

I looked for a card or any handwritten note but found none.

*Surely, it couldn't be from him. It was impossible. He would have known there was no one in the house to receive deliveries. He couldn't have found out I was coming here today . . . he just couldn't! Why? How?*

A car honked, snapping me from my thoughts. After confirming the booking, I got in the car and continued to stare at the small box. It did not have a return address. I gulped and slowly opened it. Inside were tissue papers, which I set aside. Underneath them rested a little green and blue glass marble. Gently, I picked it up and observed it up close.

*A marble? Why would he give me this? This doesn't make sense at all. What's this marble for anyway?*

48

I pushed it back into the box, but as I lifted the tissue papers to return them inside as well, I noticed a note. I retrieved it immediately, realizing that there was indeed a separate letter. Unfolding it, I read the words handwritten in blue ink.

*To my beloved son, Kei Forest,*

*This marble may be just a small, useless object for you, but always remember that not all big things bring happiness. Your father and I want you to keep this valuable marble with you so you will always remember what it symbolizes as you go through life.*

*My son, have you noticed the colors in the marble? They are similar to mine and your father's eyes. I hope this small object will help you remember us as well.*

*Just remember that no matter how much someone gives you a hard time, just look into their eyes and you'll see their true colors.*

*Don't run away, son, and don't ever forget that.*

*With love,*
*Mom*

I sucked in a shaky breath after I read the note.

It was just a gift from my parents before they died. The lawyer probably sent this to me. I thought it was from Jace.

I sighed in relief.

Well, now that I read my mother's letter, I knew that running away wasn't the solution to any of my problems. The timing was still suspect though. Seeing my mother's handwriting made me feel both sad and happy at the same time. Then I remembered her message: *Look into their eyes, and you'll see their true colors.*

I scoffed to myself. *True colors? Yeah, right.* I already knew a long time ago that Jace had already shown his true colors, and they weren't as good as what my parents believed. Jace Langlois was simply pure evil, nothing else.

49

He never cared for anyone but himself. He was selfish, cruel, inconsiderate, overbearing . . .

I could go on and on, but words still wouldn't be enough to describe his horrible personality. No matter how much the words of my dead mother stirred something inside me, Jace's horrible qualities would simply overpower them and would end up making me more irrational than anything else.

Something else about my mother's letter stirred something inside me, but I couldn't place what it was. I placed the glass marble on top of the coffee table as I tried to forget everything that had happened.

I couldn't care less about anything. Jace could be the devil for all I cared and mess with my mind, but I refuse to let him affect me in any way. I refuse to let him destroy my life. I would face the world and enjoy my life without Jace Langlois.

# CHAPTER TEN
## Husband

JACE

Kei Forest . . . or currently known as Kei Langlois.

My husband. True.

*My lover? Hardly.*

*My confidant? Not likely.*

My supposed partner in life. Gone.

He ran away from me just because he was tired of my "shitty personality" or something along those lines.

I scoffed at the thought and closed my laptop.

*Husband? Yeah right. Who cares about him?* It wasn't my fault at all. In fact, he was the one who was acting like an immature brat. We were husbands after all, didn't that mean we also had to put up with each other's less-than-stellar traits and just bear with it?

*Point is, his fleeing was frankly fruitless.* I already knew where his current location was. I had him followed the minute he rode that awful taxi. In his haste and anger, he probably did not realize another taxi had stopped and picked up one of my guards.

Silverline Apartments. Apparently, his college friends lived there. Friends whose faces and names I vaguely remembered. All I knew was that I met them once when I picked up Kei from his school.

I had expected him to return to his row house apartment, but he didn't. I had someone stationed there.

I didn't bother going over there to apologize. I was fully aware of how I treated him these past few days, but I didn't do anything that could hurt or kill him. Well, except for the *les rognons de veau*, which I may have crossed the line with that one.

I knew Kei hated veal kidney. In fact, the mere mention of it made him want to vomit, but still, I wouldn't apologize for that one either. I was just going to wait for him to open his eyes and stop being such a *bébé*[9].

I stood up from my office chair and stretched my muscles. Gazing out the large floor-to-ceiling window at the scenery below, I tore my eyes away and surveyed my office.

At first glance, the office clearly belonged to a man, evident from its dull colors. The ceiling was pure white, and the walls were gray with black lines. My mahogany lacked any personal touches, holding my laptop, a few documents, and an inclined brass plaque with my name and position carved on it: *Jace Langlois. Chief Executive Officer.*

Another thought crossed my mind—I had never brought Kei to my office before. In fact, he had never been anywhere near my building. The only place he had visited that had any connection to my work was my study at the house.

*How come I never brought him here?* The thought crossed my mind before it was immediately answered by another. Simply put, Kei hated the idea of the public knowing he was married to me. He was the type of person who abhorred having too much attention, while I, on the other hand, liked to it a certain extent. Not in a way that a typical Hollywood wannabe would obsess over it, but I dealt with it enough.

Now that I thought about it, I knew practically next to nothing about Kei. All I know about him was the fact that our

---

[9] Baby.

parents were apparently close friends, and him securing his inheritance was the only reason why we even married each other.

During that time, I remembered when I received a letter from their family lawyer. The Forest family will stipulated that I had to marry their only son for him to finally receive his inheritance.

Of course, I blatantly refused at first. After all, how could someone, much less a couple of strangers make me do something like that? I wasn't ready to marry anyone, not then and probably not even now. I was too busy managing my business, and simply didn't have the time for one measly boy's inheritance issue. I certainly wasn't going to get tangled up in that mess and marry someone like him.

The day after I received the Forest, I also received another letter from my parents, both of whom were very adamant that I marry this Kei Forest boy. The way they berated and scolded me for not honoring the will made me feel like I just committed treason. It was horrible, as if they were expecting some chemical reaction to take effect the moment I read the will. They didn't even give me time to breathe and consider. While they were usually doting parents, they could be exceptionally critical if they wanted to be, and I certainly wasn't going to be on the receiving end of their lecture any longer.

With that being said, I reluctantly searched for Kei Forest, found him, and immediately proposed—right in the middle of his class.

I shook my head at the thought. *Alright, enough with that trip down memory lane.* I needed to go through some documents first regarding internship applications. I sat back down on my desk and rummaged through the scattered papers on my desk. After I found what I was looking for, I immediately called for my secretary through the intercom.

"Diana, come here," I ordered as I skimmed through the internship applications.

The door to my office opened, revealing my forty-eight-year-old secretary, Mrs. Morris. She had been a widow for about ten years, and so far had no plans of remarrying, much to my confusion. She was also the most reliable person I know, and despite her age, she didn't seem to age much. Her hair was devoid of any gray strands, and her face sported only a few wrinkles here and there. To me, she was like my second mother.

"You called, Mr. Langlois?" she asked as she shut the door behind her and made her way toward my desk.

I nodded and showed her the requests.

She raised an eyebrow. "Internship applications?"

"*Oui.* I forgot how many openings are available," I said as I shrugged off my suit jacket and hung it on the armrest of my chair.

Diana clicked her tongue in disapproval as she took my jacket, smoothed it out, and neatly hung it on the rack off to the side and behind my desk.

"Mr. Langlois, how many times do I have to tell you to put your jacket on the rack?"

I shrugged.

She looked at me with a sigh. "And to answer your question, we always have one opening left for you to fill with your choice. The other two were already filled last week by human resources."

"Remind me why I do this?"

She sighed and, with utmost patience, answered, "The other two, chosen by HR, will be taking their internship in either HR, Finance, R&D, or whereever they are qualified. The one you choose will report to operations or IT, both of which had decided to manage closely.

I sighed, too, frustrated that she didn't understand me. "Yes, yes, I know all that. But why do I have to do it? Why not let HR handle all this . . ."

"It's what your father wanted. He believed in paying it forward. Your grandfather and father began their busines careers with an internship."

I hummed as I randomly chose one résumé and handed it to Diana, not bothering to read its contents. I didn't really care since I would not be involved with training interns, no matter how much my father wanted to delude himself. Unlike me, she read the document in its entirety and nodded as soon as she was done.

"Ryan Roberts, twenty-two years old. A computer engineering student from Santell University. Good choice, sir. IT did say they could use a few more people . . . In fact, they said that if they get an intern this year and if he's any good, they wo—"

"What did you say?" I asked and stood up from my seat.

Diana frowned in confusion. "IT could use a computer engineer to help—"

"Not that. The name you said."

She glanced down at the résumé she was holding. "Ryan Roberts?"

I ran my fingers through my hair, and looked down at the other internship résumés on my desk.

*Fuck.* Of all the things to remember, how in the world could I still remember that one name, especially when I can barely remember the name of that fast-food place Kei and I ate at?

*McRonald's? Mc—something . . . Ryan Roberts.*

I can still recall Kei and him being close as they hugged each other in front of me in that restaurant. *Were they ex-boyfriends or something? Relatives?*

"Diana, call him for an interview tomorrow," I ordered.

She nodded and trudged toward the door, but before she could close it, I called out to her, "Diana?"

"Yes, sir."

"When this Ryan Roberts comes for his interview, I want you to personally bring him here."

She looked at me askance.

I cleared my throat. "Um . . . I think it's time I take this internship—this paying forward seriously."

She smiled and said, "As you wish, Mr. Langlois."

I wasn't sure what I was doing, but all I know was that I had a bad feeling about this Ryan Roberts person.

# CHAPTER ELEVEN
## Shocking News . . . and Melon?

KEI

After settling into my house and assuring Lucy that everything was alright, I stepped out for a walk to contemplate my next steps. Once outside, I took in a deep breath and exhaled. I haven't felt this free in a long time.

Ever since that dreadful day I married Jace, my life quickly detoured down a path to hell. Soon after, my already full days were filled with endless chores that should have easily been handled by the household staff. I had to cater to whatever the spawn of Satan wanted.

Now that I was free from all that, I could return to the life I lived before I pursued more inheritance. I could do anything I wanted without caring or worrying about what others might say. It wasn't about chasing after more money anymore, despite it being the fruit of my parents' hard work; it was about finding peace of mind and enjoying life on my own terms.

I decided to get ice cream first. After that, I could go to that amusement park I saw on TV that one time. Sure it seemed childish, but I would rather have a fun day at an amusement park than drink my problems away on an alcoholic binge and suffer a terrible hangover afterward.

I crossed the street and walked toward the university campus. There was a quaint-looking ice cream shop there with the sign Creme D-Lite displayed outside. Opening the glass door, the sound of chimes echoed as I stepped inside.

There wasn't a long line at this time of the day, so I headed straight to the counter. Upon closer inspection, I nearly drooled at the sight of so many different flavors of ice cream on display.

*Wait, is that avocado?* When it was my turn, a girl behind the counter greeted me with a smile.

"Hello, sir! Welcome to Creme D-Lite! What flavor would you like today?"

I smiled at her and continued to ponder the flavors.

"For today, I highly recommend the banana-carrot ice cream! We also have the all-time favorite, chocolate ice cream, but it's not just normal chocolate, mind you! This one is mixed with crushed Oreo and KitKat! If you don't like chocolate though, I can also recommend . . ."

I tuned her out and simply stared at her mouth as she continued to talk at the speed of light.

*Seriously? What is wrong with her? Is she high or something?*

"And we also have our special purple yam-flavored ice cream which comes with sprinkles!" she finished with a wide grin on her face.

I had to admit, it was impressive how she managed to say all the different flavors without skipping a beat. I must have looked like an idiot for just standing there and saying nothing.

She glanced behind me and cleared her throat. "Sir, would you like more time to decide? I could call the next customer and come back to you afterward?"

I snapped back to reality, dumbly pointing to a random flavor.

"Ah, melon-flavored ice cream! Coming right up!" the girl exclaimed.

I blinked. *Melon?*

"Excuse me . . . ," someone said to me from behind.

I turned around and was glad to see a familiar face. As soon as my eyes met Ryan's, I immediately hugged him in greeting.

Ryan laughed and patted my back.

"What a coincidence to see you here!" I said.

He chuckled. "Same goes for you. What are you doing here?"

"Getting ice cream. Duh."

The girl called my attention and handed me my ice cream.

I grimaced when I realized it was actually melon-flavored. I hated melon.

Ryan frowned. "I thought you don't like melon."

I sighed, contemplating whether to throw the ice cream or just eat it.

*Why is there even melon-flavored ice cream in the first place? It doesn't even taste good at all.*

"How about you, sir? What would you like?" the girl asked Ryan.

Ryan tilted his head, pondering the choices.

I rolled my eyes. Every time ice cream was involved, he got all serious as if he were contemplating the next evolutionary phase of mankind. At least he didn't choose a random flavor, unlike me.

"Hmmm, I think I'll go for vanilla. Make that two, please."

I looked at him in confusion. "Two ice creams?"

He shrugged. "One for you and one for me."

I smiled at him in gratitude. He was such a good friend. Sometimes I wonder why he even puts up with me. I wasn't exactly best friend material.

As soon as Ryan got his two ice creams, he gave me the other one while I threw the melon one in the nearest trash can. Ryan led me to a two-seater table, and we sat across from each other.

I was about to start licking my ice cream when Ryan said something.

59

"So how have you been? We haven't seen each other for what, four years?"

I shook my head. "Three, actually."

"Close enough."

I grinned. "Speaking of not seeing each other . . . What's up with you? I haven't seen you in so many years, Ryan, and yet here we are meeting twice within a few days."

"Yeah, I was actually at your university that day, attending a free seminar. I thought I'd grab a bite before I go home. Then I found out that for a minimal library fee, I could access your computer engineering theses. For some unknown and possibly ironic reasons, some of them haven't been digitized, so they're not available online. And who knows, I might have even met some cute boys too."

Ryan Roberts was as funny as ever. He didn't change much . . . well, except for his body. Back in high school, he was this lanky emo guy who always got As and Bs in Algebra and Calculus. Now his physique had undergone a drastic change. His shoulders were broader, his chest firm and toned. He sported a slight tan, and his face was more chiseled. His usually long bangs were trimmed into a more flattering fringe that fell just above his right eyebrow. The emo look he once wore was gone, replaced by manlier appearance that reminded me of a certain someone I was currently trying to avoid.

"How about you? You haven't answered my question. How have you been, Kei?"

"My life's been kinda . . . difficult. I can't say I'm content with it right now," I muttered as I stared at my now melting ice cream.

"Yeah, I kinda expected that. Being married to a wealthy guy must've been hard for you."

I looked up. "What?"

He smiled. "Don't you remember the last time we saw each other at McDonald's? You were there with Mr. Langlois."

I winced. I was so preoccupied with my current problem at hand that I had completely forgotten about the last time I bumped into Ryan. I could feel myself pale at the events that happened after we hugged, when Jace told him, and everyone, that we were married.

"He was jealous of me right?" Ryan asked.

"What makes you say that?" I asked and shifted uncomfortably in my seat.

I took a bite of ice cream to give the impression that the question didn't bother me at all. It failed. Ryan didn't seem to buy my casual act one bit.

"Because no one glares daggers at someone for catching up with a friend, then announces their marriage to the public like that."

*No,* I thought with an ironic smile. *No one but Jace.*

"Sorry," Ryan quickly apologized when he noticed my expression. "It's not my place. I figured your relationship with Mr. Langlois was a private matter even if he announced it like that . . . ," he trailed off before he shifted topics. "You mentioned earlier that things have been difficult. Are you alright?" he asked with concern.

I let out a sigh and before I knew it, I was sharing anything and everything that had bothered me so far. From my pent-up issues with my marriage, to the time Jace had a fever then made me his personal slave, and to the day I finally ran away and went to the triplets' apartment.

Ryan opened his mouth, about to say something when his phone suddenly rang. He gave me an apologetic look, and I nodded.

He smiled and picked up the call.

"Hello? Yes this is Ryan Roberts . . . What? Really?

He went silent for several minutes, just listening and nodding.

"Yes, ma'am! Oh, thank you so much! I'll be there. Okay, bye!"

He hung up, his face lit up with excitement.

I raised a brow. "You look happy."

Ryan, much to my surprise, pumped his fist in the air. Okay, I was now even more curious on what happened and what that call was about.

"So who was on the phone?" I asked curiously.

Ryan looked at me with a wide grin which greatly resembled the Joker.

"Kei, I got accepted!"

I frowned. *What was he talking about?* "Accepted to what exactly?"

He rolled his eyes as if he was annoyed that I was unable to guess right off the bat.

"I sent an internship application a few weeks back, and I thought I would never get picked, but guess what?"

"What?"

"I got accepted! They just scheduled me for an interview tomorrow! Isn't that cool?" he exclaimed which earned him a few curious looks from the other customers in the shop.

I smiled at him. "That's awesome. What company did you apply in? I could go with you tomorrow if you like."

His eyes twinkled. "You sure? That would be great, thanks!"

I nodded. "So anyway, what's the name of the company?"

"Langlois Incor—" he said, and his excited grin quickly fell when he suddenly put two and two together. "Oh!"

The atmosphere of the conversation suddenly shifted.

I groaned. I should have been more careful about venting my problems with Jace. Now it's coming back to bite me in the ass.

Ryan flailed his hands in a gesture to diffuse the tension.

"I swear, man! I didn't know! I sent my request long before our meeting at McDonald's!"

I ignored him. I was internally panicking.

*What should I do? I already promised to go with him for his interview tomorrow, and knowing him, he wouldn't handle it well if I suddenly change my mind. But I also don't want to see Jace again! What if we bump into each other there? That would be crazy! Not to mention, awkward.*

"It's fine if you don't want to go with me. Really, it is," Ryan assured me, but I didn't believe him.

I knew he would be crestfallen if I wasn't there with him for this big opportunity. After all, not anyone can get an internship position at Langlois Incorporated.

"Don't worry about it." I forced a smile. "I'll go with you."

He didn't look convinced. "Are you sure?"

"I'm sure."

# CHAPTER TWELVE
## Bathroom Encounter

Nothing in this world could stop me from regretting my decision to accompany my high school friend, Ryan, to his interview.

At first, I thought I was just being paranoid. I seriously doubted I would encounter Jace in a vast building bustling with people. However, after Ryan told me that the secretary he spoke to emphasized his attendance because he would be interviewed by Jace, I began to suspect some orchestration. *I mean, what CEO interviews internship applicants?* The chances of seeing him suddenly spiked by two hundred percent, and I knew I had to keep my guard up.

"You know, judging by the way you're acting. It makes it seem like you're the one who's going for the interview and not me," Ryan whispered in my ear.

I didn't bother to acknowledge him, but instead, looked down on the floor.

After confirming his appointment with the receptionist, Ryan and I took a seat on the plush waiting lounge chairs in the building's main lobby. It was my first time inside Jace's workplace. The building was incredibly tall and expansive that even the main lobby could fit several apartments. From the outside, it appeared to have about thirty to forty floors, more or less.

Ryan nudged me gently. "Hey, don't worry. You don't have to be here with me. You can go home if you want. I'll be fine by myself."

I frowned. "No, I made a promise, and I'm gonna keep it. For your sake."

Despite the concern in his eyes, Ryan gave a grateful smile.

I returned the smile, although it felt forced, and glanced around. Behind the counter a few feet from us, were three receptionists. They appeared busy, all engrossed in phone conversations while typing rapidly on their keyboards.

"Mr. Roberts?" a female voice called our attention.

Ryan and I looked up simultaneously to face a very professional-looking woman who appeared to be in her mid-forties. She looked beautiful, elegant even. Ryan stood up and wiped his sweaty palms on the back pockets of his slacks.

"You are Mr. Ryan Roberts?" she asked.

"Yeah, I mean, yes. Yes, I am Ryan Roberts."

I chuckled inwardly at his stuttering He was totally nervous about the interview. The elegant woman extended her hand to shake Ryan's.

"I am Diana Morris, Mr. Langlois' secretary. I'm here to escort you to his office for the interview."

Ryan nodded. "I'm Ryan Roberts. Thank you for escorting me, and it's a pleasure to meet you."

Diana was about to lead Ryan away when she noticed me.

I gulped. *Oh no, does she know who I am?*

"And you are?" Diana asked.

I was about to answer when a phone rang, causing Diana to take her phone out from her pocket.

I sighed in relief. *Whew, that was close.*

Diana pressed the phone to her ear. "Yes, sir . . . yes, he's with me right now . . . we're on our way."

Hearing the word *sir* sent goose bumps down my skin. She must be talking to Jace on the phone. After the phone call ended, Diana smiled and gestured at Ryan to follow her.

Ryan faced me and gave an apologetic smile. "Hey, I have to go for the interview now? I'll catch up with you later?"

I nodded. "Good luck on your interview."

He nodded in return and followed Diana, standing a few feet away and watching me intently. As she led the way to the bank of elevators, I glanced around once more and decided to wait outside, in a small garden area. Unfortunately, my bladder suddenly felt like it was about to explode, so I hurried to the nearest bathroom, conveniently located right across the cluster of elevators where Ryan and Diana had disappeared.

I had no idea why it feel like I was heading toward my impending doom. At this time of the day, there was no reason for Jace to be anywhere the reception area of his building, let alone its facilities. Nonetheless, I still let out a sigh of relief when upon finding the bathroom was empty. After relieving myself, I went to the sink and wash my hands.

While drying my hands with a paper towel, I checked myself in the mirror and muttered to my reflection, "Oh yeah, I have to do grocery shopping. Might picked up some food for the triplets as well . . . God knows what those triplets eat with their empty fridge."

"Won't you need a ride for that then?" a very familiar voice sounded from behind.

My eyes widened as I stared straight into Jace's eyes through the mirror. My heart almost ripped itself out of my rib cage at the sight of him. I felt terrified yet giddy at the same time, for reasons I couldn't explain. All I knew was that I wasn't ready to face him. Hell, I wasn't prepared to be near his presence alone.

Through the mirror, I saw him move to stand beside me, casually turning the faucet on to wash his hands.

I gulped. *What will he do to me? Is he mad? Furious?*

Discreetly, I observed him through the mirror. Unsurprisingly, he looked as sharp as ever in that expensive suit of his. Any type of outfit would look better on him than those worn by models in fashion magazines.

He didn't look worried though. He acted as if nothing was wrong with my actions, as if running away from him wasn't a big deal at all. It had been three or four days since then, and he hadn't once tried to contact me. I wondered if he had looked for me or hired someone to search for me.

*I didn't even get a message or a phone call . . .*

I grimaced at my thoughts. Why the hell should I even care if he searched for me or not? Him not doing anything to find me was actually what I wanted, right? I hated my brain sometimes. It always had to betray me at some point.

"You seem troubled. What's on your mind?" Jace suddenly asked, snapping me back to the situation at hand.

I glared at his reflection. "None of your business."

Jace clicked his tongue. "Not even a *comment allez-vous?*"[10]

I angrily faced him but quickly regretted it when I saw him smirk in amusement.

*Oh, now he finds me amusing? What an asshole.*

"Just shut up."

Jace suddenly frowned and kept quiet. I ignored him and was about to walk out the bathroom when he grabbed my arm and forced me to face him.

"What the hell?" I yelled at him.

"Why are you here?"

I glared. "It's none of your business. Let me go!"

Instead of doing what I said, he only gripped my arm tighter. I winced, I was certain that was gonna leave a red mark.

"Why. Are. You. Here?" Jace asked again.

---

[10] How are you?

67

His tone was so low and dangerous that I wanted to escape and never look back. I gulped, mentally scolding myself for showing fear of what Jace might do to me.

"I-I came here with Ryan . . . for-for his interview," I said.

The expression in his eyes darkened at this, but immediately reverted back to normal as he let my arm go. I stumbled and rubbed my now aching arm.

Just as Jace was about to say something, the phone in his pocket rang. Quickly, he fished it out.

"Yes, I'll be there," he said coolly and hung up.

Curiosity got the better of me, and I couldn't help but ask, "Who was that?"

Jace sighed. "My secretary. It's time for the interview. Whatever you're doing here, don't bother to try and follow me."

I rolled my eyes. "Oh, trust me. I wouldn't follow you if it's the last thing I do."

I expected him to snap back at me for this, but instead, he just sighed and opened the door. Taking it as a sign that the conversation was over, I went out. As we both exited the restroom, another thought came to mind.

"Why are you even here anyway? Don't you have your own private restroom in your executive suite?"

I had never been to his office before, but I imagined that as a CEO, you wouldn't use common facilities where you might have to wait in line just to wash your hands.

He gave me a brief glance before he playfully replying, "None of your business, *mon beau*."[11]

I gritted my teeth in annoyance, resisting the urge to strangle him in public. After all, I didn't want to be accused of assaulting Jace Langlois and seeing my face plastered all over the news. Instead, I took a deep breath, huffed once, and walked away from the one man I never wanted to see again.

---

[11] My handsome.

Just as I was about to turn away from him, Jace seemed to recall something and strode toward me with a menacing glint in his eyes.

I blinked, taking a few cautious steps back. The urge to bolt surged through me, but my legs felt like lead. Before I could react to his grip on my waist—whether with a scream or a punch—I was silenced by the one thing that made me want to do the latter.

He kissed me.

# CHAPTER THIRTEEN
## I Hate You

Saying I was taken aback would be putting it mildly. It felt like all the muscles in my entire body froze in shock. Jace had already released my lips before I could even react. I looked at him with dazed eyes, still reeling from the shock of what just happened. He smirked and ruffled my hair before striding toward the elevators, likely heading to his office floor. I stood there, dumbfounded, watching him until he disappeared from sight.

"Freaking hell," I muttered to myself as I brushed my lips gently with an index finger.

This was probably the first time that Jace and I had ever kissed. During our "wedding," if we can call it that, we merely signed a couple of papers, and he handed me a ring like a candy to a child, already wearing his own.

Another realization hit me—Jace still had my ring. I had thrown it at him before I ran away . . . I shook my head. *What do I care if he returned it or not?* Our marriage was only on paper; the rings weren't necessary.

With that thought, I returned to the seating area and sat down to wait for Ryan to return, hopefully with good news.

\*       \*       \*

*One and a half hour later . . .*

"Kei!"

I snapped out of my nap and blinked a few times before I saw Ryan making his way toward me. I just realized that I had fallen asleep while waiting for him.

"How was it?" I asked and stood up.

He stopped in front of me. "Well . . ."

I frowned. "What happened?"

I sincerely hoped that it wasn't bad or that Jace hadn't tried to hurt my friend; otherwise, he would have to deal with this building being burned to the ground along with him in it.

"What's up with that expression?" Ryan asked, concerned.

My face must have looked like I was planning for a murder, ready to unleash my wrath upon Jace at a moment's notice.

I blinked and immediately relaxed. "Nothing."

Ryan hummed and started walking toward the exit, and I followed suit.

"So, what happened during your interview?" I asked again.

He seemed sheepish and confused as he scratched his head.

"Well, he sort of . . . threatened me?" he finished, sounding unsure, as if he himself couldn't believe it.

My eyes widened. "What?"

He stepped back from me at once and raised both hands, as if afraid I would lash out at him.

"Woah woah, easy there . . . it's just . . . you know . . ."

I scoffed at his reaction. I had every right to be mad if my husband was making casual threats to my friends like this. In fact, I felt the urge to march back there and give him a piece of my mind.

Whether it was my expression or caution, Ryan grabbed my arm to stop me before he let out a heavy sigh.

"Look," he began, sighing again. "Mr. Langlois just told me to uh . . . stayawayfromyou," he muttered quickly, making the last part incoherent.

"What?" I snapped, growing impatient.

71

"Oh, come on!" he exclaimed, exasperated. "Don't make me say it again!"

"Just say it," I insisted, feeling entitled to an answer.

He groaned. "Ugh, fine! He told me to stay away from you!"

My jaw dropped. What the flipping hell? Jace said that to Ryan? My best friend, of all people?

In that split-second, my nerves snap, and I made my decision. All the rage I felt toward him bubbled in the pit of my stomach, threatening to spill out. Everything he had done to me— treating me like a slave, kissing me without warning—paled in comparion to how he treated my friend. This was the final straw.

"Ryan, stay here. I have something to do," I said as calmly as possible, though the edge in my tone was unmistakable.

Before he could stop me again, I pulled away from his touch and stormed back into the building.

"Wait, what? Kei, stop!" he called out, but it was too late.

I was on a warpath, and I managed to slipped inside the elevator at the last minute. Fortunately, it was empty. I didn't want anyone to be on the receiving end of my anger, and the few employees I did pass quickly stepped aside to let me through.

Despite not knowing what floor Jace's office was on, I immediately pressed the button for the highest level, which was the thirty-third floor. I figured the CEO of the company would have his office nestled at the very top, away from the rest of his employees.

A few minutes passed, and the elevator opened once more. There were a few employees, and some of them stopped what they were doing to give curious glances. I didn't bother acknowledging them. My eyes zeroed in on a dark wooden door at the end of the hallway. It had a tempered glass on the center with Jace's name etched in gold letters.

My blood practically boiled as I stormed toward the door. Without hesitation, I pushed open the door without bothering to knock. Jace's secretary—the same woman who had led Ryan to the interview—immediately stood up from her desk as soon as she saw me. Behind her, I knew was the devil himself.

"Excuse me, do you have an appoint—" she started but stopped when she realized I wasn't going to stop in my tracks. "Oh," she said, sounding like she had come to a conclusion.

I opened the second door and slammed it close behind me, making sure to lock it so she wouldn't barge inside. I turned around and immediately faced Jace, who was sitting casually on his chair without a care in the world.

"Kei, what are you doing here?" he asked with disinterest.

The intercom on his desk beeped, and automatically, his secretary's worried voice echoed in the room.

"Sir, are you alright? I'm not sure, but I think—"

"Everything is fine, Diana. Continue your work." Jace turned off his intercom and leaned his elbows on his desk before he rested his chin on his hands. "What brings you here, *mon beau?*"

I stormed toward his desk and slammed both my palms on the surface. "Don't give me that crap talk, asshole! Why did you threaten Ryan to stay away from me?"

He raised an eyebrow. "What are you talking about? I didn't do anything."

I gritted my teeth at his fake innocent act and slammed my hands again, letting a few papers spill over to the floor.

"Didn't do anything, my ass! I didn't realize that threatening intern applicants was a part of your interview process," I said with venomous sarcasm.

His entitlement due his wealth was suffocating. Just because he was a billionaire didn't mean he had the right to threaten anyone without consequences. It was disgusting.

Jace sighed tiredly. "I didn't threaten him. I just told him to stop getting close to you."

"That's not what he said to me earlier."

He mockingly gasped, and clutched his chest in exaggeration. "And you believe him more than your own *époux*?[12] *Je suis triste.*"[13]

I rolled my eyes at his antics. His attractive French accent wasn't going to quell my rage, even though I had a thing for French men when we first met. This was a serious matter, and his money and attractiveness weren't going to excuse his behavior.

The thought that I was even remotely attracted to him made me gag now. *How could I feel attracted to him now?* Even when he spoke to me in French, I always felt like I was beneath him, and he knew that I wasn't fluent enough to understand every single word he said.

I pointed a finger at him. "Shut up."

Much to my frustration, he grinned. "It feels like déjà vu."

"You know what? Fuck you. I'm leaving."

There was no point in trying to argue with someone who wasn't going to listen to you. I just came here to let him know that he wasn't going to threaten my friend without me standing up for him. No way.

As I stepped away from his desk and was ready to turn around, he called out, "Wait."

He stood up from his chair and walked over to me.

I stepped away, my fight-or-flight response kicking in. Instinct warned me to be cautious about what he might do next. Suddenly, the image of his lips on mine from earlier replayed in my mind, and I felt myself freeze.

Jace stopped a few inches in front of me, his lips mere inches away from mine. He was close enough that I could feel his minty breath fanning over my face. Then, he put his hand inside his suit pocket and fished out something.

I looked down, and on his finger was the wedding ring he hadn't taken off since that day, not even after I left. The light from

---

[12] Husband.
[13] I am sad.

outside seemed to peek into the room, reflecting off the silver band. He opened his palm, and sitting on it was my own wedding ring. He grabbed my left hand, and much to my utter surprise, gently slipped the ring on my ring finger.

I looked up and saw him smirk.

"You need to have a ring on your finger before you go outside, *mon beau*," he said cheekily.

I scowled and snatched my hand away from his grasp. Why I didn't bother to rip that ring off and throw it at his smirking face again, I'll never know . . .

"I hate you," I said instead as I started to walk away from him toward the door.

Just before I could open the door, he called out once more, "Kei."

I turned around impatiently. "What?"

He smiled. "See you back at home."

Unexpectedly, and for reasons I will never understand, my heart skipped a beat.

# CHAPTER FOURTEEN
## Welcome Home


"You sure you're gonna be fine, Kei? I still don't think you're ready to go back to . . . you know," Summer asked in concern.

I didn't answer and instead just gave her a tight hug, grateful that she cared so much. Earlier today, I told her and her brothers that I would be heading back to Jace's place, she had been worried about whether or not I would be okay.

To be honest, I wasn't even sure myself. I held out another day before returning home to Jace, and I still didn't have the answer as to why I decided to go back, especially knowing Jace would just revert to his old, evil ways of torturing me with endless chores and whatnot. Maybe I felt guilty with bumming around, or maybe there was a part of me that wanted to see where this was going.

I briefly wondered if I was a masochist . . .

"Dude, if something happens, you know who to call." Autumn clapped me on my back, strong enough to make me stumble forward and nearly fall on the sidewalk.

I gave him a smile in return and replied cheekily, "Yup, 911."

Summer chuckled while Winter tried not to smile too widely. Even though I knew I would see them around the university, I couldn't help but feel emotional. They were such great friends.

"I'm serious, man. If that lousy douchebag ever does anything to you again, don't hesitate to call me," Autumn said seriously.

"Yeah, yeah," I replied.

Summer hugged me again. This time even tighter than before which nearly made me lose my breath. Fortunately, Winter pulled her away from me.

I nodded to him in gratitude.

"I'll see you around," I said and waved goodbye, just in time for a sleek black car to pull up right by the sidewalk where we all waited.

A man in a black suit, whom I recognized as one of Jace's bodyguards, got out of the driver's seat and walked around the vehicle to open the door for me. I felt a slight disappointment that Jace hadn't picked me up himself.

The triplets waved. "See you! Take care!"

I got inside the car, and the driver closed the door for me. Without another word, he went back to his seat and drove me to Jace's house in silence.

*　　　*　　　*

"Welcome home," Jace greeted me at the front door of his huge house.

I rolled my eyes and walked past him into the familiar-looking living room. As I gazed at the maroon-colored couch, I noticed that its matching cushions were tossed and scattered around the white carpet. Wondering how the kitchen might look, I sighed inwardly at the housework waiting for me.

I looked at him with a raised brow. "What did you do to the house while I was gone?"

He merely shrugged and instead strutted toward me to ruffle my hair.

I swatted his hand away with a scowl. "Stop that!"

"What?" he asked innocently before giving me a devilish grin. "Old habits die hard."

"Uh huh, sure," I replied dryly.

I headed toward the long staircase with the intricately designed railings and went straight to my room—or rather, our room. Opening the door, I was immediately greeted by Jace's familiar musky scent, as well as the mess that was his belongings. The bed wasn't even made.

"Miss the bedroom? We can have some fun if you want," Jace teased in a low and sultry voice behind me.

I resisted the urge to smack him and ignored him instead. I went to the bed and sat on my side of the mattress.

"The silent treatment, eh? I can live with that," he said as his weight caused the mattress to dip from his side.

I stood up and made my way to the bathroom. Perhaps a shower was what I needed. A thought stopped me in my tracks.

"Hey," I called out and slowly turned around to face him.

Jace merely looked at me, his expression already bored.

"If you think that I'm just going to go back to following your every command, then you can go fuck yourself. I'm no one's pathetic servant, especially not yours. If you ever treat me as weak or worthless, then kiss this marriage goodbye." I ignored the sudden image of his lips on mine at the word 'kiss' and continued, "I also have the right to make my own decisions. You cannot order me around simply because you're Jace Langlois. You may be the boss of thousands of people in your empire, but you're not the boss of me. We're husbands, and I expect you to fully understand that we have to treat each other as equals. Got it?"

It felt good to finally let those words out. Sure, we may never have the most loving marriage in the world, but there should at least be some level of decency here. My words may be harsh, but I was speaking from the heart. I really do wanted to make this work.

My fists clenched at the memory of my mother's note that came with the small glass marble. *I had to.*

Jace merely stared at me, and it felt like an eternity. The dark look in his eyes made me nervous about what he could possibly be thinking.

*Were my words really that harsh?* I supposed I would have to deal with the consequences, but I don't regret saying them. I had to stand my ground, and I refuse to let him boss around me for fun. Those days were over.

Jace got up and took a few steps toward me, making me involuntarily flinch. He stopped a few inches from where I stood as I continue to look into those dark eyes.

"*Ça va. C'est bien,*"[14] he finally said with a nod.

I frowned. "Fine, what?"

He sighed in exasperation, and I couldn't help but smirk.

He groaned. "I meant that I'll comply to your wishes, and I'll try not to give you a hard time from now on."

I crossed my arms over my chest. "Say you're sorry."

Jace scrunched his nose like I just asked him to eat slugs. "I won't."

I rolled my eyes. *Prideful as ever, but hey, it was worth the shot.*

I figured that was the end of it. Now that we had come to an understanding, I really hoped there wouldn't be any more problems coming our way. I could only take so much drama and struggles in my life.

"Now that that's settled," Jace announced as he headed to his closet, "change into something formal."

I blinked. "Why? Where are we going?"

"I want you to meet a few acquaintances of mine."

"And who are they?" The curiosity was getting to me.

"Just some close friends," he said vaguely.

I scoffed. *Acquaintances? Friends?* "Is it too much to ask for some details? Geez . . ."

"*Dépêchez-vous.*[15] The party starts at seven."

---

[14] Okay. It's good.

I glanced at the digital clock on the bedside table. My eyes widened when I realized that it was already six-thirty.

I turned back to Jace and realized the reason he looked freshly showered and attired. From the closet, he emerged holding an expensive-looking suit. It was a slim-fitting black suit with a matching dress shirt with a gray collar. The jacket featured a short silver chain link that dangled from the front pocket, accentuating the exquisite stitching tastefully.

"When did you buy this?" I asked, stunned at how a suit could look so expensive yet subtle.

Jace shrugged. "Not too long ago. Now hurry up and go change. I'll be waiting for you downstairs," he said, placing the clothes on the bed before he left.

I watched the suit for a minute, still stunned at the fabric, stitching, and everything about it, before snapping back to reality. The idiot didn't even give me the courtesy of time to shower. Hurrying up, I stripped off my clothes and changed into the suit. Afterward, I spritzed some *Eau de Vert Eau de Parfum*, a wedding present from Jace.

After fixing my hair for a couple of minutes, I hurried downstairs and was met by the person who had picked me up from school. I knew he was one of Jace's bodyguards, but the fact that I still didn't know his name embarrassed me, even though I have been living here for almost as long as I have been married.

"Mr. Langlois is already in the car, sir. Please allow me to escort you there," he said formally.

I just nodded and let him lead the way.

It wasn't the same black car earlier. This time it was a sleek black limousine that waited at the front steps. I resisted the urge to just stand there and admire the vehicle, knowing Jace was in a hurry.

---

[15] Hurry up.

Carefully stepping inside as the bodyguard opened the door for me, I was stunned by the interior, which alone made my jaw drop.

I was vaguely aware that Jace had a limosine, but I had never seen it before. Trust Jace Langlois to get a limousine with the finest interior—luxurious carpet, wood-trim features, and plush leather-upholstered seats.

*I could live here . . .* I thought in awe.

My eyes landed on a Jace, who was already seated inside. A smirk was apparent on his face, and I quickly deduced it was because he saw me practically drooling over the interior of the limo.

Not long after I took a seat, the bodyguard settled beside the driver behind the wheel, who activated the privacy panel before driving off. No Harry this time, just his bodyguards whose names I didn't know. It would be a few more days before the house staff returned to work, but at least Lucy would be coming back in the morning.

I couldn't help but glance at Jace and his attire. Even though I hated his guts, there was still one thing I liked about him: he could wear a suit so well. We had been married for nearly a year, and strangely enough, I never tired seeing him in one. The suit he wore now resembled mine, but the jacket's front pocket lacked a chain. The dress shirt underneath was also black, with a white collar. As usual, he filled out the suit impeccably, looking like he was born to wear it, while I felt awkward in mine. Despite its slim fit, I probably looked like a random kid playing dress-up next to him, and I couldn't help but feel envious.

"So where exactly are we going?" I managed to ask.

"You'll see."

# CHAPTER FIFTEEN
## Ralph . . . What?

After what felt like forever, the limousine finally stopped at the Luxuria, one of the five-star hotels in the city. The bodyguard made it a point of opening the door for us. Stepping out of the vehicle and through the revolving door into the lobby, my jaw instantly dropped at the opulence of it all.

I raised my eyes to the ceiling and beheld a large chandelier at its center, its brilliance in gold tone and crystal glory enhancing the grandeur of the place.

Unlike me, Jace didn't seem to care and simply led us through the lobby. The confidence in his strides led me to believe that this wasn't his first time here, and judging from the respectful nods from the concierge and other front desk associates, I was right.

We continued to walk in silence until we approached a pair of double doors, where a couple of attendants stationed at the entrance pushed them open for us. What I saw beyond the doors made me want to run away again.

Here I was, an average college student nobody, while beyond those doors were several members of high society: women in gorgeous ball gowns and men in designer suits, socializing around the hall. I wondered what sort of event was drawing the elites of the city to the grand ballroom of the Luxuria tonight.

"What the hell is this place?" I whispered at Jace.

Jace looped my right arm around his elbow, causing me to flinch. I looked at him curiously.

"Ask questions later. For now, just behave," he ordered.

I was about to retort when three people approached us: two men and a woman. The men wore expensive tailored suits, while the woman was dressed in a dark red gown with a thigh-high slit.

*"Bonsoir, Monsieur Langlois. Comment allez-vous?"*[16] greeted one of the men.

Jace smiled. *"Très bien, merci."*[17]

*"Qui pourrait vous être?"*[18] The woman looked at me curiously.

I gave a sheepish smile. *How the hell am I supposed to answer her?* While my understanding of the language was improving, I couldn't speak French—I couldn't form sentences. Much to my relief, Jace came to my rescue.

*"C'est mon mari. Il s'appelle Kei,"*[19] Jace said.

On second thought, I could have just told her my name, sans description.

Both men took turns shaking my hand, all the while continuing their conversation in French. I merely smiled at them, congratulating myself for understanding some of the words they uttered, even though some flew over my head.

While they talked, I accepted a glass of cocktail and some canapés from the waiters in white tuxedos who were walking around, carrying silver trays of refreshments—water, champagne, various types of hors d'oeuvres, and anything else the guests desired.

*To hell with being rude. I'm a growing boy attending school, and I'm hungry as fuck.*

After Jace's acquaintances left, I thought that would be the end of it, but the woman remained. Her expression of disgust

---

[16] Good evening, Mr. Langlois. How are you?
[17] Very well, thank you.
[18] Who could you be?
[19] This is my husband. His name is Kei.

caused my smile to fade. When I raised a questioning brow at her, she left in a huff.

I tugged at Jace's sleeve. "What were you talking about?"

I was not paying attention to what they were saying, and I continued to pretend to Jace know that I don't know his language.

Jace sighed. "They just asked about you."

"And what did you say?"

"I said, 'This is Kei, and he's a drag queen.'" He winked mischievously.

I pretended to gasp and pinched his arm repeatedly. "You did not!"

Instead of wincing in pain, he merely laughed it off.

"I was kidding. I told them that you're my husband."

I knew what I had heard earlier, but for unknown reasons, for a moment, I could have sworn that I stopped breathing. My heart felt frozen in place, and yet, I couldn't help but feel . . . warm?

I frowned again. *Why am I feeling this way?*

"Are you hungry?" Jace asked, and as if on cue, my stomach rumbled, and I blushed.

Jace chuckled. Just as he was about to signal for one of the waiters carrying hors d'oeuvres, dinner was announced. We were guided to our assigned table, where conversations in French continued, although some of them were conducted in low voices, making eavesdropping impossible. Tuning out everything else, I focused my senses on the food.

After the four-course dinner, I was beginning to feel disappointed by the lack of after-dinner sweets when Jace led me to an impressive spread of delicious-looking dessert. The sight of the chocolate fountain immediately won my attention.

Without even thinking, I pointed to it. "I want that one."

Jace looked at the fountain skeptically. "Chocolate?"

I stubbornly shook my head and unclasped my hold on Jace's arm before heading straight to the chocolate fountain, the dark liquid and luscious fruits making my mouth water. Tempted to have a taste, I reached for a dessert teaspoon displayed on the table, but stopped when another hand reached and beat me to it.

I looked over to see who it was, and there stood a man as equally tempting as the chocolate. To say that he was gorgeous would be an understatement, and like any idiot, I stood frozen on my spot.

*"Qui es-tu?"*[20] he asked in the deepest and richest voice I had ever heard in my entire life.

I couldn't speak, much less understand what he said so I probably looked like a zombie.

*"Es-tu seul? Ou avec quelqu'un?"*[21]

Finally, I snapped from the trance I was in and immediately shook my head. "Uhm, I . . . I don't speak French, sorry," I said sheepishly.

I was embarrassed beyond relief and was about to tell him who I was with when I realized Jace was not at my side.

Subtly, I searched for Jace, but he was nowhere in sight. Nervously, I wiped my hands on the back of my pants. Feeling disappointed and angry that he had left me hanging out to dry, I couldn't help but mentally plan a murder attempt on my husband.

*So much for a fresh start on our marriage. Seriously, why didn't he even tell me about this gathering of rich people in the first place? And what's with all the French people? Doesn't anybody speak English?*

"Kei!"

I sighed in relief when I saw Jace coming our way, but that did nothing to relieve my disappointment and rage when he simply ignored the deadliest glare I could muster. Jace was staring at the man beside me who grinned at his presence.

*"Copain,"*[22] Jace!"

---

[20] Who are you?
[21] Are you alone? Or with someone?
[22] Friend/buddy.

Jace nodded and put an arm around my waist. However, when I looked at him again, he didn't bother to acknowledge my existence and instead engaged in conversation with the other man in French.

"*Ça fait longtemps, mon frère!*"[23]

"*Comment allez-vous, Ralph?*"[24]

"*J'ai été bon. Comment l'entreprise fait?*"[25]

I mentally groaned in annoyance. *Is it too much to ask for some of them to speak English for once in their rich lives? Escpecially when I'm still slow on the uptake.*

Jace shrugged and tightened his hold on my waist.

The man noticed Jace's gesture and smirked.

"*Bon á savoir. Est-ce votre secrétaire?*[26]" the man teased.

Jace scoffed and glared at the man in front of us.

"Oh, shut up. *Tu sais très bien qui il est.*[27] This is Kei. I've told you this a million times already. *Je t'ai même envoyé des photos.*[28] Kei, this is Ralph Faucher."

I tilted my head. *Photos what?* "Ralph . . . what?"

Suddenly, Ralph let out a loud laugh, catching the attention of nearly everyone around us. It lasted for a few moments before they eventually returned to whatever they were doing, after figuring out that it was nothing serious.

"I apologize for my behavior earlier, *mon minou.*[29] I am Ralph Faucher, Jace's older brother. I thought I would introduce myself when my brother was not doing his job," Ralph said with a toothy grin.

---

[23] It's been a long time, my brother!

[24] How are you, Ralph?

[25] I've been well. How is the company doing?

[26] Good to know. Is this your secretary?

[27] You know very well who he is.

[28] I've even sent you photos.

[29] My sweetie/darling/kitty/kitty cat.

His French accent was very thick, but I could still understand every word, causing my eyes to nearly popped out of their sockets.

*Wait, what? Jace's brother?*

"You have a brother?" I asked Jace in disbelief. *And you've told him about me and sent him my photos while I got nothing!*

Jace sighed and pinched the bridge of his nose with his thumb and index finger, as if he was already getting tired of the situation. Nevertheless, I was curious and waited for him to start explaining.

*Why had Jace never told me he had a brother, and if they really are brothers, then why couldn't I see any resemblance?*

"Jace," I demanded, already growing impatient.

Ralph clapped Jace's back with enough force to make Jace and me stumble forward slightly.

"Ralph is my older brother. He's a doctor in Strasbourg," Jace explained nonchalantly.

Ralph nodded enthusiastically. "*Oui, oui!* It's a city in France, *mon minou.*"

I gave him a skeptical look. He seemed overly hyperactive and enthusiastic, which made it hard to believe . . . he was older than Jace.

"But why is his last name . . . ," I trailed off, not bothering to mention his surname.

I could not even remember what it was, much less attempt to say it. Meanwhile, the brothers were talking again, and I caught the words hospital, going on vacation, and I think asking Jace to stay with us in our house. Jace answered with an adamant no, reminding him of his big empty house. Ralph replied that was exactly why he wanted to stay with us, because it was empty.

Until Jace loosened his hold on my waist and shoved Ralph away, I didn't even notice he was getting too close for comfort. Ralph seemed intent on lingering in our space until he finally gave up and left, but not before mentioning that he'll see us again soon.

Jace merely ignored him.

Once he was out of earshot, Jace turned to me and explained, "His last name is Faucher, and technically, he's my stepbrother. He's my mother's son from her first marriage, where his father tragically died during a bank robbery on the day Ralph was born. She loved him dearly, so much so that even after she married to my father and he legally adopted Ralph, she didn't want to change his last name."

I blinked and nodded. It was my first time learning about his family's history. I had met Jace's parents a few times before our marriage, but during our wedding, there was no attempt at making connenctions. They were kind and decent people, especially Jace's mom, which made it hard to believe that she had such a tragic past. It made me feel sorry for her, and to an extent, I felt somewhat sorry for Ralph as well.

"How come you never talk about these kinds of things?" I finally muttered after what seemed like a while.

"I thought it wouldn't matter to you, since you were never really fully accepting of our arrangement," he replied, his tone devoid of any emotion.

I looked into his eyes. I wasn't sure what he was feeling exactly, and try as I might to gauge and label some emotion behind his expression, there was only one feeling I could detect but couldn't quite place a finger on. As I continued to look into his eyes, I felt my chest tighten, and I frowned when my heart started to beat rapidly against my chest.

I sucked in a breath, trying my best to ignore that sensation.

As I glanced back into his eyes once more, the same rush of sensations flooded back.

*What the hell was happening to me?*

# CHAPTER SIXTEEN
## We Meet Again

Overall, the entire event was filled with more socializing and more conversations in French, mostly shop talk, which was all the same to me. As I had said before, I had no head for business. Plus, the fact that none of the guests bothered to speak English pissed me off to no end, leaving me in a sour and bored mood for the entire evening.

Jace picked up on that quickly and promptly found a way to excuse us both so we could head home. Despite his tendency to drag me around, it was a thoughtful gesture from him. The night seemed endless when all I wanted to do was to go home and sleep.

The weekend ended soon after and Monday arrived as expected, which means I have to face another day of boring lectures from boring professors. Like clockwork, I woke up early and made Jace breakfast: eggs and bacon—with caviar, of course—while he slept.

After I was finished, I swung my bag over my shoulder and went outside. Today, I didn't bother to use Jace's car, and since Harry wasn't back yet to drive me to school, I opted to ride in the bus instead.

Once I got to my stop, I stepped off the bus and walked toward school's the wrought iron front gates. Despite the bustling presence of cars and students on campus, I paid them no mind, heading directly to the familiar spot where the triplets often hung out before classes. This area, adjacent to the administration building, boasted several species of trees, offering ample shade—a perfect retreat from the sun.

"Kei!" Summer called out the moment she saw me.

I smiled and sat down on the soft green grass beside her. Across from us, Autumn and Winter were busy scribbling notes in their binders.

"What's with them?" I asked Summer.

Summer flipped her hair. "They didn't take notes in philosophy class last week. Luckily, I had some notes and let them copy."

I nodded and observed Autumn and Winter as they worked. Even though we have been friends for a while, the fact that they were so synchronized without effort never failed to amaze me. Their matching brown hair, similar expressions, and identical builds made them look like reflections of each other.

"Winter, stop hogging the notes and scoot closer, will you?" Autumn said in annoyance.

Winter said nothing and merely followed Autumn's wishes so the latter could take a good look at Summer's notes.

As I watched them continue to work, it reminded me of how some people often thought that the two were a bit "too close for comfort." The fact that they were so comfortable with each other often gave people the impression that they were a lot closer than siblings should be, but that wasn't the case at all. They had just grown up relying firmly on each other, a fact that Summer told me a long time ago.

"Sometimes, I get jealous of them," Summer said quietly as she watched her brothers with a smile.

I gave her a side glance. "Why?"

She shrugged. "They always stick together in whatever they do, while I just stay in the shadows and watch them. Sometimes, I feel like they forget about me."

"Now that's where you're wrong. They love you just as much as they love each other, Summer. Trust me," I assured her.

"I know. I'm lucky to have them as my brothers. Well, except for Autumn." She groaned as if she just remembered something horrible.

I smirked. "Why? What did he do?"

Summer threw a heated glare at Autumn, who was totally oblivious to his sister.

"He's messy as hell. He always throws his stinky clothes in my hamper. My hamper, Kei! It's so disgusting. And you know what's worse?"

I shrugged.

"He never changes his toothbrush. Like, the one he's using now hasn't been replaced in years."

I grimaced at that. "Uh, good to know," I muttered dryly.

Summer gave me a goofy grin, and I smiled back.

She was just about to say something else when Autumn's sports watch suddenly beeped, signaling that their first class was about to start. The triplets stood up and waved goodbye to me.

I waved back at them as I sat there alone, watching them leave. Checking my watch, I realized that I had about five minutes before my first class began.

I decided to start walking toward the building when someone said, "*Bonjour, mon minou.*[30] We meet again."

Jace's older brother, Ralph—*something*, greeted me with a dazzling smile. For the life of me, I couldn't remember his last name, except that it was hard to pronounce.

"Do you mind if I sit here with you?" he politely asked.

I forced a smile. "No, I don't mind at all, but I'm actually on my way to class."

---

[30] Good day, sweetie.

Ralph smiled again, his perfectly white teeth on full display. He casually sat beside me on the grass and leaned against the tree behind us.

*"Ce que tu lis?"*[31]

I shook my head apologetically. "Sorry, I don't— I mean, say that again?"

Ralph blinked in surprise. *"Merde!* [32]I am sorry, *mon minou.* I'm not yet fluent in English."

"It's okay. Jace sometimes forgets to speak English as well, so no worries," I assured him, although I couldn't help but regret bringing Jace into this conversation.

"Ah, I see," Ralph said.

An awkward silence fell between us. I wondered what he mean by "Ah, I see." Eventually, I remembered that I needed to head to class, and just as I was about to do so, Ralph grabbed my wrist, stopping me.

"Yes?"

"Do you want to eat lunch with me later? My treat," he offered.

"Uh, I don't know," I replied hesitantly.

I wasn't sure why I was hesitating in the first place. After all, Ralph was Jace's brother. It wasn't like he was some stranger or some sadistic monster like a certain French billionaire I know.

Instead of answering, I asked him a question, "What are you doing here anyway? On campus, that is?"

"Ah! I have people to see here, and hopefully, I will be finished with them before lunch, hence the invitation. What a happy coincidence, is it not, *mon minou,* that I see you here before I head to my meeting? *Alors, qu'est-ce que tu en dis, mon minou?*[33] I promise you will enjoy it. I will take you to any place you want," he reassured.

---

[31] What are you reading?
[32] Shit!
[33] So, what do you say/think about it, sweetie?

After pushing my doubts aside, I slowly nodded.

"Okay, sure."

Ralph grinned widely, making me stare at his perfect teeth again. I knew it was weird and creepy, but I liked how his teeth looked. They were so white and clean.

*"Kei? Mon minou?"*

I snapped back to my senses and gasped when I realized my class had already started. I scrambled to my feet and excused myself from Ralph.

"I'm late for class now. I guess I'll see you . . . later?"

Ralph nodded and ruffled my hair before heading to the administration building. I let out a tired sigh as I hurriedly walked to my first class.

It seemed that even though Jace and Ralph didn't look like brothers, they both shared the same habit of ruffling my hair—a gesture I detested. Another similarity between them was their knack for getting what they wanted, despite my protests.

*Great. Double the trouble.*

# CHAPTER SEVENTEEN
## Lunch Date

JACE

"*Bonjour, mon frère!* Are you busy?"

I groaned when Ralph's obnoxiously cheery voice disturbed my thoughts. I slammed the papers that I was signing onto the table and glared at him as he made himself at home in my office.

He ignored my glare and just flopped down on the black chair in front of my desk.

"Why are you here? Shouldn't you be at your hospital? On vacation like you were talking about? Or in Strasbourg? Get out of here. I'm busy," I grumbled.

Honestly, I didn't have time for him. I had a lot of necessary paperwork to sign, and to make matters worse, Diana had been on my tail about informing our stockholders regarding the next big investment in another company—which, much to my chagrin, must be done within the day.

*Honestly, how in the world was I suppose to manage all that when I wasn't even finished with half of what I was doing?*

Diana could sometimes go overboard in her role as my secretary. Needless to say, I was not in the mood for pleasantries or idle chitchat.

Ralph laughed. "As what the Americans say, *chill*. Get a day off. Relax. Or better yet, take a vacation."

"I don't have time for that. Now, please leave. *Tu me prends la tête*,"[34] I shooed him off.

Ralph sighed. "Suit yourself. I guess Kei and I will have fun by ourselves today."

My eyes widened. *"Qu'est-ce que vous avez dit?"*[35]

Ralph smirked. "I invited Kei for a lunch date today, and oh . . . look at that! It's almost time for me to pick him up. *À tout à l'heure!"*[36]

*Since when did he and Kei become friendly? And why didn't I know about this until now?*

This was absurd. I had known Ralph for a long time, and I knew I wouldn't like what would happen if this lunch date occurred without me.

*"Attendez!*[37] I'll come with you."

Without thinking twice, I stood up from my seat, grabbed my suit jacket from the rack, and put it on. I didn't even spare a second glance at the unfinished paperwork waiting to be signed. I left them scattered on the office desk.

"Well, well . . . look who's coming out of his shell. I'm proud of you, *mon frère!*" Ralph teased.

I ignored him and followed him in silence to the elevators. Once we reached the basement, we continued to his car.

"Where is your car?" Ralph asked.

*"Ça ne vous concerne pas,"*[38] I grumbled before I slipped inside the passenger seat.

When we finally arrived at the parking lot of Kei's college, the designated meeting place, most of the students were already emerging from the buildings for their lunch break.

---

[34] You're giving me a headache.
[35] What did you say?
[36] See you later!
[37] Wait!
[38] That does not concern you.

I got outside the car before Ralph had a chance to do so, earning an eye roll from him. I scanned the bustling students, searching for Kei.

"Oh, there he is! *Mon minou!*" Ralph shouted unashamedly.

I followed his gaze, and sure enough, Kei was walking toward us with a backpack loosely slung over his right shoulder. I couldn't help but stare into his eyes until he stopped and awkwardly stood before us.

"Uh, why is Jace here?" he asked Ralph, completely ignoring me.

I crossed my arms across my chest. "Now that hurt my feelings, *mon beau.*"

"My baby brother here was being a . . . well, a baby. He insisted on joining us for lunch," Ralph explained.

Kei hummed in response, still giving me a suspicious look.

I frowned at him and hopped into the car.

Once we buckled up, Ralph drove off to wherever he wanted to take us for lunch. Unfortunately for him, I didn't like his choice of restaurants. Instead of fine dining restaurants, he always preferred fast-food chains or pastry shops. It wasn't that I disliked sweet foods, I just didn't care for the aftertaste, which is why I preferred savory over sweets.

We were now back at the central business district, not far from my building. With all the unfinished job I left, the CEO in me couldn't help but think it would have been more efficient if Kei had driven himself here. Although, I wasn't sure he had taken a car today. He often preferred the relaxed status of a passenger to driving and navigating the road.

"Here we are. The Pittoresque Bistro," Ralph said as he parked the car right in front of the restaurant, where a valet stood by.

Kei gave a faint gasp of amazement as we entered the bistro. I couldn't blame him. The French restaurant was charming and had an old-fashioned aesthetic that was appealing. The word *pittoresque* means quaint in French, and the restaurant truly lived up to its name. It wasn't too extravagant and eye-catching from the outside, but once inside, it was inevitable that you would want to return.

I had been here a few times myself, either with Ralph or with my business clients. As per our request, the hostess seated us at a table located far from the entrance and away from the noisy lunch crowd.

When Kei examined the menu, he furrowed his eyebrows in curiosity. I couldn't help but smile at his expression.

"Ugh, French words again. Seriously, why can't you guys just drag me to a place that didn't have an alien language?" he complained and placed the menu back on the table.

"Take a French class then," I said bluntly.

Ralph snorted. "Now that would be hard for Kei here. He's literally a beginner. Right, *mon minou?*"

Kei wore a peculiar expression on his face, nodding and smiling in an odd manner that caused me to clench my fists under the table.

*This can't be good.*

If Ralph and Kei got too comfortable with each other, then I certainly wouldn't like what happens next.

The waiter arrived at our table, holding a small notepad and a pen, waiting for us to place our orders.

Glancing at the menu, I decided to order my usual.

"I'll have *le hachis parmentier*[39] with white cheese," I said, then glanced at Kei, who was sitting next to me

He looked like he was having a hard time deciphering the menu, so I leaned closer and held the other end of the menu. This made him flinch for a microsecond before he composed himself.

"What do you want to eat?" I asked gently.

---

[39] A traditional French dish that consists of a layer of cooked, seasoned minced meat (usually beef) topped with mash potatoes.

Kei stared at me for a moment before glancing back at the menu. "Uh, I don't know. Can you order for me?"

Pleased, I nodded and pointed to one of the dishes in the lunch section of the menu. I was sure Kei would like this one.

"Does *filet mignon* with *aligot* sound good to you?"

He frowned. "What's that?"

I knew he knew what filet mignon was, so I pointed to the English description of the side dish and let him read. It stated, "It's a traditional dish in French cuisine, originating from the Aubrac region. It consists of mashed potatoes mixed with melted fresh tome cheese, often with butter and garlic. The result is a creamy and stretchy texture, commonly served as a side dish with meats, especially beef or pork."

After he finished reading, he said, "Sounds delicious to me. I'll have that one, and with beef."

I added, "Do you mind fries as an appetizer? Here, they served it with aïoli, a sauce similar to mayonnaise made with garlic, olive oil, egg yolks, and sometimes lemon juice."

Kei smiled at Ralph, then eagerly nodded at me. Just as I was about to reciprocate his enthusiasm, I noticed the waiter looking at Kei with intense malice. That look alone sent an uncomfortable feeling through me, and before I knew it, I cleared my throat loudly to grab his attention.

That seemed to do the trick, as the waiter quickly snapped out of his thoughts and appeared visibly embarrassed. He then averted his eyes to his notepad in feigned innocence.

For some reason, that wasn't enough for me. Something inside me wanted to ensure the waiter understood his place.

"My *husband* would like to have filet mignon with the aligot, please," I said with authority as I narrowed my eyes at the waiter.

He gulped. "Y-yes, sir. Right away, sir."

Ralph whistled. "And I'd like the pasta and chicken with red wine sauce."

The waiter frantically nodded, then ran off with our orders. Feeling satisfied, I casually leaned back in my chair and glanced at Ralph.

He smirked at me knowingly. "Well done, brother. Well done."

Kei scoffed. "Am I missing something here? Because I hate it when I'm being left out."

"Nothing to worry about, *mon minou*," Ralph said with a wave of his hand.

Just as Kei was about to say something else, another person approached our table. It became apparent that this lunch date was going to be more challenging than I had anticipated when I instantly recognized who that person was.

"Whoa, Kei! Nice to see you here!"

I struggled to hide my grimace as Kei abruptly stood up from our table and greeted the person with a huge smile.

# CHAPTER EIGHTEEN
## Craving Caviar

KEI

"Hey, Ryan!" I greeted my friend gratefully.

Smiling broadly, he said, "Hey, Kei! Hello, Mr. Langlois." He then gave a tiny smile to Ralph.

Thank God, he came over. The awkward tension between Jace, Ralph, and me was just too heavy for my liking, and I still wondered why Jace was here with us.

"Are you here for lunch, Ryan?" I asked.

"Yes, what is he doing here? Jace muttered, then in a louder voice said, "*Il semble apparaître partout où nous sommes.*"[40]

Ralph chuckled, looking intrigued, and I elbowed Jace.

"I'm here to confirm a booking. Someone at work double-booked a dinner reservation and couldn't cancel it online. The restaurant requested someone to come in person to fill out a form because there's an issue with their system."

Ralph cleared his throat, drawing our attention. He looked at Ryan and said, "I'm Ralph. Would you like to join us for lunch?"

"Ryan," he said, offering his hand to Ralph, who accepted it without standing.

---

[40] He seems to appear everywhere we are.

"Pardon me for not standing—we're all friends here," Ralph said, clearly enjoying himself.

Ryan grinned at him, gave me a pat on the back, looked at the French siblings, and asked, "Can I?"

I nodded and gestured for him to take the vacant seat beside Ralph.

He happily complied, but when he finally noticed Jace giving him a hard look, he cleared his throat and quickly shifted his focus to the menu.

"Aren't you expected back at work, Ryan?" Jace asked.

I jabbed Jace's hip with my elbow which made him grunt under his breath. Nevertheless, Ralph noticed and chuckled at the gesture. I gave him a smug smile in return.

"Ugh, it's my lunch break, Mr. Langlois, sir."

"So, Ryan, how's your job as an intern so far?" I casually asked.

Ryan briefly glanced up from his menu and gave a shrug. "It's early days. I'm not trusted with any systems yet, so I'm relegated to manual or unskilled tasks."

I snickered. "Such as ordering food."

"Pretty much." He snickered. "I get coffees and lunches everyday. Cool thing about it is I get to keep the change. Boss said I should." He chuckled, then sobered. "I'm really hoping they would let me in on the writing or debugging codes. I'm not hoping for something terrible to happen to the system, but it would be awesome if I could help with troubleshooting."

The waiter finally arrived with our appetizer, and Ryan politely added his own order before the waiter walked off.

The *aïoli* smelled good, and I couldn't help but dig right into my food. Ralph chuckled before he started on his own appetizer—quiche.

"Do you like it?" Jace asked.

I nodded, my mouth full of fries.

Jace smirked, clearly satisfied with my response. Then he too began eating his quiche, one-handed. I was so engrossed in enjoying my meal that I only just noticed his arm casually draped around the back of my chair.

*Wait, when did that happen?*

I looked up just in time to see Ralph shake his head.

"So *mon minou*, do you have any classes after this?" Ralph said.

I put my fork on the table and gave him my full attention. "Nope, but I do have an essay to write that is due tomorrow."

Ralph pouted. "Well, that sucks."

Unexpectedly, Jace started choking on his food, which caught all of our attention. It was so unlike Jace to react that way. After he recovered by taking a sip of Ralph's red wine, he cleared his throat and wiped the corner of his mouth with a napkin.

"Sorry, I was just shocked," he admitted.

"Shocked of what, exactly?" Ralph asked.

Jace glared at his brother. "Since when were you familiar with American expressions?"

I blinked when I realized what he meant. Yeah, he had a point, alright. From what I had observed, Ralph spoke with a heavy French accent and barely used common American phrases except the one he just said a while ago.

"After my meeting in your *mari's*[41] school, I stayed for a while and walked around the campus. College boys always have useful mouths," he explained.

This time, it was Ryan who choked on his drink.

Ralph merely flashed him a teasing grin, just in time for the waiter to bring Ryan's order. Ryan thanked the waiter before he took another sip of water.

"You okay?" I asked in concern.

He nodded. "Yeah, I'm okay."

---

[41] Husband's

"So, Ryan," Ralph started, "tell me about yourself or why you all seem to know each other."

I couldn't help but notice the slight teasing tone he used. I wasn't sure why, but I had a sudden feeling that this lunch wasn't going to be what I expected.

Ryan sat up straight and said, "Yeah, Kei and I have been friends since high school."

"He's an intern at Jace's company," I informed Ralph.

Ralph raised an eyebrow, intrigued. "Really? That's nice. My brother hasn't been giving you a hard time, has he?"

Jace responded by pointing his fork dangerously close to Ralph's face. However, Ralph didn't seem to care or even blink. He simply ignored Jace and kept his focus on Ryan, as if he was trying to figure him out.

"At first, it was kinda hard to adjust. People in business sorta makes me feel small, I guess," Ryan said.

I smiled in agreement. "I know what you mean, Ryan. Businessmen just have that particular aura around them like they look so intimidating and kinda condescending."

Ralph snorted, "Condescending? Well, that fits my brother's personality very well."

I couldn't help but laugh in agreement. It was true. Ever since I married Jace, he had this tough exterior, and everything he did used to piss me off endlessly. Even though he has changed somewhat now, I still hated his attitude. The memories of why I ran away from him and how he technically threatened Ryan to stay away from me were still fresh in my mind.

"Just shut up, Ralph," Jace commanded.

Ralph shrugged nonchalantly before digging right back into his food.

I was about to bring up another topic when I noticed Ryan fidgeting in his seat. It wasn't that obvious, but it was enough to make me curious.

I leaned toward him and asked in a whisper, "What's wrong?"

"Huh? Oh, n-nothing."

"Are you sure?"

"Yep."

I frowned. I didn't believe him, but for his sake, I ignored it and turned to Jace instead. He was currently playing with his food with a fork.

"What are you doing?"

He glanced at me. "Eating."

I rolled my eyes at him. "Sure, you are."

Ralph chimed in, "He's got a point, *mon frère*. You should eat up."

Jace glared at his brother before turning his attention back to his own plate. "I'm craving—"

"Oh! Ryan, I almost forgot. Can you fix my laptop for me? I can't write my essay if my laptop's broken." My eyes widened as I immediately thought of the essay I had to write.

Ryan chuckled. "Why? What did you do to break it?"

"I dunno. The cursor blinks very fast then disappears for a few seconds. Every time I open a new tab, the screen shuts off, then it lights back up after a little while."

Ryan hummed thoughtfully. "Yeah, I think I can fix that. Where's your laptop?"

"At home. I'll just call you so you can come ov—"

Jace suddenly cut me off. "I'm craving caviar."

Much to my surprise, both Ralph and Ryan grimaced in disgust.

I smirked to myself. Well, well, it looked like I wasn't the only one who hated Jace's food choice. That certainly cheered me up a bit.

I shifted on my seat to face Jace properly. "Can't you just order here?"

I raised my hand to call the waiter, but Jace pulled it down and didn't let go. I turned to glare at him, but he kept a neutral expression. I didn't know why, but I had a feeling he was angry with me.

"What's wrong with you?" I asked, unsure if I wanted to know.

Instead of answering, he stood up, placed a couple of hundred dollar bills on the table, and grabbed my hand to pull me up.

Turning to Ralph and Ryan, who wore matching bewildered expressions, he announced, "I think it's about time that Kei and I leave."

"What?" Ralph asked in surprise.

I frowned at Jace, but he ignored me. I looked back at Ralph and Ryan, but Jace was practically dragging me out of the restaurant. His grip tightened, and it seemed he had no intention of letting go anytime soon.

"What the fuck are you doing? What do you mean it's time to leave? What about your brother? And Ryan? And the food! I was looking forward to eating that filet and aligot!"

He took his phone out and made a call, speaking a few words that I couldn't quite catch.

I continued trying to pull my hand away from his tight grip, but my efforts were futile. Eventually, my frustration turned to fury, and I waited for either Ralph or Ryan to come and get me. Turning to face the restaurant, I immediately spotted the two engrossed in animated conversation, as if nothing happened.

*Unbelievable! It's like they didn't just saw Jace drag me out of there against my will, and my beef and potatoes!*

Knowing that neither of them were going to come and save me, I continued my feeble attempts to pull my hand away from Satan himself. After a several minutes of grappling with Jace, his black car arrived. As soon as it stopped in front of us, he opened the door, practically pushed me inside, and followed suit before the car drove off.

"Are you insane?!" I hissed at him, rubbing my sore wrist with my other hand as he finally let go. "What did you do that for? I have half a mind to punch you in the face right now!"

He ignored my threat and simply leaned back on the leather seat before he crossed his legs like a king.

"Like I said, I'm craving caviar."

My jaw dropped in utter disbelief. "What the hell? You kidnapped me just for that? And wasted excellent food for a caviar?"

"It's not kidnapping, and caviar is food of the gods."

I rolled my eyes at the implication.

"It definitely is kidnapping, smart-ass!" It took every strength in me not to strangle him. "And why the hell are you craving caviar? You could've just ordered it at the restaurant, dipshit. Are you PMS-ing or something?"

He didn't spare me a glance and just looked straight ahead.

"Let me rephrase, *mon beau*. I'm craving your caviar."

I blinked. "What?"

# CHAPTER NINETEEN
## Aprons and Kisses

"You left your brother and Ryan in the restaurant, you wasted excellent food, you kidnapped me, and you brought me back home just so I could cook something for you? Are you sure you're not as mad at that Candace girl from *Phineas and Ferb*?" I ranted as I paced in front of Jace, who was currently sitting on a kitchen stool like a very impatient German shepherd.

He put his elbow on the island counter and rested his head on it.

"*Mon beau*, quit yapping and start cooking. I'm hungry."

I gritted my teeth in pure rage. That fucker . . . if it weren't for his good looks, I would have beaten that goddamn face until the brain in his skull turned to dust.

I closed my eyes to calm myself down for a bit, then opened them again only to see Jace smirking at me.

"I'll put poison in your caviar omelet, you jerk-face," I muttered before grabbing a pan and turning on the stove.

He chuckled. "We'll see about that."

I ignored him, though I really wanted to stab him with a butcher knife. As I cracked some eggs, I heard Jace stand up from his chair and walk toward me.

"Need a hand, *mon beau*?" he whispered in my ear, making me shiver.

I pushed him away with my hip, but he just laughed.

107

"Keep it in your pants, booger-head," I scolded as I chopped up some onions.

He looked at me in amusement before he stepping close again. He rolled up his sleeves to his elbow, grabbed a bottle of olive oil, and poured some into the pan.

I gave him a curious look, and he smirked when he noticed.

"Everything tastes good in olive oil."

I crossed my arms across my chest. "As if I don't know that. Just wear an apron, dumbass. I don't want your germs all over the food."

I swatted his hand away and pushed him toward where the aprons were hung.

Just as he was about to grab the plain white one, a brilliant idea struck me. It always amused me to see one of the female house helpers wearing their ridiculous aprons. A devious smile spread across my face as I snatched the pink frilly one with black polka dots. To top it off, it had the words, *'Mama's cooking, bitch!'* emblazoned on the front.

I nearly died laughing when I saw Jace's expression as I handed the apron to him.

*"Non. Non, merci,"*[42] he blurted out.

"Oh, come on! Just wear it! You'll look good in it!" I urged, pushing him to wear the girly apron.

He shook his head. "How do you know if I'll look good in it?"

"Imagination does a lot of things," I explained.

He raised an eyebrow. "I don't know what creeps me out more . . . you imagining me in an apron like this or the apron itself."

I rolled my eyes impatiently. "Ugh. Just wear the freakin' apron, Jace. If you don't, there will be no caviar omelet for you."

He shot me a suspicious look before donning the gaudy apron and tying it around his waist. I resisted the urge to laugh, but

---

[42] No. No, thank you.

108

his embarrassed expression alone did it for me. Before I knew it, I was laughing so hard that my stomach hurt. Tears streamed down my cheeks, and for a moment, I couldn't catch my breath.

"Oh my God, look at your face! It's priceless! Wait! Let me get a camera."

I sprinted to the living room before he could stop me. Jace was following me and yelling at me to get back. I grabbed my phone from the coffee table. A second later, he grabbed me by the waist and tackled me onto the nearby couch. I was still laughing, and in the midst of our scuffle, my phone fell onto the carpeted floor.

Jace managed to pin me on the couch, his expression was unreadable.

Eventually, my laughter died down when I noticed his eyes traveling from my eyes to my lips.

"Jace?"

Without another word, and in one swift motion, where he nearly had me fall off the couch, he pressed his lips against mine. His tongue pushed itself roughly into my mouth, making me gasp in shock. In a split second, it slipped inside as he deepened the kiss.

I tried pushing him away, but his strong hold kept me in place. I tried speaking, but my words ended up being muffled by his sinful lips. The kiss was hard and rough, and as much as I tried to resist, I eventually melted into it.

He was definitely a great kisser. If there was an award for best French kisser, Jace Langlois would win it by a mile.

After a few minutes, my lungs felt like they were about to burst, so I urgently tugged on the collar of his shirt, hoping that he got the message—which he did.

He pulled away, breathing hard against my lips, making me smell his wine-scented breath.

Hesitantly, I gazed into his eyes. If I hadn't known pure, unadulterated desire before, I certainly knew it now. His eyes held a heated promise that only he could fulfill, maybe . . . only for me.

*"Tu as de très beaux yeux,"*[43] he whispered against my lips.

"Huh?"

He kissed me once, twice, then paused to gaze into my eyes as if searching for my soul.

"You have very beautiful eyes, *mon beau*."

I blushed madly at his compliment. *Was that even a compliment?* With Jace Langlois, you could never be sure. But deep inside, I felt warmth spreading through my body, making my heart race.

We remained in that intimate silence for a while, him on top of me while I lay beneath, neither of us saying a word.

To be honest, I kind of liked this. Him not being an arrogant, egotistical asshole was rather nice.

My arms started to numb after a while, so I gently nudged him away. But he tightened his embrace, circling his arms around me. A silent gasp escaped me as his hot breath brushed against my exposed neck.

"Jace, the omelet . . ."

He grumbled under his breath but held onto me even tighter, snuggling his head under my chin. Seeing him like this made me imagine him as a baby, but now . . . an overgrown baby.

"Let's stay like this for a while," he mumbled.

I hesitantly put my hand on his head and played with his hair. It was surprisingly so soft and very well-maintained. I expected gel or wax, but instead, the musky yet fruity scent of his shampoo wafted through my nostrils.

"Jace, get up."

"Five more minutes."

"Jace, I'm hungry. And I know you are too. Let me go so I can cook for the both us."

Silence.

"Jace?"

---

[43] You have very beautiful eyes.

Then I heard soft snores escaping his mouth, their gentle vibrations I felt against my neck. *Shit, he's asleep.*

I didn't want to disturb him, so I stayed still and let him rest, running my fingers through his hair as I stared at the ceiling, letting time pass.

As much as I hate to admit it . . . lying here with Jace on the couch, it almost felt we're starting to act like a real married couple.

*Fuck! Could it be that I'm actually looking forward to it?*

*Could our relationship work?*

Not sure of the answers to either, I suddenly remembered something that made me chuckle quietly to myself.

Jace was still wearing the apron.

# CHAPTER TWENTY
## Burn

I fell asleep but had no idea for how long. Jace was still on top of me, but he had shifted slightly, with only half of his body covered mine. After several futile attempts to push Jace off me, I finally managed to shove him away by pushing my entire weight sideways until he fell onto the carpeted floor.

I stood up, shaking my arms as I started for the kichen. My watch indicated I had been asleep for about an hour. No wonder my arms had gone numb from Jace's weight.

*Man, he's so heavy.*

My stomach grumbled, reminding me that I missed lunch. I realized that Jace missed lunch too, so I decided to cook him his omelet and wake him up when it was done. I threw away the eggs I had cracked earlier, then cracked a few more into a bowl and mixed them with caviar. The pan had already oil in it, reminding me that Jace had poured the oil earlier. It was a good thing he had turned off the stove before following me to the living room.

After I poured the disgusting mixture into the pan, I opened the fridge and took out some leftover lasagna. I gave it a quick sniff to check if it was still safe to eat before putting it into the microwave.

I was stirring the eggs, thinking about the time I had wasted sleeping when I still had an essay to do, when my phone rang. I sighed in annoyance and made my way back to the living room where Jace was sprawled out on the floor, still fast asleep.

An idea came to mine as I grabbed my phone. Without bothering to check the notifications for why it rang a few seconds ago, I opened the camera app and took a few pictures of Jace before receiving a text message from Ryan.

> *Yo, Kei! Just wanted to tell you that Ralph dropped me home.*

I frowned.

> *Since when were you on a first name basis with Jace's brother?*

It didn't take long before Ryan replied.

> *So he's Mr. Langlois' brother? Cool! Who's the big bro?*

I texted back.

> *Ralph is the older one.*

I was composing a message when his reply came.

> *Damn, I can't believe it. They don't look like brothers though.*

Before I could finish my message and reply to Ryan's latest text, the microwave beeped, signaling that my lasagna was now ready to eat. I tucked my phone into the back pocket of my jeans as I sauntered into the kitchen.

I nearly drooled at the smell when I pulled my lasagna out of the microwave. Grabbing a fork, I took a mouthful of the mouthwatering lasagna before settling comfortably on one of the stools around the island counter. Then, I took out my phone to read another message from Ryan.

*By the way, when can I fix your laptop?*

I had nearly forgotten about my broken laptop. We were talking about it at the restaurant when Jace so rudely interrupted us and got bitchy before essentially kidnapping me. No matter how much he would try to deny it, it was clearly a kidnapping.

I grumbled at the memory. He should be grateful I wouldn't press charges. That jerk was lucky that he was my husband. The thought of Jace, mixed with a scorched smell, reminded me of the omelet I was cooking. I went to turn off the stove and sighed at the ruined omelet.

Letting out another sigh, I returned to my food and phone and finished typing my reply.

*This weekend maybe.*

*Is Saturday fine with you?*

*Yeah, sure.*

We exchanged a few more text messages, during which I would take a few bites of my delicious lasagna, moaning at how heavenly the dish was.

My God, Garfield was right. Lasagna really was the food of the gods. I could practically live off lasagna for a year—well, with a few fast-food picks here and there. After all, I do like greasy food.

"If I were you, I'd stop moaning like that or else I'd regret it."

I nearly fell off my stool in shock. Jace was leaning casually against the kitchen doorway. His hair was ruffled, giving him that oh-so-sexy-bed head look. His clothes, now without the ridiculous apron, were rumpled too, but instead of looking like a slob, he looked even more attractive than normal.

I pushed out the memory of our earlier kiss out of my mind and stood up from my stool before pointing an angry finger at him.

"You, sir, should stop scaring the hell out of people. Jesus! You could've at least cleared your throat or something!"

Jace didn't say anything. Instead, he just stared at me with his deep, piercing eyes, which made me very uncomfortable. His gaze traveled from my head down to my feet, then back up to my face, lingering on my eyes for a bit.

I just stood there, not moving a muscle, as a wave of uneasiness washed all over me. After a moment, his eyes widened.

"Kei . . ."

"What?" I asked.

He swiftly walked toward me, or rather, zipped past where I stood. A second later, my eyes widened as I saw Jace holding the pan.

*Oh shit! I should have thrown away the evidence of my crime.*

Jace stared at the dish for a while, as if it would somehow come to life before he turned to me with a grievous expression.

I raised both hands in surrender. "Sorry I forgot."

He frowned. "Kei."

"I swear I forgot! I was eating! I was so hungry, I forgot! And I was worrying about how to do my essay since my laptop's throwing a tantrum . . . much like you right now," I muttered the last part.

"You should have at least—"

"Ah, so now it's my fault?"

"I didn't say it's your—"

"Oh so now you're denying it? Well, bravo for you."

"Will you just—"

115

Suddenly, out of the blue, Ralph barged into the kitchen with what looked like a takeout food bag. He was looking back and forth between Jace and me with an amused smirk.

"Wow, look you two. You're already acting like an old married couple," he said.

I rolled my eyes at him as he sat down on a stool. Then, he noticed the burnt food in the pan that Jace was still holding and grimaced.

*"Qu'est-ce que c'est?"*[44]

Jace replied tiredly, "Food."

"That does not look like food at all."

"Well, it doesn't matter. I'll just order something."

Ralph slammed the food bags onto the island countertop with a smug grin.

"Good thing I brought takeout. Does Japanese sound good?"

With no other options, Jace and I just gave up and sat down.

Ralph happily handed us chopsticks.

I frowned. "Uh, I don't know how to use these things," I muttered sheepishly.

Ralph was leaned forward and was about to teach me how when Jace interrupted with an annoyed *tsk*.

I glanced at him. "What?"

"If you try to burn the house down, tell me. I'll just cook it myself. At least it'll be safer that way."

I scowled at him in disbelief. "Yeah, sure. I look forward to it. Oh, that reminds me. If someone were to choose who is safer—me, who actually knows how to cook, or Mr. Langlois, who doesn't even know how to crack an egg? Then yeah, I can totally see the answer."

"Burn," Ralph snickered behind his hand.

---

[44] What is it?

Jace glared at his brother before angrily picking up a roll of sushi and put it inside his mouth.

I held up a finger and gasped mockingly.

"Oh yeah! I almost forgot. Jace, if you ever try to cook something and blame it on me, just remember I have something that will make you cringe."

I took out my phone and showed Ralph the picture I took of Jace sleeping in an apron a while ago.

Ralph couldn't help but laugh out loud.

"Jace, *copain*, if these get posted on social media, you'll be toast." Ralph chuckled.

Jace was practically fuming when he caught a glimpse of the images I took before I tucked my phone back into my jeans pocket. I just smiled triumphantly at him.

"Don't you dare post those pictures, *mon beau*," he warned.

I shrugged carelessly. "That'll depend on how you act toward me."

Ralph was still laughing obnoxiously, and I couldn't help but laugh along with him.

God, I had never felt so victorious before, and damn, it felt good—especially because Jace was now the butt of the joke instead of me.

# CHAPTER TWENTY-ONE
## In Love

I groaned in annoyance as the incessant sound of the alarm clock blared from the nightstand behind me. Reaching blindly for the stupid device to turn it off, I was beaten to it by someone else.

I mumbled a thank you before snuggling deeper under the thick comforter.

"Remind me to destroy that thing later," Jace grumble, moving on the bed beside me.

I turned around to face him but still didn't bother to open my eyes.

*Damn it! I was so fucking tired. I feel like I could sleep all day today.*

Jace's brother was to blame for how I felt.

Yesterday, on a Sunday of all days, I had to go to campus for some pre-planning activities for an exhibition we would put up after spring break. When I got home from school, exhausted and ready to sleep forever after a hectic week before the short vacation, I found Ralph had just arrived with takeout food. Then, he requested—no, *demanded*—that we have a movie marathon, which lasted all night.

When Jace joined us later, I had expected to get another chance to make fun of him since Ralph put on a horror movie, but fate had other plans, and I became the scaredy-cat of the night. It was especially embarrassing when I made a fool of myself by literally jumping off the couch and running away to hide in the bathroom.

*Great, I just practically humiliated myself in front of two other guys. How embarrassing was that?*

After Ralph went back to his penthouse, Jace was obviously frustrated with me while we tried to sleep. The reason? Because I kept hogging the blankets and refused to turn off the lights. This went on until 4 AM, and when I finally managed to get to sleep, so did Jace.

Now it was already nearing noon, and I still wasn't determined to get up and get ready for the day.

"We should get out of bed. It's already quarter to twelve," Jace said as he slowly got up.

"Ten more minutes."

"*Non.* Now, come on. Wake up. We have plans today."

I opened my eyes at this and looked at him. He was already combing his bed hair with his fingers, and the gesture alone made him look incredibly hot. Discreetly, I pulled the sheets up higher over my body, just in case I formed a tent or something.

"What plans?" I asked.

He didn't answer and instead just went straight to the en suite bathroom, closing the door behind him.

I glared at the door. "Jerk," I muttered.

I sighed and looked around the bedroom I shared with Jace.

When we first got married, his mother insisted that I sleep in the same bed with Jace. She said, and I quote, "You're husbands now. It's your lifetime obligation and responsibility to sleep next to each other."

I wanted to refuse because, come on, who the hell sleeps with a man you just met and married for convenience? It just didn't make sense at all. Still, his mother was adamant, so I reluctantly just went with it. Now, almost a year later, I was already used to waking up with Jace snoring like a cow beside me.

"I snore like a cow?"

I jolted from my thoughts and shifted my gaze from around the bedroom to the open bathroom door where Jace stood, clad

119

only in a navy blue towel loosely hanging around his hips. Instantly, my eyes fixed on his chiseled abs and traced down to his V-line, then further—

"Liking the view, *mon beau*?" Jace teased.

I snapped back to my senses and quickly averted my gaze. Sensing Jace moving toward the bed, I slowly backed myself up against the headboard. The mattress dipped as he sat down, and I flinched when his hand gently touched my arm.

"You didn't answer my question, *mon beau*." His voice went an octave lower, and goddammit, my body decided to betray me and reacted.

I clenched my fists and tried to get out of bed, but Jace pushed me back down onto the mattress. In a split-second, he was on top of me, his thighs resting between mine.

I froze as his eyes bore into mine. Nervously, I licked my lips, regretting it when his eyes darkened, following the same movement. Then, without warning, he pressed his lips roughly against mine.

I didn't know what came over me. It was as if I were possessed because almost instantly, my arms moved on their own, winding themselves around Jace's neck.

Jace groaned and slipped his tongue out into my open mouth.

I couldn't understand why I was letting him do this to me, but I hated to admit it . . . I liked it. It felt right—the sensation of lying underneath Jace, our lips moving together, the warmth from our shared tension, Jace's hands exploring . . .

My eyes widened when I felt Jace's hands slide down to my bare chest. His touch was gentle, caressing my skin lightly, moving up and down over and over again.

I couldn't help but moan against Jace's rough lips. Just as my hand started to travel down toward the towel around Jace's hips, he stopped.

He released my lips but remained on top of me.

120

"What's wrong?" I asked.

Instead of waving me off dismissively, as was his practice, he merely smiled and ruffled my hair.

I grunted in annoyance and swatted his hand away.

He chuckled and tried to ruffle my hair once more.

I glared at him. "You're an idiot."

He moved closer so that his forehead touched mine, then he pecked my nose. "But I'm your idiot."

I blushed.

Jace sat up and slipped out of the bed, disappearing into his large closet.

A warm feeling coursed through my body as I lay there. My chest tightened, my fingers tingled from touching Jace, and my lips yearned for more of his kisses.

I frowned to myself. He barely left, and I was already missing his touch.

*What's happening to me?*

*You're falling in love, dimwit.*

I mentally scolded myself. *Shut up.*

*You shut up. Just admit it already.*

*Admit what?*

*That you love Jace.*

*I do not!*

*Uh huh, sure you don't.*

I shook my head. I couldn't believe I was talking to myself in my head. I must be going crazy.

*It's just one of the perks of being in love.*

I groaned and covered my face with a pillow.

"Shut up, shut up, shut up!" I screamed into the fabric of the pillow.

Then I heard Jace call out, telling me go get ready because we were going out.

Slowly, I pushed the pillow from my face, and when I saw him in his suit, my cheeks flushed redder than ever.

121

*Kei and Jace sitting on a tree. K-I-S-S-I-N-G!* My stupid subconscious obnoxiously sang.

Instead of arguing with it, I found myself silently wishing for Jace to kiss me again.

*I'm falling in love, aren't I?*

# CHAPTER TWENTY-TWO
## Surprises

"Where are we going?" I asked Jace for the hundredth time today.

"Be patient."

I huffed and slumped into the leather seat of Jace's car. I had been asking him the same question one too many times, and he still thought it was a good idea not to answer.

"Jerk."

"You're immature." He glanced at me before he faced the road again.

I just scoffed at him and decided to ignore him for the rest of the drive. Well, not entirely ignore, because every once in a while, I stole quick glances when he wasn't looking. I couldn't help but blush every time I did.

Jace looked incredibly attractive when he was driving, and even more so when he wore suits designed to fit his proportions perfectly. Each suit, likely costing a fortune to tailor, was worth every penny. I loved seeing him in them. He exudes a blend of class and sexiness that was irresistible.

*Wait . . . I'm just blatantly staring now, am I?*

"Ugh!" I groaned in annoyance.

"What?" he asked.

I blushed again and immediately hid my face in my hands.

*Damn it, being in love sucks balls. I hate this. I really do.*

After a long, awkward drive, the car finally stopped.

I hurriedly hopped out of the car and looked around. We were standing in a neighborhood that looked like it had seen better days.

*Somehow . . . this place looks familiar . . .*

"Why did you take me here?" I asked Jace as he locked his car before he walked toward me.

*This was getting too much . . . even the way he walked screamed, "sexy."*

I resisted the urge to yell at him not to get too close, afraid I might blush to death.

"Just follow me."

I ignored the nagging voices in my head and reluctantly trailed him. He headed toward a few yards away from us.

As we drew nearer, it was obvious that the home was abandoned. The picket fence in the front yard looked as though it had been eaten by termites and could collapse at any second. The lawn was now dead and dull in some parts, overgrown with weeds and bushes in others, and the porch where one would sit and enjoy the breeze was falling apart . . .

I nearly stopped in my tracks at the realization of what this place was.

*How could I forget? I haven't been here in years . . .*

"Jace . . . this house . . ." I couldn't finish my sentence as he opened the door and hurried me inside.

Once we were in, I could barely contain my tears.

While the outside of the home looked unkempt and abandoned, the inside looked exactly as it once was. It was like I had stepped into a time machine and was transported back to my childhood.

To when my parents were still alive . . .

The living room . . . the kitchen . . . hell, even the stairs looked the same. It was as if I had never left.

My old home, the same place where I once lived with my parents, still appeared perfect. But outside, everything had gone to hell. Increasing criminality had brought a once happy neighborhood to its knees. I blinked away the memories of how my parents died—attacked during their regular after-dinner stroll in a community they loved.

I blinked away my tears. "Jace, w-why—" I quietly gasped when I turned around and saw Jace holding a husky puppy.

"W-what the fuck . . ."

*Talk about a rollercoaster of emotions.*

Jace's smile grew wider. "Happy birthday, *mon beau.*"

The little puppy yipped, as if also to offer his greetings, which made me laugh.

"Thank you! I actually forgot that today's my birthday," I muttered as I stepped closer to Jace.

I was only reminded that today was my birthday during our brunch earlier when I received a tiny gift and a bouquet of flowers from Lucy.

The puppy's tail wiggled in excitement, and to an extent, his bottom as well, which made him all the more adorable.

I didn't even think Jace knew the date, which made his gift even more precious.

Carefully, Jace handed the little pup to me. As I got neared, the puppy wagged its tail. I gratefully accepted him and carried him in my arms.

"How come I didn't notice this cute little guy?"

Jace shrugged. "After I bought him, I let Ralph take him here."

"When did you buy him?"

"That day Ralph met you at your college. I bought the puppy online for your birthday. I wanted to surprise you," he replied.

"And when did Ralph brought him here?"

"Earlier today. You didn't notice, but we actually met his car on our way here."

I laughed as the puppy wiggled in my arms, which forced me to let go of him and let him scamper around the house.

I turned to Jace with a smile. "Thanks, Jace. It was nice of you. I can't believe I even forgot my birthday."

He smiled back. "You're welcome."

We just stared at each other like that for a few good minutes before I realized it was getting terribly awkward. I cleared my throat and averted my eyes.

"So, uh . . . what's the puppy's name?" I asked.

Jace seemed to notice my discomfort because he stepped away from me and leaned against the stairs' railing.

"You can name him. He's yours after all."

I contemplated that for a while. *What could be a good name for a cute puppy?* I shrugged, giving up after I couldn't come up with anything.

Jace frowned. "What's the matter?" he asked. He must have noticed my expression.

"I can't think of anything good."

Jace went silent. He walked away from the stairs and went into the living room. I followed suit.

Right in the middle of the room was the nameless puppy himself, rolling around on the brown rug. His bright eyes widened when he saw us, his tongue lolling out of his open mouth in glee.

I grinned and sat down on the floor next to the pup.

Immediately, he stopped rolling and crawled to my crossed legs to make himself at home. My smile grew wider as his little pink nose nuzzled against my hand.

Jace sat down on the couch across from us.

I looked up at him. "Can you name him for me?"

He scoffed. "*Non.* I don't even like dogs."

My jaw drop. "Then why the hell did you give me one as a present?"

He shrugged. "I know you love dogs, and it's your birthday."

I rolled my eyes at him, despite the fact that I was practically jumping around and squealing like an excited teenage girl in my head. The urge to actually do that in real life was strong, but I managed to hold back and stay calm.

I nearly jumped when the puppy sneezed, then went back to wiggling in my arms. His excitement was evident, and it seemed that he couldn't stay still for even a second. It was like he was eating sugar behind our backs.

"He's way too hyper," I commented out loud.

Jace chuckled. The low tone of his voice made me blush. "He is, isn't he?"

I ignored him and focused on the puppy instead.

Ever since we got here, my heart had been beating faster, and I couldn't help but wonder how I was going to show Jace I was thankful for what he did. Saying "thank you" wasn't enough, at least for me, and a part of me felt like I should return the favor in some way

*But what?* I stayed quiet for a few minutes, my brain going into overdrive as it tried to come up with ways to repay him.

Suddenly, Jace stood up and announced that it was time to go home. Glancing out the windows, I saw that the sun was already low in the sky. I didn't even notice how much time had passed since we got here.

I got up as well, still carrying the excitable husky puppy in my arms as we left the house. Jace locked the door before heading to his car. He fished out the keys from his pocket and quickly unlocked it.

I placed the puppy inside, lowered the windows to let in fresh air, and closed the door. I slowly turned around and faced Jace, who was about to open the car door.

"What is it, *mon beau?*"

I anxiously bit my lower lip. "Um . . ."

127

The puppy yipped impatiently, as if he was already aching to go home.

"Jace, I just wanted to tell you that I'm thrilled. For the dog, for . . . for everything. I appreciate it a lot."

He smiled and ruffled my hair. "It's no problem, *mon beau.* As long as you're happy."

Just as he was about to slide into his seat, all inhibitions left my mind. I grabbed his tie and pulled him close to me.

His eyes widened at this. "Kei, what . . ."

Instead of answering him, I pressed my lips against, covering his mouth with mine in a searing kiss. I knew I wasn't as experienced as he was, but I wanted to show him how happy he made me today, and kissing him seemed like a brilliant idea.

And God, what an idea it was.

This was the best birthday ever. I swear.

# CHAPTER TWENTY-THREE
## Food Fight

JACE

I just stood there as Kei pulled away from my lips and hurriedly climbed inside the car without a word. I blinked once, twice, then shook my head before I climbed into the driver's seat.

*Why did Kei kiss me?*

I knew it was a strange question to ask. After all, we had kissed before. Earlier today, when we made out in our bed, my lips pressed against his, I couldn't help but think about how his sweet lips tasted.

Still, I was shocked. Kei wasn't the type of person to initiate something, much less an intimate gesture like that.

*So why?*

I started the car, but not before glancing at Kei. He had leaned his head against the car window, purposefully avoiding my gaze. I kept quiet and turned the radio on to ease the tension.

Just as I turned up the volume, a song I was unfamiliar with started playing. I scrunched my nose, about to change the channel when the lyrics echoed throughout the car.

*Just a kiss on your lips in the moonlight,*
*Just a touch and the fire is burning so bright,*
*No, I don't wanna mess this thing up,*

*I don't wanna push too far . . .*

I frowned at the lyrics. *What in the world was this song? Who composed this?*

I was about to find another song when Kei stopped my a hand. I glanced at him briefly, curious as to why he did that.

"S-sorry. Don't change the channel," he quietly said.

I returned my hand to the steering wheel and focused back on the road ahead. "Why?"

I sensed him shift a bit on his seat before he leaned comfortably against the headrest.

"I like the song."

I didn't say anything after that.

The silence continued throughout our drive. As soon as we arrived home and I parked my car, Kei immediately grabbed the husky from the backseat and practically ran into the house.

Locking the car, I followed Kei inside, and to my surprise, Ralph was already there, casually sitting on the leather couch.

And Kei was frowning in confusion. "A what now?"

"Ralph," I greeted with a nod.

Ralph grinned goofily. "I mean a puppy, *mon minou. Un chiot.*"

I stood near Kei and glared at Ralph.

"Ralph, I think it's best if you not speak French in front of Kei."

Kei elbowed me in the hip, making me groan. "Then teach me how to speak French, idiot."

All of a sudden, Ralph clapped his hands. "Oh right, I just remembered! *Joyeux anniversaire, Kei!*"[45]

Kei smiled. "Thank you, Ralph."

He noticed the wiggling puppy in Kei's arms and laughed. "Ah, I see that you like him! What did you name him?"

---

[45] Happy birthday, Kei!

I was about to tell him that we haven't come up with a good name yet, but Kei beat me to it.

"Frenzy."

Both Ralph and I looked at him in disbelief.

"Why Frenzy?" I asked.

The puppy yipped and wagged his tail, as if to to show his approval of his new name.

Kei laughed and carefully let go of him.

Unsurprisingly, the pup, now named Frenzy, scampered off toward the kitchen, as expected.

Ralph snorted. "The new name definitely suits him. He's always in a frenzy."

I rolled my eyes at him.

Kei came to my side and looked up at me. I couldn't help but stare into his warm brown eyes, the same eyes that captivated me during our so-called wedding.

"Hey, I know I've said this like a million times, but thank you. I'm so glad that I get to celebrate my birthday with you," he said softly.

My eyes widened. "What?"

Kei blushed tremendously, as if he just realized what he had said.

"Oh, I—I mean, I'm glad that I get to celebrate my birthday with you and . . . and Ralph! Yeah, with Ralph and Frenchy!"

I couldn't help but smirk in amusement.

"Frenchy?"

He blushed even harder in response and slyly turned his back to me.

"I m-mean Frenzy. Frenzy, the, y'know, the puppy," he corrected himself.

I glanced out of the corner of my eye and saw that Ralph was long gone, probably looking for Frenzy. I then turned my attention back to Kei, who was now making his way toward the kitchen.

I silently followed him. For some reason, I couldn't seem to suppress the big smile on my face as I watched him move around the kitchen, where the household staff were busy preparing his birthday dinner.

During the first few days after meeting Kei, my initial impression was that he was immature and unlikely to adapt to my lifestyle. Of course, my early treatment of him didn't help. I was aware of how I acted—it was a test to see if he was going to be a suitable life partner, even when he was already my legitimate life partner. That was it really. Nothing more, nothing less.

Frankly, I expected our marriage to crumble within the first few months, but as time went on, I realized he was too good to be true. Kei was very independent and had a soft heart for everyone— well, everyone except me.

"Jace!"

Kei's irritated voice brought me back to reality and saw him holding a bag of flour and a tray of eggs.

"Jace?" Kei repeated.

I cleared my throat and sat down on one of the stools around the island counter.

"*Desolé*. I was just thinking. What were you saying?"

Kei gave me a suspicious look before he set down the items he was carrying.

"I was just telling you that I'll make some cupcakes for us. If you don't mind?"

"*Mon beau*, it is your birthday. You can do anything you want. I won't get mad," I reassured him. "But, you should know that the staff had already baked a birthday cake for you. In fact, Lucy said it's your favorite, the one your mom always baked for your birthday."

His eyes twinkled and widened further, accompanied by a devious grin. "Really? I can do anything today?"

I nodded without thinking. *"Oui."*

Without warning, he reached into the bag of flour and threw a handful over my head. My eyes widened at what had just transpired, but as the flour settled on my head, I closed them tightly and tried hard not to sneeze.

Not a minute later, Ralph came in, carrying Frenzy in his arms.

*Oh no.*

"Food fight!" Kei and Ralph shouted in excitement before they chased each other and threw flour at everything, causing everyone to scamper away, including the puppy, who was now sneezing.

I groaned. *Dieu aide-moi.*[46]

---

[46] God help me.

# CHAPTER TWENTY-FOUR
## Take Me to Palawan

KEI

Ralph and I somehow made a huge mess of the entire kitchen, and the supposed cupcakes were long forgotten. The kitchen floor was chalk-white from the flour, and I could have sworn I saw egg yolk dripping down the side of the fridge.

*Fuck! It would have been hell to clean up. What the hell was I even thinking? Thank God for the house staff . . .*

Right now, I was sitting next to Ralph on the couch in the living room, while Jace stood in front of us like an angry parent. It seemed that his anger had only intensified instead of calming down during the time Ralph and I took to clean ourselves up.

*I swear, there's not a single spot on my body that wasn't covered in flour . . . I think it even got into my ears.*

"Uh, so how about that dinner?" Ralph nervously said.

Jace gave us heated glares. *"Tais toi."*[47]

Ralph quickly shut his mouth. Okay, never mind. Jace wasn't just angry. He was furious.

"A dirty kitchen is one of the things I hate the most, yet you two deliberately—" Jace stopped, as if the extent of the chaos had momentarily stunned him into silence.

---

[47] Be quiet. or Shut up.

I slumped my shoulders. "Sorry, Jace."

"I'm sorry too. I promise it won't happen again," Ralph added.

Jace let out a sigh before gesturing for me to get up. I gave him a curious look, but he didn't answer as he turn around and headed toward his study.

"Ralph, just go home. I have something I need to do," Jace told his brother, not once looking behind him as he continued on his way.

Ralph looked at his brother's retreating form for a second before finally leaving, closing the door behind him.

I inaudibly gulped. Without Ralph, I was suddenly feeling very nervous, and my mind was racing with questions.

*What's Jace gonna do to me? Is he really furious with what Ralph and I did?*

Nevertheless, I kept quiet as I followed him to his study. The last time I had been in here was when Jace overworked himself to the point of passing out.

I grimaced at the memory.

*And some time after that, he made me cook that vile veal kidney for him . . .*

"Sit."

I snapped back to the present and saw Jace casually sitting behind his desk. Slowly, I made my way to the armchair in front of his desk and sat down. Once settled, I looked up at Jace, and before I knew it, my hormones started to kick in. It didn't help that he looked hot, sitting there all regal-like. He looked like a king . . . a hot and sexy king.

*So that would make me his . . . queen? Hell no.*

"Where's the dog?" he suddenly asked.

I blinked. "Oh yeah, I saw Frenzy going upstairs. Why?"

"Nothing. Anyway, did you enjoy today?"

I smiled. "Very much so. Thank you again, by the way."

Jace just nodded.

135

I frowned at him. He was acting weird, and it was creeping me out.

"What do you think of Palawan?" he suddenly asked out of the blue.

"Should we have dinner now? I said almost at the same time.

I cocked my head in curiosity. "Pala-what?"

Jace's mouth twitched into a small smile, but he covered it with a cough. *Aw, cute.*

"Palawan. It's an island in the Philippines. I've heard there are plenty of beautiful places there."

My eyes widened. "Oh yeah, I remember now! I once saw online that there's an underground river there, and it seems that we can go kayaking too. Are you going on a business trip to Palawan?"

Jace shook his head. "No."

I frowned again. "Then, what . . ."

Jace took something from his drawer.

I leaned forward to see what it is, but then he flicked my forehead.

"Ow! Jerk." I pouted.

He just smirked, then stood up and walked around his desk to throw something on my lap.

I looked down and frowned. Noticing my reaction, Jace leaned against his desk and reached out to ruffle my hair. Normally, I would have hated it, but his touch feels nice.

"As my second birthday present to you—"

I cut him off. "Second? I thought Frenzy was my present?"

He flicked my forehead again. "No, *mon beau*. I have another present for you."

I had been in a state of heightened excitement throughout the day, but it ramped up even more with his statement.

*Oooh, what could be his next present for me?* God, Jace was starting to spoil me a lot, and I loved it!

Jace's hand remained on my head, occasionally running his fingers through my hair. I couldn't hide my blush as I felt his hand gently massage my scalp. As strange as it sounds, the gesture felt intimate.

I nearly closed my eyes at the touch of his fingers but restrained myself. I didn't want Jace to know how I feel about him; it was simply impossible for me to show.

"My second present for you is in those papers," he said.

I raised said papers to my face, which turned out to be brochures and reservation documents for a resort in the Philippines.

Frowning in confusion, I stared at Jace, who smiled at me like the cat that got the cream. *I don't get it. Was Jace trying to sell me something? Why on earth would he . . . Wait, what? . . . Is he? Oh shit . . .*

"Jace, these are printed out reservation papers!"

"I'm aware," Jace replied, amused.

I read the details on the papers and nearly fainted. This couldn't be real. Surely, Jace was playing with me again, right? This must be another prank or something because there's no way . . .

"You're taking me to Palawan?" I asked in disbelief as I looked up at him.

Instead of answering, Jace merely gave me a dazzling smile, confirming my guess.

Suddenly, and without a second thought, I reached over to pull down his tie and closed the distance between us with a kiss. He grunted in surprise, but I ignored it because all that mattered right now was this moment. Jace was slowly pulling on my heartstrings, and he didn't even know it. How cruel yet incredible was that?

I felt him move from the desk and helped me stand up. After a bit of maneuvering, without breaking the embrace or the kiss, I found myself sitting on his lap with my arms wrapped around his firm neck. Our lips were meshed together, neither of us even bothering to gasp for air.

The kiss was . . . *I don't even know how to describe it.* Like the kisses before this, it was incredible beyond words. Before I knew it, my feelings for Jace became stronger than ever, making my chest ache as all the pent-up emotions inside me just exploded.

Jace's hands moved to my hips as his thumbs gently caressed my sides. We pulled apart for a second before kissing again. I could feel his tongue press against my bottom lip, and I parted my lips in response, allowing him full access to my mouth. His lips were soft against mine, and I wound my arms tighter around his neck, careful not to strangle him as we deepened the kiss. The sensation of his wet tongue made me lose all touch of reality.

It was like we were the only two people in the world. Nothing else mattered because we only had each other.

I moaned at the taste of his tongue.

*He tasted like . . . like . . .*

"What are you thinking about?" Jace murmured against my mouth, his tongue still licking me.

My eyes fluttered at his deep voice. "You taste very sweet. Like candy."

He quietly chuckled. "Well then, *merci.*"

I grinned. "You're welcome."

He continued to kiss me, and I quickly gave in. Why should I resist when I loved everything about him? I could overlook his imperfect attitude as long as he was smiling at me right now and as long as my feelings for him were still there.

Jace gently pulled me away from him.

I frowned. "What is it?"

Jace smirked. "Let's enjoy your birthday dinner and cake before you go pack your things. We're going to Palawan. Tonight."

# CHAPTER TWENTY-FIVE
## The More the Merrier

"What the—" I muttered upon entering the plane, or rather, Jace's private jet.

"Hi, *mon minou!*" Ralph said from his lounging position, wiggling his fingers at me.

*I can't believe this. I thought this trip was only for us two.*

"Hold that thought for a moment," I told Ralph.

I should have known his brother would be coming with us. Turning around, I grabbed Jace by the hand and dragged him with me behind the curtains across the cockpit.

"Why is Ralph here?" I hissed at him.

He raised both hands. "I didn't invite him."

"Then how the hell did he know?"

Jace just shrugged. "Don't blame me. I didn't even know he knew, let alone that he was coming with us."

I groaned in frustration. He was acting like he didn't care at all and it bothered me. I was expecting for this trip to be a private moment between Jace and me, like a honeymoon. I wanted us to be lovey-dovey together, even though it sounded childish. But how could we do that when his brother was here?

"Look, let's just ignore Ralph and enjoy the whole trip. Okay, *mon beau?*" He cupped my face with both hands.

I sighed in defeat. "Okay, but you owe me a massage when we get there."

He laughed and planted a kiss on my forehead.

I blushed. *What did that kiss mean? Was it a friendly kiss or something else?*

Shoving the curtains aside, Jace said, "Let's go see the capt—"

"Kyaaa!" A shriek echoed inside the plane.

I shoved Jace away in surprise. That ear-damaging shriek sounded oddly familiar. I turned around and saw what nearly made me want to throw Jace off the plane and leave him in pieces.

"What the hell are you doing here?" I exclaimed.

The Winston triplets were all standing in front of me, each sporting a wide grin. Autumn and Winter, as usual, wore matching clothes in different colors, while Summer wore a summer dress and a pair of sunglasses resting on her head. They all looked like they were dressed for a tropical vacation.

Summer suddenly jumped into my arms. "Kei, I hate you! You didn't tell me you're going on a trip to the Philippines with your hot husband!"

Autumn snorted. "Hugging him while saying you hate him doesn't make sense."

Jace looked at the three siblings in curiosity. "How did you get here? I don't recall inviting you."

"Um, Ralph invited Ryan and told him to invite Kei's best friends from school, and that's us. So here we are!" Summer explained in excitement.

I face-palmed myself. *Oh my God, so the whole gang is here?*

Autumn clapped me on the back which made me stumble forward.

*Damn it, couldn't he control that strength of his?*

"How come you look like you don't want us here, Kei?"

I shook my head frantically. "I didn't say that!"

Summer smirked and elbowed Winter beside her. "I get it. Kei doesn't want us to interrupt his honeymoon with his hubby. Isn't that right, Winter?"

Winter just shrugged and stayed quiet.

Like instinct, I immediately defended myself when Summer pointed that out. After all, I didn't want Jace to know what I secretly wanted. Not only would that be embarrassing for me, but it would also inflate Jace's ego even further.

"I-I don't know what you're t-talking about, Summer. You're crazy," I stuttered.

Autumn and Summer merely laughed. Those jerks!

"Sir, the captain said we need to prepare for takeoff in ten minutes," an attractive man said to Jace.

He was probably the copilot. Summer was ogling at him, which almost made me feel sorry for the poor man. Nevertheless, I approached Summer and pinched her cheek.

"Ow! What did you do that for?" she yelped in pain.

I rolled my eyes at her. "Don't torture one of Jace's pilots, Summer."

Autumn laughed in agreement.

Jace and the copilot went to the cockpit, probably to make sure that everything was in order and that there weren't any technical problems or anything.

I was just about to find my seat when I suddenly remembered something. "Wait a second . . . Didn't you say Ryan is coming with us too?" I asked Summer.

She nodded, and just like that, Ryan emerged from the plane's restroom as if to finally make his appearance.

"Hey, dude!" he greeted with a grin. "I'm going to Palawan with you."

*You've got to be kidding me.*

\*     \*     \*

*A few hours later*

"How long before we get there?" Summer whined.

141

The rest of us groaned in annoyance at Summer's question. Ever since the plane took off, Summer has been constantly asking the same questions nonstop.

*"Are we there yet?" "How far is the island?" "Are we close?"*

Needless to say, it was irritating as hell, especially given the navigation system clearly indicating real-time information about our flight. But it was especially irritating for Jace, sitting right beside me, wanting to fall asleep but couldn't because of Summer's annoying questions, and it was clear he was becoming cranky.

"Maybe I should have put my food down and not let them come," Jace grumbled beside me, his arms folded on his chest.

"If you had done that, then you would have owed me another birthday present," I said.

He scoffed. "You already have Frenzy and this—" He flapped his hand, unable to continue.

"You're immature."

"No, I'm not." He scowled.

"Are too."

"Am not."

"Are too."

"Hey, lovebirds! Quiet down, will you?" Summer yelled from the front part of the plane.

"Says the one who creates noise pollution!" I yelled back.

"Oh, you are so dead!"

*"Tais toi!"* Jace impatiently exclaimed.

Summer and I shut our mouths in an instant.

After that, except for the hum of the plane's engine, the rest of the flight was spent in pure silence. Finally, everyone had settled down and fallen asleep.

Jace and I, however, were unable to sleep, sitting tensely beside each other. I hesitantly glanced at Jace, who was rubbing his temple with an index finger. He noticed me watching him, and I quickly looked away. After a while, I felt his hand on my head as he gently played with my hair.

142

I faced him again.

"I'm sorry I yelled at you," he apologized in a whisper.

I just smiled at him, but internally, I was doing everything within my power not to spazz out. Damn it, how was it possible that he could be hot and adorable at the same time? It should honestly be a crime. In fact, his face alone should be illegal. I honestly couldn't handle it.

"Nah, it was my fault in the first place anyway." I shrugged.

Jace smiled before he leaned in to kiss my cheek.

As usual, I blushed to the tips of my ears. His kisses alone could make me do that. Hell, even his presence alone could incite a reaction from me.

I looked into his beautiful eyes, which seemed to outshine everything. It was strange how everything changed between us. The first time we met, I didn't have any deep feelings for him. He was annoyingly overbearing, his ego was as big as his bank account, and he never really cared about me, but now . . .

I too had made myself comfortable and slept—though I had no idea for how long. All I knew was that my head was on Jace's shoulder and he was waking me up.

"Lady and gentlemen, this is Captain François Dumont speaking. We are now beginning our descent. It's a beautiful day outside, as you can see from your windows. The temperature is approximately 31°C—that is 87.8°F for our American guests. We anticipate landing in approximately thirty minutes, at Pamalican Island, north of Palawan Island, in the Philippines. Please fasten your seatbelts," the pilot said through the speakers.

Jace ruffled my hair. "We're almost there, *mon beau*. Would you like to use the toilet first?"

I nodded and went to relieve myself. While there, I decided to wash my face and brush my teeth. Sometime during the flight, I had been awakened from my sleep when the flight attendants began serving food, but I promptly returned to sleep afterward. Glancing at my watch, I calculated that I might have slept uninterrupted for more than six hours, leaving me feeling both light and heavy at the same time.

When I returned to Jace's side, he fastened my seatbelt before his own, which made me blush.

As the plane safely landed on the runway, a decision cryztallized in my mind. It was a choice that could either make my heart soar in bliss or shatter into a million pieces. It was a risk I was willing to take, and strangely enough, I wasn't afraid of any of the consequences.

Deep down, I knew tI had to do it during our stay in Palawan. Despite the possibility of failure, I was determined to try.

I was going to tell Jace I loved him.

# CHAPTER TWENTY-SIX
## Let's Play Beach Volleyball

*Note to self: Don't go on a trip with your husband if your friends are present.*

Ever since the plane landed on renowned Palawan island in the Philippines, Summer decided to drag me along with her, disrupting my plans to stay with Jace as I had intended.

I considered telling her I had other plans, but the girl came prepared, immediately countering with a threat that could make anyone question her sanity.

*"If you don't stick with me, I'll stitch your butthole with dental floss so tight you won't be able to produce babies with your precious hubby."*

Yep, she was definitely crazy.

After clearing customs, completing immigration procedures, and ensuring all paperwork was in order, we immediately proceeded to an exclusive-looking resort set amidst trees. There, we checked into a four-bedroom villa that Jace had reserved for an entire week.

Naturally, I expected that Jace and I would share the same suite. However, there was one tiny problem . . .

"Kei! You have to share a room with me!" Summer declared after everyone had done a mini-tour of the immediate surroundings and settled down in the spacious living room.

I gaped at her. "What?"

She grinned deviously. "I wanna share a room with you. Is it alright with you, Jace?"

*Since when were they on a first-name basis?*

I turned to face Jace, who stood beside me. A part of me half-expected him to disagree with Summer. It was also the part that wanted to know whether he wanted to share a room with me or not, because if I had a choice, I would definitely share a room with him. That way, I could enjoy all the attention I could get from him in peace.

"Sure, it's fine," Jace casually replied, shattering my fantasies of being alone with him.

"Winter's gonna be with me," Autumn announced, lazily propping his feet on the wooden table at the center of the living room.

Ralph yawned but not before he also chimed in, "Then *mon frère* and I will share a room."

I chuckled at the mortified expression on Jace's face. "*Non.* Why don't you sleep by yourself?" he suggested, a hint of desperation in his tone that I caught onto.

"Oh, come on. I'll even read you a bedtime story."

Jace obviously didn't like the idea, so I came to his rescue.

"Guys, how about this? Autumn and Winter will be in the first room. The second room will be shared between Ralph and Ryan, and Summer and I will take the third room."

Jace wrinkled his nose. "Then that leaves me alone in a room."

Ralph laughed. "All the better. The master shall sleep in the master's bedroom. By himself."

Everyone else seemed to be okay with that decision except Jace, who looked less than pleased that he was being outvoted.

Summer clapped her hands to get our attention. "Now, who's up for some swimming at the beach?"

\*　　\*　　\*

146

"This place is amazing!" Summer shrieked, her eyes sparkling as she gazed excitedly at the crystal-blue ocean.

No one said anything to the contrary—we were all in agreement. The beach resort was nothing short of breathtaking. Villas nestled among tropical tress, some bearing fruit, while palm trees lined the shoreline just a few feet away from the water. Scattered across the pristine white sands were lounge chairs under beach umbrellas, inviting relaxation. A few were occupied by other resort guests soaking up the sun's warmth, finding respite from its midafternoon intensity, while others enjoyed a swim in the water. Not too far away, a group of teenagers played volleyball.

*"C'est le paradis,"*[48] Ralph said with his arms wide open.

Again, we nodded. I glanced to my side and saw Jace sprawled lazily on a beach chair under the shade of a palm tree. I nearly drooled at the sight of him. It was the very first time I had seen him in swimming trunks, paired with a white unbuttoned shirt that perfectly showed off his firm chest.

"Yes, *mon beau*? Do you need something?" Jace suddenly asked.

*Yeah, I need you.* I almost said that aloud, but luckily, I bit my tongue just in time. I didn't need to make a fool of myself in front of Jace.

"Nothing," I replied.

Jace hummed in response and put his sunglasses on.

I sighed. He was acting normal ever since we arrived. Too normal.

Just as I was about to sit beside him and strike up a conversation, Summer called out and urged me to play volleyball with them. Reluctantly, I left Jace alone and joined the rest of the gang.

As I walked over to them, Autumn was already holding a ball in both hands. He was standing on the other side of the net with

---

[48] It's paradise.

Ryan and Ralph, while Winter and Summer were on the side closest to me.

"Don't you think our side has a hundred percent chance of losing to those three?" I said to Summer as I stood by her side.

I already knew we weren't going to win this game since Ryan had been playing volleyball since middle school. He had even managed to win a few trophies at the time.

Summer snorted. "Pffft, nonsense! We can totally win this! Plus, we have our trump card."

Now that got me excited.

"Really? What is it?"

Summer merely winked at me before she took a predatory-like stance in the center.

I frowned. She was acting weird, and I didn't like it. For all I know, she could be hatching some evil plan that could backfire and drag me down with it in the process.

"Aw, look at wittle Wummer twying to act scwary!" Autumn teased his sister as both Ralph and Ryan laughed.

I expected Summer to lash out at them with a barrage of curse words, but much to my surprise, she merely smirked.

*What the . . .*

"Here I go!" Autumn yelled as he threw the ball toward us in a spike serve.

I barely managed to hit the ball toward Summer before she set it to Winter. My eyes widened when he jumped up high and spiked the ball with such brute force that the ball might as well be on fire.

I looked at our opponents on the other side, and their reactions were similar to mine.

We got the first point.

"Way to go, Winny!" Summer cheered for her brother.

The game continued in this manner, with Winter scoring point after point. The heat of the sun didn't bother me, but moving

148

around in the sand proved challenging. Beach volleyball was a lot harder than I expected.

The score was now 6–2, thanks to Winter.

After a couple more sets, Autumn yelled in defeat. Summer and I high-fived while Winter just smiled in victory.

"Since when did you learn how to play volleyball?" Autumn asked as he approached his brother.

I decided to leave them to argue and walk straight back to Jace, who was now standing up with his sunglasses perched on his head. I held in a smile as he yawned.

"Took a short nap, old man?" I teased once I got close to him.

He playfully flicked my forehead in response. Instead of getting mad at him, I just looked at him with a smile.

"Wanna go for a swim?"

"Sure."

I frowned. "You don't sound enthusiastic."

"I do."

"Oh really?"

"Yes."

I crossed my arms over my chest. "Then prove it."

I immediately regretted saying it because in an instant, I found myself in Jace's arms, bridal style. My face heated profusely, and I could have sworn it had nothing to do with the sun.

"Put me down, Jace! People are watching!" I hissed at him.

He ignored me and continued walking toward the water.

"Go, Kei! Skinny-dip with your hubby!" Summer yelled behind us as the other guys laughed.

I gave them a death glare behind Jace's shoulder.

*Some friends they are.*

# CHAPTER TWENTY-SEVEN
## Kisses

I screamed as I suddenly felt myself airborne. Jace had thrown me into the deep part of the ocean. I felt the impact as my body hit the water, sputtering as I began to sink. Before long, I propelled myself back to the surface.

Jace was grinning smugly; his shirt now long gone, giving me full access to stare at his jaw-droppingly toned, wet chest.

*Gulp.*

"Having fun, *mon beau?*"

I snapped back from my short fantasy and splashed at him. "You asshole! I could have drowned!"

He just laughed as he swam closer to me, but I kicked my feet to keep away from him. He didn't catch the hint and continued swimming toward me until his arms were wrapped around me under the water.

I stared into his eyes, and goddamn if I didn't pop a boner right then and there. He was too handsome for his own good—attractive, beautiful, gorgeous, sexy, and hot as hell . . . like a god.

"Jace, I . . ." I ran out of words as I continued gazing straight into his eyes.

Then, it felt like we were the only two people left on this island, and my body turned to jelly at his touch. I hadn't expected falling in love to be so . . . hard.

*"Mon beau?"*

We leaned closer to each other in slow motion, just like in the movies. In that moment, I ignored everything else—the blaring sun, the cool ocean wind, the gentle waves that came with a calm and peaceful day, and the joyful sounds of people on the beach.

Time seemed to slow down, and after what felt like forever, I could almost feel Jace's lips when—

"Kei, watch out!"

*Too late.*

I fell backward into the water after getting hit on the head by a volleyball. I could vaguely hear Jace calling out for me before everything started fading to black.

*       *       *

"Kei? Kei!"

My eyes fluttered, and immediately I coughed, forcefully expelling water until the sensation of drowning subsided. Gradually, I felt my lungs clear, allowing me to finally breathe in the fresh air.

"Kei! Are you alright?"

"Please say something, Kei!"

"Is he still alive?"

"Idiot, of course he is! Shut up!"

As I slowly regained all my senses, I looked around. I found myself lying on a beach chair with the whole gang fussing about, each firing question after question as they anxiously wondered if I was okay. My eyes widened when I caught sight of Summer, whose eyes looked red and puffy as if she had been crying.

"W-what happened?" I mumbled hoarsely.

Someone handed me a glass of water, but I ignored it as Summer knelt beside me, wiping her tearstained face.

"Oh my gosh! I'm so sorry, Kei! I didn't mean for this to happen."

I frowned. *What did she mean by that?*

Glancing around, I see Ralph and Ryan looking sick with worry, while Autumn and Winter were quiet.

"Where's Jace?" I asked, noticing his absence.

Ryan scratched his head. "We, uh, don't know."

This caused me to stand up, but I immediately regretted it because my head started to spin, making me feel nauseous. Luckily, Summer helped me sit back down again, while Ralph handed me a glass of water.

I thanked him and gulped it down until the glass was empty.

"Where's Jace?" I repeated.

Ralph came forward. "We really don't know, *mon minou*. He just walked away without saying anything after Ryan saved you from drowning."

I didn't need him to continue. My heart hurt as I imagined Jace blaming himself for what happened. I was sure he was wandering off, his mind filled with unnecessary guilt. I wondered if he would do something self-destructive.

Hurriedly, I stood up to search for Jace, determined to prevent anything bad from happening. My head was still spinning, and I could faintly hear the others yelling at me to stop, but I just ignored their pleas.

Despite not knowing where I was going, I kept walking until Ryan caught up with me and grabbed my hand. I turned to glare at him.

"Kei, stop. You don't know where he is. Nobody knows," he said in concern. "The resort is vast, Kei."

I shoved him away. "I don't care. I have to find him."

"Kei—" He stopped when he saw the determination on my face which made him sigh in defeat. "Still stubborn as ever. I hope you find him then."

I turned around and resumed my search for Jace. Even though I was feeling a bit woozy, I pressed on, earning a few strange looks from the people around me.

*Damn it, Jace. Where are you?*

It was getting dark, so I stopped walking and decided to rest for a bit. Glancing behind me, I realized I had already walked a long way, though I could still vaguely see my friends at the end of the beach.

Squinting at the ocean to my right, I watched people playing with the waves.

*Lucky them*, I thought bitterly.

As I sat down on the soft sand, my thoughts drifted back to the day when Jace and I signed our wedding papers.

\*　　　\*　　　\*

*"Congratulations. You're now officially married," announced the judge from across the long business table.*

*I just sat there, trying my best to ignore everything.*

*The man beside me, whom I had recently come to know as Mr. Jace Langlois, put his pen on the table after signing the papers—the same papers that sealed my fate. Or should I say, a death warrant?*

*Whatever. All I knew was that I was doomed to spend my life with a stranger.*

*"You look upset. I expected you to say 'thank you,' at least. Your inheritance is finally yours, you know," Mr. Langlois suddenly said once the judge and the witnesses left the room.*

*"Thank you, Mr. Langlois." I forced myself to say, though the words tasted bitter in my mouth.*

*He chortled. "Mr. Langlois makes me sound old. Call me Jace."*

*I looked at him. He was joking, right? Why should he complain about names? Apparently, he was way older than me. I didn't even know his age.*

*"I'm only twenty-eight," he said, as if he had read my mind.*

*I averted my eyes from him and focused on something else instead, like the plain white walls of the room.*

*"Married at the age of twenty-eight, and here I thought thirty is the right age to marry," he said to himself.*

*"Then why did you agree to this arrangement? You should have just thought of something else. Marrying a man I barely know is just stupid," I grumbled.*

*As he stood beside me, he laughed, but I didn't make an effort to look at him. To make things worse, he was actually French, and I had a certain weakness for French guys.*

*He shrugged. "I don't even know why I considered your parents' instructions, let alone went through with all the legalities. Maybe I want to give myself—this . . . us a chance. Who knows?"*

*A chance, huh?*

*       *       *

The silence of the beach and the darkness of my spot away from the resort snapped me back to the present. I hadn't realized how late it was getting, and Jace was still nowhere to be found. With that thought in mind, I stood up and brushed the sand off my shorts.

*"Mon beau?"*

I jolted, whipping around toward the voice. There he stood, on the white sand that shimmered under the moonlight. The ocean behind us sparkled with the reflection of the stars, casting a magical glow over the entire beach.

"Jace," I whispered.

I was shocked when he suddenly ran to me and hugged me tightly.

"What . . ."

He hugged me for a couple of seconds before pulling away, his eyes searching my entire face with a worried expression.

"I've been looking everywhere for you."

I frowned. "Looking for me? I was looking for you. Where were you?"

Now, it was his turn to frown. "I went to lick my wounds."

"But they said—"

154

"When the ball hit your head, instead of making sure you were alright, I was too busy getting angry at your friends, glaring at them that I did not even realize you had gone under. Even seeing Ryan sprint across the beach toward us failed to inform me of the danger you were in."

He shook his head, gently touched my face, before he hugged me tightly again.

"It doesn't matter now. You're here," he said.

I kept quiet, internally debating on whether to return his hug. In the end, my heart won, and I wound my arms around his back, feeling his chest against my face. I breathed in his scent, a mix of musk and the ocean.

God, I never would have admitted back then that hugging him would be the safest thing that I have ever felt. It just felt right being in his arms like that. I snuggled closer to him, feeling his heartbeat.

His hand traveled softly up and down on my back, while his other hand played with my hair. I smiled dreamily when I felt his lips on my head. For the first time ever, I felt content.

"Jace?"

"Hmmm?"

I gulped. "There's something that I wanna tell you."

He didn't let go even as I said that, so I swallowed the massive lump in my throat and hugged him tighter. I just couldn't let go, even if I tried. His embrace served as my strength—the strength that I needed to I tell him everything.

*"Desole,"* he suddenly said against my hair.

Reluctantly, I pulled myself away from him and stared into his eyes. As expected, the expression behind them was filled with guilt.

"Jace, don't—"

He shut his eyes close. "I should have saved you from drowning. I should not have let my anger at their intrusion into the vacation I had planned for us get the better of me. I should have—"

I placed a finger on his lips to quiet him. He opened his eyes.

"None of what happened is your fault. You don't have to apologize. Look, I'm fine. I'm right here, okay?"

He didn't reply. Instead, he kissed me firmly on my forehead before hugging me again.

I was about to say something when his hands began to shake.

"Jace? Are you okay?" I dared to ask.

He silently shook his head.

My heart soared at this surprising revelation. He was scared for me. He was worried about what would happen to me, and he blamed himself for it. My smile grew even wider, and I failed to suppress my laugh.

Jace heard me and gave me a curious look.

"What?" he asked.

I laughed a little more before I cupped his face with both hands. I stared into his eyes longingly. "I never thought that you would be worried about me."

He chuckled. "Then, I succeeded."

I blushed as his lips softly brushed against mine, his hot breath fanning against my mouth and sending goose bumps erupting on my skin.

"Succeeded on what?"

At long last, his lips deepened the kiss, and I closed my eyes in bliss, loving every second of this moment. His kisses never ceased to amaze me. His lips expertly danced with mine as I moved my arms from around his back to his neck. I had to stand on my toes just to press our mouths closer together, while his hands ran down to my waist and held me close.

From slow and gentle, the kiss became more passionate and wantoned. In the past, I would have killed myself if I acted like this with another guy, but Jace wasn't just any other guy. He was my

156

world. I loved him so much, and I would do anything for him—and him alone.

Jace pulled away first as we gasped for air. "I succeeded in giving us a chance."

I smiled happily at his words.

He remembered.

# CHAPTER TWENTY-EIGHT
## Too Much Doubt

Jace and I stayed on the beach, enjoying each other's company. I didn't even know what time it was, but at that moment, I didn't care. The world could have ended right then and there, and I still would have clung to Jace like my life depended on it. Literally.

A long silence passed between us, except for the occasional sounds of the crashing waves against the shore, the soft ocean breeze, and my thumping heart.

I sat on the sand with my back against Jace's chest, my head resting on his shoulder. For the first time, I felt genuinely happy.

I felt Jace move behind me, making me tilt my head back to look at his face. He looked even more handsome now that the moonlight illuminated it. I couldn't resist the sudden urge to caress his stubbled face.

He blinked twice before staring deep into my eyes.

"What?" he asked, confused by my gesture.

"You're so handsome."

As expected, he smirked. "I know."

I pinched his nose, but not too hard. I wouldn't want to see his beautifully sculpted face with a broken nose.

"Cocky shit," I muttered before leaning back to his chest.

His arms wrapped around my torso, making me blush.

"By the way, what were you gonna say to me?" he suddenly asked.

I frowned but didn't face him. "What are you talking about?"

"Before I said sorry, you told me there's something you wanted to tell me. What is it?"

I sucked in a breath.

*Shit.*

I slowly untangled Jace's arms from around me, then scooted several inches from him. He looked more confused as I avoided his eyes, which seemed to be staring straight into my soul.

"Um, I was just . . ." I suddenly realized that I had no idea how he would react if I told him. Sure, I had encouraged myself to tell him now, but I didn't think it was a good idea. Despite telling myself that I was going to be brave and just get on with it, my heart couldn't take any more feelings.

Honestly, I was just scared of how Jace would take it. So I sighed and reluctantly gave him a forced smile.

"Nothing."

He raised an eyebrow. "You sure?"

Despite the nagging feeling I felt in my stomach, I gave him a smile before I stood up and pulled him with me.

"Yeah, I'm sure. Let's go."

*     *     *

I was pretty sure that Jace and I had made some small progress in our "relationship" yesterday. I assumed that it was gonna be all right despite me not confessing my true feelings to him, but now . . .

"Where's Jace? He was supposed to take us to his rented yacht today," Summer said as I sat on one of the beanbags.

It was 10:30 AM, and everyone was lounging in the living and dining pavilion. Autumn and Winter were playing a board game, Ralph was watching gags on YouTube, while Ryan sat in the far corner of the room, tapping away on his laptop, which reminded me that he had yet to fix my broken one.

"*Mon frère* had some business to attend to. He will probably be back by noon," Ralph said, not averting his eyes away from his device.

Summer scowled. "He's working? I thought this was supposed to be a vacation!"

"Well, he *is* rich. He's got to work all the time to make loads of money," Autumn said after winning the game, making Winter pout.

"But still!" Summer whined.

Even I had to agree with Summer. *What the hell was Jace thinking?* He said we were gonna spend this vacation together, but no, he just had to up and leave us here to work his ass off, which by the way, was completely unnecessary. I was sure he already had zillions of dollars saved up in his multiple bank accounts. Why would he need to work in the middle of a vacation? He was wasting his time.

"Do you know where he is?" I asked Ralph, who was laughing at a video of a cat jumping on a trampoline.

*Yeah, I know. Hilarious. Please note the sarcasm.*

Ralph looked at me. "He did not give any details. Just said he had some people to talk to."

I sighed in defeat.

"Why don't you just call him?" Ryan suggested.

"I did call him. Ten times, and all of them went to voice mail."

Summer groaned. "This sucks! I wanna be on a yacht so bad! Ralph, do something!"

"Don't look at me! I have no idea about any yacht. Why don't you go to reception and ask about it?"

As they bantered, I quietly went outside and closed the door. I decided to take a stroll around the beach and explore the

160

whole resort. I didn't want to stay in the house without Jace. Despite my friends' presence, it still wasn't the same.

At the beach, I couldn't help but smile. With the silky sand under my feet and the cool gentle breeze against my skin, I couldn't help but admire the stunning scene—the waves of the blue ocean, and the multitude of palm trees that danced against the wind.

I really liked this place. Despite Jace being gone for a while, I was still grateful that he brought me here.

Continuing my walk along the sandy beach, I occasionally smiled at people who greeted me with their own smiles. As I walked, doubtful thoughts came flooded my mind, especially concerning Jace.

*How could he work in the middle of a vacation? If he really had feelings for me, which I doubted, why would he leave me here? Did he love his work more than me? Was that it?*

Somehow, that last thought hurt my feelings. My chest tightened, and I immediately felt my heart drown in unimaginable pain. Thinking about Jace not caring for me at all hurt. Everything hurt.

Some would say I was overreacting, but nobody knew how difficult it was for me not having Jace by my side. What would you do if the person you love chooses to work instead of spending time with you?

It hurts, but I won't let my feelings take over. I won't let the tears fall. Crying doesn't solve any problems, and I learned that the hard way. If anything, it only makes me feel worse.

"I'm just gonna wait for him," I said to myself as I looked at the ocean.

Waiting is probably a good idea for now.
*Probably.*

# CHAPTER TWENTY-NINE
## Oh Shit

It had been a week and three days since Jace left us in the island to meet some people. Since then, he hadn't showed up once. It had also been a week and three days without me seeing him or even hearing his voice.

Later, when I returned to the villa, hungry, thirsty, and hot, no one was there. I had assumed everyone had done their own exploring and that Jace still at his meeting. Later that night, however, after I had strolled the island alone, wondering if Jace felt the same I did, he was still a no-show, worrying everyone, including Ralph, who had not heard from him either.

Early the next morning, Ralph told us that we were flying back to America that day. Jace had taken off by himself the previous day, so we would have to take a commercial flight instead.

Summer argued for us to say, what with the villa already paid for, but Ralph wanted to leave, and I was just devastated.

*That night we got . . . personal, was the last night he was on that island.*

Nevertheless, to say that I was furious as well as heartbroken when I heard the news would be an understatement. I became dead set on finding out the reason Jace left without a word, and maybe then I can give him a piece of my mind.

"You're making that face again."

Sighing heavily, I looked up at Ryan sitting across the small round table. He was holding a cup of espresso, dressed in a gray hoodie with black skinny jeans, and his look was completed with a pair of dirty white Doc Martens.

I couldn't help but smile wryly at the fact that he looked like he had prepared his outfit of the day, which seemed to go perfectly with the rainy weather outside the coffee shop.

As for me, I wore a navy blue sweatshirt and torn jeans with brown Converse shoes. I didn't bother to style my hair this morning, so I wore an old beanie to hide my bed hair.

"What face?" I asked with a frown.

"The face you make when you're thinking about killing someone."

I gave him a blank stare, not bothering to deny his observation. It was true. I was thinking about killing a certain someone who had yet to show up. I didn't even bother to look for him anymore because I knew he wasn't in his office. I knew this because Ryan told me. Apparently, everyone knew Jace was around, but very few actually saw him. As far as the department heads were concerned, Jace might as well have been absent—they had all been turned away. No one had been graced by Jace's presence since the day we left for Palawan. Meanwhile, the gossip mill churned out a hundred different versions of Jace's whereabouts.

"Jace again?" he guessed.

I nodded with a frustrated sigh.

Ryan chuckled and shook his head before he took a small sip of his coffee.

I just sat there, not saying anything until "Sparks" by Hilary Duff rang from Ryan's phone, resting on the table.

I raised my eyebrow at his choice of ringtone.

He playfully stuck out his tongue and picked up the phone.

"Hey," he said gently.

I gave him a curious look.

He threw an empty packet of sugar at me. "Yeah, my day off is today. Busy? Actually, Kei is with me."

I frowned.

"Yeah. We're at a coffee shop just a couple blocks away from Rosemary Hospital. Why?"

A blush creeped from his face to his neck. I couldn't help but smirk knowingly.

*Now, who could that person be?*

I gave him a mischievous wink. In response, he flipped me the bird, and I just laughed.

"I don't know. Maybe next time. What? Are you kidding me? Ralph, shut up! I'll hang up. Bye!" Carelessly, he shoved the poor phone into his satchel.

I smirked. "So you're phone buddies with Ralph now, huh?"

He blushed even harder. "What are you talking about?"

"No need to deny anything. I know you and Jace's brother have some chemistry together," I teased.

He was about to retort but thought better of it, choosing to remain silent instead.

I just grinned at him as I leaned forward, resting my forearms on the table, waiting for him to share things he had yet to share. I let him take his time, not saying a single word in case he chickened out on me.

Back in high school, he was the kind of guy who would always give great advice to others but rarely shared anything about himself. I remembered he even avoided the girls who wanted his attention because he believed they loved to ask too many personal questions.

A couple seconds of silence passed before Ryan sighed. "I dunno if Ralph and I, y'know . . ."

I raised an eyebrow. "What? You two not dating yet?"

He nodded in response.

"Well, you have each other's numbers, so that's progress enough as it is."

He slumped forward on the tabletop and groaned tiredly. "But it's really confusing as hell. He keeps giving me these—these fucking mixed signals, and I'm wondering if I'm overanalyzing stuff or what."

I observed his confused yet amusing state. It was funny how Ryan had been this lanky, silent guy in school so many years ago, but now, with Ralph's presence in his life, he had changed a lot. As Ryan's best friend, I was proud of his transformation.

"Initiate the first move then," I suggested.

He raised his head a little bit to glare at me. I stared back, silently letting him know that I wasn't joking this time. His eyes widened when he realized my seriousness.

"Oh shit, I can't! That's embarrassing!" he yelled, causing the other customers to turn their heads toward us.

Ryan blushed and bowed his head sheepishly.

"What did he say on the phone?" I asked.

"Why are you asking me now?"

"I asked you first."

"I won't tell you."

"Ryan."

A pause.

"Fine. I'll just go back home then." I was about to stand up and leave, but Ryan grabbed my wrist and forcefully pushed me back down into my seat.

"He wants to take me out for lunch, but I said maybe next time," he explained.

I groaned. "Oh come on! You were supposed to say yes and go with him!"

He looked at me as if I had just grown two horns. "What? And leave you here?"

I snorted. "I don't mind. Now, call him!"

Ryan didn't budge and merely sat there stubbornly.

165

I let out another groan and slumped backward on my chair. Geez, I didn't think Ryan could get any more stubborn than before.

"Enough about me, Kei. I think that *you* should be making the first move."

"Why would I hit on Ralph?" I asked incredulously.

"Not Ralph, you idiot. I meant your husband, who also happens to be my boss, of course."

I ignored Ryan's suggestion, yet just the mere mention of *his* name made my heart skip a beat.

*Not cool, Kei.*

"Is he still AWOL?"

I only managed a nod.

"Well, that sucks."

"Gee, thanks," I sarcastically said.

Ryan laughed. "Hey, I'm your best friend. I shouldn't be giving you helpful advice."

"Then what are best friends supposed to do, anyway?"

"Make fun of my best friend's current situation."

We just sat there, locked in a somewhat impromptu staring competition before bursting into laughter. Honestly, it felt good to laugh. After everything that had happened, sometimes we just needed a nice release. We laughed so hard that we didn't even mind the other people in the café.

Gradually, our boisterous laughter turned into occasional chuckles. Tears formed in my eyes while Ryan's cheeks were as red as a tomato.

"Man, that was funny," Ryan said once we both calmed down.

I nodded. "Yeah, it sure was."

Ryan downed the last of his espresso and wiped the corner of his mouth with his hand before he looked outside the window.

Meanwhile, I just held the cup of choco fudge coffee in my hands, not bothering to drink it all up because it wasn't warm anymore.

"Oh shit!" he said.

"What?"

I frowned at Ryan as he continued staring at whatever it was he saw outside. I tugged at his arm to get his attention, but he didn't budge. As I followed his gaze, what I saw made my jaw drop and my heart freeze.

"Is that—" He didn't need to continue because what I saw was definitely real.

There, just across the street, stood Jace with a woman in his arms. They were laughing at something, and all of a sudden, the woman kissed Jace on the lips.

"Oh shit! Kei . . . ," Ryan said.

And what hurt the most was that Jace, my husband, just let the woman kiss him like that.

*Oh shit, indeed.* But I ignored Ryan and just continued watching the man I love kiss someone else. And not just another person. A woman. A fucking female.

Watching their intimacy hurt.

I could feel my heart crack and slowly shatter into a million pieces.

# CHAPTER THIRTY
## His Ex

"Kei, are you alright?"

Of fucking course, I wasn't all right! Who would come out of that feeling well after seeing their husband kiss another woman? Because if there was such a person, I would give them a gold medal.

*I swear I could've punched Ryan for asking that stupid question in the first place.*

"Maybe it's not what we think it was," Ryan said, although his face clearly showed disapproval of Jace's actions.

Jace and the woman had already left, which surprisingly made me grateful because I knew I couldn't bear to look at them acting all intimate and so close together for another minute.

*Do you know that feeling you get when you already feel down because you haven't seen the person you loved in a while? It hurts, but before you know it, you'd give anything to get that feeling back, because somehow, something worse comes along. If you haven't felt that at all, consider yourself one of the lucky ones, because my already injured heart feels like it just been soaked in acid.*

After another minute of sitting in the café in silence, Ryan and I slowly made our way out. He offered to drop me home, but I declined. I didn't want Ryan to get involved in whatever situation Jace and I were in now, that is, if there ever was one.

A part of me wanted to believe that maybe, just maybe, I was simply overanalyzing the things the things I had with Jace, but as that kiss he had with that woman replayed over and over again in my mind like a movie, the stubborn part of my brain won.

So with newfound determination, I went straight home to deal with the problem head-on. *That is, if Jace has already decided to go home.*

*   *   *

As soon as I opened the front door, an unfamiliar fruity scent greeted me, catching my sense of smell by surprise, and I frowned. The mansion had never smelled like this before.

"Jace?" I called out as I headed toward the living room; my frown disappeared when I saw Jace sitting alone on the couch.

He stood up and greeted with a peck on my cheek.

Despite the anger I felt, I couldn't help but blush. That brief moment of warmth quickly faded as I remembered that he hadn't shown up for over a week, nor had he given me the courtesy of text or a phone call. With considerable self-control, I shoved him away.

"Where were you?" I demanded, not wasting any time.

His smile faded.

"You fucker," I cursed at him, unable to hold back.

I had every right to, considering how he had been acting. He didn't deserve my forgiveness. I shouldn't give in to him that easily. Hell, he deserved a whole lot more than just curse words from me.

"Where the hell were you, Jace? Huh? Tell me!" I demanded.

Jace just stood there in silence. He looked calm, but judging from the thin line of his lips, I could tell he was tense.

I gritted my teeth, ready to yell at him some more for being an inconsiderate asshole, when a woman's voice stopped me.

"Jace?"

I turned around and saw the woman who had been Jace earlier, her face filled with concern. Now that I could see her up close, I could honestly say that she was a very beautiful woman. Her slightly tanned face, wavy brown hair cascaded down to her upper back, and eyes were a strange shade of gray. She carried herself with undeniable elegance, wearing a formfitting lilac turtleneck dress which fell just an inch or two above her knees.

Simply put, she was a goddamn model, and right there in that moment, I wasn't sure whether to admire her for being so beautiful or hate her for kissing Jace.

"Jace, what's going on?" she asked as she stepped stepped inside the living room.

"Nothing, Bridget," Jace replied calmly.

I simply watched Bridget as she stopped beside Jace. Her gray eyes flitted between Jace and me, and I didn't miss the quick once-over she gave me, which honestly creeped me out.

"Oh my, is this the husband you've been talking about, Jace?"

My eyes widened at her statement—her pretense of not knowing who I was and the subtle bitchiness in her tone.

Jace gave me a brief glance before shifting his attention back to Bridget.

"Yes, how rude of me. Bridget, this is Kei, my husband. Kei, this is Bridget."

"I'm Jace's ex-fiancée," she added with a smile as she casually draped her arms around Jace.

*Ex-fiancée* . . . I pressed my lips tighter. Well, that did it for me.

Jace must have noticed my reaction because he quickly removed Bridget's arms from around him and walked over to my side, causing us to face his former fiancée together.

I held in my irrational urge to punch Jace in the face. No, scratch that. I wanted to shred him to pieces with no mercy.

Suddenly, Jace grabbed my shoulders and turned me to face him, but I avoided his eyes. I knew I would give in and fall too deep just by looking at them. Hell, I couldn't even bring myself to look at him, and even if I could, I didn't want to.

"*Mon beau*, she's actually here to—"

With a fake smile plastered on my face, I cut him off, "Honeybunch, why don't you join our visitor on the couch while I go and grab some refreshments?" I emphasized the words honeybunch and visitor while I gave Bridget the fakest smile I could muster.

Jace gave me an incredulous look, but thankfully, didn't say anything.

I gave an innocent shrug and pressed my lips against his, making sure to grasp Jace's neck in a possessive grip. At first, he didn't move a muscle, but eventually, he gave in and kissed me back with equal fervor.

I opened an eye discreetly and saw Bridget silently fuming at the display before she somehow managed to control her reaction by clearing her throat.

Slowly, Jace pulled away from the kiss; his eyes boring into mine.

"Hurry up then, *mon beau*," he said softly, his hot breath fanning my face.

I responded by giving him a playful yet very hard pinch on his butt. He winced in response, while I gave a look that clearly said, 'We'll talk about this later,' before I sauntered off toward the kitchen.

As soon as I stepped inside, I immediately hid behind the wall near the fridge to eavesdrop on their conversation. I knew it was wrong, but I couldn't help it.

"Bridget, what the hell? I told you to stop calling yourself my ex- fiancée," Jace said sternly.

I heard the clacking of heels on the maple wood floor.

"Well, it's the truth. I was your real fiancée, hence now your ex-fiancée. You just ended everything between us because of a damn letter."

171

I frowned. *Letter? What letter was she talking about?*

"Bridget, that letter was important and held valuable information from a close family friend. My father requested me to adhere to what's in it," Jace explained.

"Don't tell me it involves that . . . *that boy*! I can't believe you, Jace. Of all people, *him?*"

"Don't use that tone with me, and that *boy* is my husband. I married him because I wanted to and not because of a single letter!"

My jaw dropped at the revelation. *Oh my God.*

"I don't care if you married him on your own free will or whatever, but remember this: if I don't get what I want, you know full well what will happen to your father's valuable company," Bridget warned.

I strained to listen closer but couldn't make out the words. After trying and failing to eavesdrop some more, I finally decided to stop. I was about to leave my hiding place to prepare the beverages, planning to join them and openly show my discontent toward at Jace and the woman, when Jace said the following words that made my heart flutter.

"Go ahead, I dare you. I'm not afraid of whatever it is you're going to do. As long as Kei stays with me, I don't care about anything else."

# CHAPTER THIRTY-ONE
## It's Called Witty Banter

A myriad of emotions flooded through my entire being the moment I understood Jace's words. The overwhelming feeling of elation, relief, anxiety, and everything else combined, continued to course through me, making it harder and harder to breathe. Everything else in my body felt numb except for my heart and brain, which were locked in a fierce match because of Jace and Jace alone.

For a while, I just stood there, until my hand slowly reached up, making a soothing motion on my chest. I closed my eyes and silently counted to ten before exhaling deeply. Pushing myself away from the wall, I made my way to the cupboards. I opened one of them and grabbed a can of tea leaves.

While waiting for the water to boil, I prepared the small silver tray, arranging the porcelain teapot, cup and saucers sets, and silver flatware on it. Next, I decanted milk into a tiny porcelain milk pourer and placed sugar in a dainty porcelain bowl.

As the leaves steeped, I grabbed a cup of frozen yogurt for myself and briefly considered adding food suitable for tea, but decided against it. Then I placed my frozen treat on the tray, disposed of the tea leaves, and returned to the living room without haste, as if I hadn't just eavesdropped on a major part of their conversation.

They stopped what appeared to be a heated discussion when they saw me. The two were seated on the couch, though Jace seemed to make a point of keeping his distance from her. It was as if he wanted to maintain a polite distance without being rude.

Carefully, I placed the tray on the coffee table and invited them to help themselves to tea. Jace gave me a dazzling smile before silently gesturing for me to come sit beside him on the couch.

I would have liked to serve Jace his tea just the way he likes it, but at the same time, I also wanted to observe their interaction closely.

While Jace poured tea for the two of them, I glanced at Bridget, who still wore her fakest smile proudly.

*Bitch.* I nearly spat, but kept that to myself.

Heeding Jace's wishes, I sat down. I made sure not to leave any space between Jace and me, despite the couch being big enough for five people.

"So, Kei, I hear you've been taking the job of Jace's husband seriously," Bridget said, her tone clearly patronizing.

Jace twitched beside me as he lifted his cup to his lips.

I smiled at Bridget. "A job you say? I suppose that's one way to put it," I said calmly.

She opened her lips to say another word, but I cut her off, "I notice that you don't have a ring around your finger. I suppose you're not married?" I asked, keeping my tone casual and friendly.

She seemed taken aback. "No." She managed to say as her hand twitched.

"Hmmm," I hummed, crossing my arms over my chest. "I suppose that makes you unemployed."

"Excuse me?" Her frown deepened.

"Considering that you referred to being a husband as a 'job,' I think it's only fair that I call you unemployed since you're unmarried," I said snarkily.

Jace stifled a laugh at this and took another sip of tea.

Ignoring his reaction, I lifted my head high to let Bridget know that I wasn't going to play her games. It was time for Kei

174

Forest-Langlois to step up and metaphorically slap the arrogance out of her with words.

Even though I was still mad at Jace, I didn't bother to interrogate him. There were other pressing matters, one of which was in the form of a female model sitting elegantly on the couch across from us.

"Anyway, to what do I owe the pleasure of your company?" I asked innocently and grabbed my frozen yogurt.

Jace sat up straight. "Well, she's here to—"

"I'm not asking you, Jace."

He shut his mouth.

"Actually, I'm only here for a visit. It's been a while since I last set foot in America. Come to think of it, my last visit was when Jace brought me here on my birthday," Bridget said with a smug smile.

I smiled back, concealing the urge to stab her with a butcher knife. I swear, this woman could give me wrinkles at an early age.

"Oh really? How did that go?"

She sighed and daintily placed a hand on her chest as if the memory she had with Jace was something she'll cherish for life.

"Oh, it was wonderful! I remember Jace giving me a bracelet and a bouquet of roses. He was such a romantic. Right, Jace?"

I glanced sideways to gauge Jace's reaction. He didn't say anything, continuing to sip on his tea.

"He never left my side the entire day. I even remember him asking me if it was okay for him to stay in the same hotel where I was checked in. I refused, of course. We weren't engaged at that point." She laughed.

Jace cleared his throat. "That's enough, Bridget."

"Oh, but why? Kei and I were having such a warm conversation," she said.

I patted Jace's thigh, keeping my eyes fixed on the she-devil. "It's okay, honey."

175

Bridget glared at me, a look I completely ignored.

"Anyway, what did Jace do for your birthday?" she asked, crossing her long legs, causing the hem of her dress to ride up her thighs. "I doubt he did anything for you, what with his job as CEO of his father's company keeping him busy and all. Am I right?"

I glared at her. *What is she doing? Is she trying to seduce Jace?* I almost laughed at that thought.

Then I remembered her remark about my birthday, and I struggled to respond while resisting the urge to knock her teeth out.

"Oh, he did something, alright." I leaned closer to Jace, who looked startled at my sudden gesture. "He treated me to a trip to the Philippines—to a five-star resort—and gave me a puppy. He's even more romantic with me, I believe."

As if on cue, a loud bark echoed from behind the stairs.

I grinned as Bridget's eyes widened in panic, just as Frenzy ran happily toward Jace and me. I picked him up and turned him face Bridget.

Jace reached out and patted Frenzy's small furry head.

"Frenzy, meet Ms. Bridget! She's here to play with you," I said, standing up to hand him over to Bridget.

Jace moved as if to intervene, but Bridget hastily stood up, holding both hands up in alarm. She was apparently afraid of dogs, which made me grin in satisfaction.

"Oh my, l-look at the time! I'm gonna be late for my reservation. Jace, could you have your driver drop me off?" she quickly said.

I stepped in front of Jace and answered for him, "Sure, I'm sure you've already met Harry . . . you can tell him yourself. I'm also sure you know where he can be found."

Jace made a noise, probably in protest at the rudeness I showed his former fiancée, but I glared at him.

Bridget threw me one last nasty glare before storming out of the mansion in anger. Once she was gone, I let out a tired sigh and sank back onto the couch, releasing the puppy.

Frenzy barked and wagged his tail in excitement before he ran off into the kitchen.

An uncomfortable silence settled over us. The Bridget problem was resolved, but another issue lingered. Neither of us spoke, and the room's atmosphere grew tense.

Not wanting to be the one to break the silence, I shoved a spoonful of froyo into my mouth.

"That was awkward," Jace finally said.

I snorted. "Awkward? Jace, it's called witty banter."

Jace chuckled and was about to put his arm around my shoulders, but I shoved it away and gave him my deadliest glare.

He gulped.

"Now, how about that talk?"

# CHAPTER THIRTY-TWO
## The Talk

JACE

"Now, how about that talk?"

The way Kei said that one sentence almost made me want to go hide in my office. I never knew he could be so . . .

Instinctively, I gulped nervously and watched as he stood up and paced in front of me. It was clear that he was gathering his thoughts and taking his time.

Slowly, I sat back down on the couch. Despite wanting him to sit beside me, I decided to keep that request to myself and keep my mouth shut.

Besides, he had every right to be mad at me. After all, I ditched him in the middle of his birthday trip to the Philippines without even telling him where I went or why I left. Although it seemed that I just up and left without an explanation, truthfully, I had my reasons for doing so—billions of reasons.

$$* \qquad * \qquad *$$

I had planned to have another talk with Kei that day, but that plan quickly flew out the window when Bridget called. Apparently, she had just arrived at the airport and had something very important to tell me—something that I should hear in person.

Knowing Bridget, it wasn't going to be good, and after alternating between listening to her or completely ignoring her, I decided to do the former and agreed to meet her. I was abroad at the moment and couldn't pick her up at the airport.

I had hoped that it would be a quick trip. I would meet Bridget, listen to what she had to say, then head back to the Philippines and hopefully find another opportunity to spend time with Kei.

That was the plan until Bridget dropped the news.

By then, I was already in hot water. I couldn't even make up some lies to explain my actions and behavior. Time was running out and the longer I was away from Kei without a word, the more he would worry and undoubtedly get angrier.

But Kei, and our relationship, would have to take a back seat. Bridget's grandfather wanted my father's company.

Not just the company and its assets, but everything—including the building and the land that the company stood on. Whatever the reason was, it simply flew over my head because the moment she said those words in the airport, an emotion I was never familiar with grew within me and multiplied.

Panic.

Her announcement caught me off guard. Not only was her grandfather threatening my father's legacy, but it also extended toward me, the current CEO who would undoubtedly face the heat and humiliation should his plans were to succeed. It was up to me to devise a plan that could hopefully prevent my father from knowing anything about this so-called siege.

After picking her up at her hotel, Bridget and I went straight to my office to have a private meeting with her grandfather via the company's communications system—an app we developed that has earned the company a huge amount of money.

To say that it was a 'meeting' would be the understatement of the century. If anything, it was a full-out impromptu verbal onslaught where we debated, negotiated, and even attempted to see through each other's point of views on the terms, conditions, and other stipulations of his plan.

Whatever the case, there was no way I was going to let him bury my father's legacy, not when he worked so hard all his life to make a name for himself. It was up to me to protect his life's work.

However, the negotiations were going nowhere, and I decided to ask him the one simple question that had been brewing at the back of my mind.

"Why do you want my father's company?"

The answer I would get wasn't so simple. Bridget's grandfather, a stern and usually direct man, was also sly. He simply replied that I needed to look into some very important documents before he unceremoniously disconnected.

Days passed, and I studied every document of the company that I had little to no knowledge about, and reviewed those I was very familiar with, but there was still no lead to what the answer might be. That is, until a new set of papers came. They held all the answers to the questions in my mind except the one thing I wanted to know the most: *Why?*

Bridget didn't know the answer, but she seemed perfectly content with how things were going and insisted that I just agree to her grandfather's terms and conditions.

I couldn't do it. I wouldn't. Yes, I would do anything to save my father's company, but agreeing to such conditions would be unethical. His conditions were reminiscent of— I shook my head, cementing my decision in my mind.

Whatever happened next, I knew I wasn't going to take this out on Bridget. No, she wasn't exactly in charge of her grandfather's ambition, but still, perhaps if we discussed these things, then maybe, just maybe there would be a compromise between our families.

\*      \*      \*

And that was what I had been doing the last ten or so days: looking for compromises, heading off Bridget's grandfather, getting answers from my father, seeking solutions, consulting with the board of directors, asking advice from my successful businessman brother, meeting with lawyers and financial advisors, assessing my own personal liquid assets . . . dodging Bridget's attempts to reconnect . . .

But today, I was unable to say no anymore, so I invited her for a meal. It was hard to stay mad at Bridget. After all, we had a history together, and even though I don't feel anything for her romantically anymore, it felt good to laugh especially after her grandfather tried to stab me in the back.

When we arrived at the restaurant, I opened the car door for her. After she stepped out and straightened her impeccable clothes, she leaned upward and kissed me.

I pulled away. *No.* This wouldn't do. It wasn't supposed to lead to that. Whatever Bridget felt, I wasn't going to give her false hopes, so I quickly stepped away. She noticed the ring on my finger and immediately put two and two together.

"You're still married?" she asked in disbelief.

I nodded. I couldn't imagine why she thought I was already divorced. She couldn't believe that I was still married. She didn't know Kei and I had been through so much together, which was hard of course, but after everything that Kei and I went through, and after that amazing kiss in Palawan, I wanted to make it work with him.

"Let's go to your place," Bridget suddenly suggested, sliding back into the still-open car door.

"Why?" I asked, already not liking this one bit. *What in the world is she thinking?*

She didn't answer. She already had her seat belt on, and knowing Bridget, I had to go along to get the answers myself. So I drove us home, and not long after we arrived, Kei came back from college.

Whatever stress and anxiety I felt these past few days instantly evaporated the minute his warm brown eyes met mine. I wanted to hold him and apologize profusely. I wanted to tell him everything that happened and why I had left without a word. I wanted to express how glad I was that he was still here and how much I had missed him.

Of course, I couldn't do that. Not when Bridget was still here and things unfolded the way they did.

Whatever game these two were playing, I had never anticipated that Kei would act like this. He was never the publicly affectionate type, but whether it was because Bridget was here or not, I realized that I actually liked this side of him. After all, he never behaved like that over the course of our marriage. He had never shown any tender feelings for me, let alone any romantic feelings for me, but after that kiss in Palawan, maybe . . . just maybe, his feelings would change.

*     *     *

"What are you waiting for, asshole? Talk."

Kei's angry voice snapped me from my thoughts.

I cleared my throat. This was my chance to clear the air, and without any further distractions, I immediately told him everything—from the day Bridget called me to inform me she had something important to discuss in person, to the moment he arrived home to find Bridget here. I recounted everything that had happened since then with complete honesty because I wanted Kei to trust and believe me.

No, I *needed* Kei to trust and believe me.

He listened to every word without interruption, his expression passive all the while. Once I finished, he stayed silent, and the atmosphere was tense yet again. Nevertheless, I waited for some sort of reaction from him.

Funny, I used to be impatient with him all the time, but now I was certain that if he asked, I would simply wait forever.

After a couple of minutes of silent torture, he finally said, "I saw her kiss you."

I stood up immediately. "I'm sorry, *mon beau*. I didn't mean for that to happen. It honestly took me by surprise as well. Also, I deeply apologize for leaving you without explaining things. You deserve to know everything, but I—"

He looked me in the eyes. "I believe you."

Relief filled my entire being, but then he followed it up with the words that would leave me stunned.

"But I don't forgive you, Jace."

"What?" I asked, completely shocked.

*     *     *

KEI

"You left without a word, and it hurt more when you didn't even bother to call or leave a message."

Despite not intending for it to happen, my voice cracked as I struggled to say the last three words. I cleared my throat and turned my back to Jace, taking in a deep breath before I finally lettig it all out in a slow exhale.

"I need time to think."

Jace sighed before he softly saying, " I understand."

I closed my eyes. I didn't want to look at him because I knew that when I did, my heart will scream at me to stop being a stubborn idiot and to run straight into his arms.

I knew I wanted to. I wanted nothing more than to do that. I missed him terribly, yet my mind insisted on keeping my distance from Jace and treating him coldly. My heart and brain continued to battle like wolves, and I couldn't handle the conflict.

I never knew that loving a man while hating him at the same time could be such a struggle. Every emotion I felt drained my energy, and my chest hurt. My head felt heavy with countless nonstop thoughts. My heart roared with demands to be listened to, but in the end, its attempts were futile. I decided to go with my brain for today.

"I'm gonna go to the triplets for a while. Don't follow me," I said, heading toward the front door.

My heart ached with every step I took because he knew I left a piece of it behind with Jace. As I stood alone outside the house, I told myself that what I did was right. Distancing myself from Jace for now was a good idea, even though I wanted to give in so badly and just let Jace embrace me.

I wanted to forgive him, but life and its choices were never meant to be painless. He had every opportunity to contact me, even if he was extremely busy, even though he was with her, and he chose not to. He made his decision, and now I was making mine. Now, I had to live with fact that the painful choice I made would hopefully keep me rational so I can learn something for the future.

*This is for my own good . . . I can't let my emotions get in the way.*

I let out a sigh. I wished life came with a book that told you what to do when you fall in love, what to do when your heart breaks, and what to do if the person you love comes back after being away for a while. Life would be so much easier that way.

I shook my head to try and erase those thoughts, then grabbed my phone and dialed Autumn's number.

After a few rings, he picked up. "Hey, Kei. 'Sup?"

"Can I come over?"

There was a pause before Autumn said, "Sure. What happened?"

"I'll tell you later. I'm on my way."

"Whatever you say."

I ended the call and looked up to the sky. The sun was about to set and a few stars had appeared earlier than usual. Pink and orange hues painted the vast canvas above, which would undoubtedly turn black before the moon emerged.

Even though I knew it was good to leave Jace for a while to have some space to think, I couldn't help but feel a pang of regret.

*Did I do the right thing?*

# CHAPTER THIRTY-THREE
## Je T'aime

"You what?!"

I winced at how loudly Summer and Autumn screamed at me.

"Kei, are you nuts? Why would you do that?" Summer demanded, clearly displeased.

I had arrived at their apartment half an hour ago and immediately told them about the events that transpired at the mansion. Of all the reactions to expect, I didn't anticipate that one at all.

Autumn and Winter nodded.

I pouted. "I thought you'd be on my side."

Summer rolled her eyes. "Well, obviously not after the way you left him."

I frowned. "I didn't leave him. I just—"

Autumn snorted and cut me off. "Uh huh, right."

"Hey, I'm not at fault here! He left without a word, and after more than week or so of no contact, I saw him kiss a girl. I have every right to stay mad at him!" I exclaimed as I tried to defend myself.

"Yes, but he also had his reasons, Kei. You said it yourself that Jace never meant for that kiss to happen," Summer said patiently.

I huffed and slumped down on a beanbag. I hated that she was right. Summer sat on the armrest of the couch, while Winter and Autumn occupied on the seat cushions. Autumn's legs were draped over Winter's lap.

"Besides," Summer continued, "what are you so mad about anyway? Jace already apologized didn't he?" Summer asked.

"I dunno," I said lamely.

Autumn rolled his eyes. "Yeah right, you're obviously still mad about the whole kissing thing. What we don't understand is why you would you about that? We all know Jace doesn't swing that way, plus he's already married to you, so women aren't on his wish list."

My jaw dropped at this.

Summer laughed in agreement. "Yeah, he seems to prefer to play for the other team."

I shifted my focus to her, my expression still in shock. "What in the world are you talking about?"

It was Autumn who answered, "Kei, Jace is a whole lot more than what you think he is. Sure, we don't really know what his exact intentions are, but I do believe they're good. Not just for his sake, but for yours as well."

Autumn looked serious, his expression devoid of any lies or jokes. A few minutes of complete silence fell between the four of us. I sat there, contemplating my earlier actions. When my heart and mind were in constant battle, I honestly thought that following the rational part of my brain would make everything easier. Now that I had time to think, the feelings of regret came crashing back tenfold. They were the same feelings I had tried to ignore until now.

Yet despite all the conflicting emotions I felt, all I could think about was how much Jace meant to me.

He was the financially independent man who gave up his freedom for me, a stranger, so that I could gain financial windfall.

Simply put, Jace Langlois was one of the richest men in the country. His aura exuded the power and authority of an alpha male whenever he was in business mode, and to top it all off, he also had the looks of a Greek god. His perfectly chiseled face, strong arms and legs, and firm chest put him on several leagues above everyone else. The way he carried himself and flashed me his smiles were honestly as exquisite as his collection of Italian leather shoes.

Despite having all the options and choices, he sacrificed his ability to choose his own life partner for me, someone who had not even been thinking about partnerships of any kind.

When I first saw him, I honestly thought that he was an angel sent from heaven, but that impression quickly soured when his true personality emerged. If anything, his behavior was the exact opposite of his appearance. Not only was he annoying and overbearing, but he ordered me around as if I were his slave. It didn't help that he also had a knack to piss me off without effort.

In a way, it wasn't a surprise when I ended up hating him. After signing those papers, my days as Jace Langlois' husband were filled with struggles and dread. Even though my parents insisted that he would be a loving husband, the universe seemed to have other plans for me, and I ended up running away.

Then things changed.

After I gave him the ultimatum to treat me as a spouse rather than a slave, Jace genuinely honored his promise. Even though he still had a possessive streak, his behavior was better than before, and it didn't take long for my feelings of hatred to turn into something else . . .

Not only did Jace change, but so did I. Whenever I was away from him, I often found myself missing his smiles and cute laughter. The way his eyes crinkled at the corners when he found something amusing made me yearn everything about him.

*His gentle touch . . .*

*The way he kissed me . . .*

*His warm embrace . . .*

"Are you all right?" Winter's soft voice interrupted my thoughts.

188

Looking up, I saw all three siblings watching me with concern. I tried to give them a smile, but it felt futile, and I gave up that notion altogether.

"Have you changed your mind?" Winter asked, once more interrupting my thoughts.

I didn't answer but pursed my lips, looked down at my hands, at the silver wedding band on my finger reflecting the light, and before I knew it, I was brought back to our wedding day.

I remembered the first time Jace gave me this ring. It was during our wedding, and he gave it to me in the least romantic way possible. If there was a way to compare his gesture, it was pretty much like a kid being forced to give candy to his little brother. That was how Jace gave the ring to me.

Nevertheless, I had never really complained about it. We both knew why we got married. For my sake, I only did it to fulfill my dead parents' wishes as well as get my inheritance.

It had almost been a year since our wedding, and now that I have received my inheritance, there really was no reason for me to stay.

*But is that really the case now?*

I looked at my wedding band once more. The conflicting thoughts and feelings slowly came to a halt, and I knew why I was still with him.

Because I had learned to love Jace. That was why I chose to stay.

He wasn't perfect by all means. He was anything but, yet he was enough for me. I knew my heart couldn't take it anymore if he wasn't here by my side.

I closed my eyes as I contemplated once more on the events that transpired. Now that Bridget was in the country, it was apparent now more than ever that leaving Jace was a huge mistake, especially after she just blatantly threatened him. What's worse was that she might even take this as an opportunity to snatch Jace away from me.

189

The possibility of things growing worse by the second just increased if I just sat here and moped all day.

I opened my eyes. With one last look at my wedding band, I knew what I had to do. It was a risk, and I didn't know what the consequences would be, but in a way, love was like that. If there was an inkling of hope that things would work out, a person in love would take all the risks they could get just to grasp it.

After my heart and my mind finally agreed on a decision, I stood up and immediately headed for the door.

"Kei! Where are you going?" Summer called out.

I stopped at the opened door and gave them a grin over my shoulder.

Both Summer and Autumn sported confused looks, while Winter, the only sibling who seemed to know where this was going, gave me an encouraging nod and a thumbs-up.

I laughed before I called out, "Wish me luck, guys!"

*    *    *

"I don't think I can do this . . . ," I muttered nervously to myself as I stood in front of Jace's mansion.

I had been standing in front of the door for about ten minutes now, unable to summon enough courage to enter and confront Jace.

"Okay, you can do this, Kei. Don't chicken out," I repeated to myself to calm my nerves.

I raised a hand and was about to turn the doorknob but quickly withdrew.

"Damn it!" I hissed at myself.

I was about to turn away when a loud bark behind made me stop. Slowly, I turned around, expecting Frenzy to wag his tail in delight before undoubtedly jumping into my arms. Instead, I was confronted by Jace's tall frame, with Frenzy nestled in his arms.

My curiosity was piqued when I took in Jace's state. His white dress shirt, usually clean and ironed to perfection, was now covered in dirt and muddy paw prints. His black jeans were torn on the left side just below his knee, making me think that he must have snagged them on a tree branch or something. His hair was also a mess, which almost made me want to rush over to and fix it immediately.

*Almost.*

"You're back," Jace said.

I swallowed nervously and hid my shaking hands behind my back.

"Oh . . . uhm, yeah. I was gonna tell you something, but . . . uhm . . . yeah, I sort of . . . forgot? Yeah, yeah, that's it . . . yeah," I rambled on.

My cheeks flamed at the fact that I probably sounded like a blathering idiot.

*This is so embarrassing.*

Jace didn't respond, which made me even more nervous.

I averted my eyes to Frenzy, who was covered in twigs, dried leaves, and mud. I frowned at the sight, and instinctively went closer to get a better look.

"What the hell happened?" I asked as I brushed away the dirt from Frenzy's fur.

Jace, who had been watching me intensely earlier, just shrugged.

"When you went out and left, he tried to follow you, so I went to after him. He ran off and probably thought it was a game, and before I knew it, he fell into the small but deep pit just behind the trees near the gate."

"Then why do you look like fell in too?" I asked.

"I climbed down to get him. Unfortunately, climbing back up was much harder than I thought."

Frenzy, whose tongue lolled out as he panted for air, started licking Jace's arm. I couldn't help but chuckle at Jace's immediate

191

reaction—a strange noise in his throat. Despite knowing he wasn't a dog person, I didn't bother to take Frenzy away from him. Seeing Jace Langlois carrying a cute little husky was both rare and adorable.

"You're not mad at me anymore, are you?" he asked, his eyes boring into mine.

I blinked and stepped a little closer to him, leaving just enough space so Frenzy wouldn't get squished between us. I took in a deep breath and bravely looked into Jace's eyes. I could see a swirl of unnamed emotions behind them, so I reached out to swipe my thumb across the skin at the corner of his left eye.

I gave him a shaky little smile before I opened my mouth to speak.

"Jace, I—"

"I love you."

My movements stopped. *Wait, what?*

"I love you, Kei," Jace repeated, a little bit louder this time. *Oh my gosh! Jace Langlois loves me? Is this for fucking real?*

"You too?" I blurted as the words slowly sunk in.

Jace's eyes widened a bit before his lips curled upwards.

I mentally kicked myself for what I had just done. So much for my plan of making a dramatic confession of my feelings.

"You love me too?" he teased with a smile.

I shut my eyes in frustration. *What did I just do?* This wasn't supposed to happen. It was meant to be a serious yet romantic conversation, with maybe a few intimate hugs and kisses. But this— this was just wrong.

I mentally berated myself further before I felt a warm sensation pressed against my lips. I quickly opened my eyes just as Jace pulled away, staring at me with such raw emotion that I almost wanted to drown in it.

Frenzy was yipping impatiently at us, but I ignored him as if he were mere background music. Somehow, it felt like we were in another universe, just the two of us against the world.

"You're an asshole," I said dazedly because I didn't think I would be able to form proper words right now.

"You know you love me." Jace smirked as he wrapped one arm around me while his other arm kept Frenzy in place.

I grinned. *God, I bet I look like an idiot right now.* I was sure my heart would literally break through my rib cage because all I felt in that moment were butterflies and an unfamiliar wave of happiness I hadn't felt in a long time.

Jace leaned closer and kissed me once more. His teeth grazed and tugged gently at my lower lip. I sighed and wound my arms around his neck. He smiled against my lips before pulling away.

"I love you, Jace. So much," I whispered, blushing.

*"Je t'aime, Kei."*[49]

---

[49] I love you, Kei.

# CHAPTER THIRTY-FOUR
## Paranoid

"How long?" I asked Jace as we brought Frenzy into our en suite bathroom to wash up.

I turned on the faucet and added some dog shampoo into the water. As the bubbles formed, Jace carefully placed Frenzy into the tub. Strangely enough, Frenzy didn't seem to mind the bath as much as most dogs would.

It didn't take long for him to get soaked in bubbles. Every so often, he would let out a little bark when a bubble landed on his nose.

I reached out to thoroughly wash him. I held back a smile as Jace rinsed Frenzy's head afterward. Jace looked so hot and adorable at the same time, and now that I knew he loved me as much as I loved him, I couldn't ask for more. Besides, we were already married, so that was a plus.

"Hmmm?" Jace hummed in response, not quite hearing my question over Frenzy's constant yipping.

"How long have you been in love with me?" I repeated, leaning closer to the tub beside Jace.

Jace stopped washing Frenzy and looked at me. He leaned forward to give me a kiss. I let him, but not before letting out a grin. The kiss was slow and gentle, as if we had all the time in the world and there was no need to rush.

Jace pulled away first and then grabbed Frenzy, who was about to climb out of the tub. His body was still dirty, and his paws needed more scrubbing.

"I don't need to answer that," he finally said.

"Why?"

"What matters is that we love each other. That's all."

I opened my mouth to retort but decided against it. He was right. We loved each other just the same, and that was what mattered. Talking about the hows and whens could be a topic for another day. Right now, I just wanted to indulge myself and enjoy watching Jace dry Frenzy's wet fur with a towel.

Jace grimaced in disgust when the puppy licked his nose and mouth, which made me laugh.

I asked, "How come you hate dogs so much?"

Jace stood up, but not before he made sure to carry Frenzy in his right arm as pulled me up with the other.

I took the puppy from him, and together, we walked out of the bathroom and into the bedroom, where another towel was laid out on the bed for Frenzy. I carefully placed the puppy on the towel before sitting down on the bed, patting the space next to me for Jace to sit.

He complied and gave me another light kiss on the lips. "It's not that I hate dogs. I just dislike the idea of them licking and pawing at me for attention," he explained.

"But what if I do those things to get your attention?" I smirked.

Jace playfully narrowed his eyes at me. "Then, I don't have a choice but to give in, do I?"

"I was kidding, you asshole." I laughed.

Jace laughed as well.

\*       \*       \*

"So is it official now?"

I just nodded in response to Summer's question. As soon as I got out of my photography class, the Winston triplets didn't waste any time bombarding me with questions about Jace and me. Of course, Summer went in for the kill with her question about our relationship.

"Wow, congrats, man!" Autumn cheered, giving me a high five.

"Thanks," I said with a smile.

"So now that you and Mr. Jace Langlois, aka Mr. Sexylicious Hunk, are finally lovey-dovey together, I suggest we celebrate!" Summer exclaimed.

Autumn and Winter nodded simultaneously, while my face scrunched up in disapproval. I already knew what kind of celebrating Summer was talking about, and I knew I wasn't going to like it.

Summer noticed my face and pouted. "Oh, c'mon. Today calls for a celebration!"

"Uh, I'm not too sure about that, Summer. Maybe some other time," I said.

Autumn scoffed. "Bullshit. Come on, Kei. We're just gonna have a couple of drinks down at a bar a few blocks from here."

I shook my head. "No, besides, why go to a bar to celebrate? We can just hang back at Jace's place. He's got even more expensive wine there than at a sleazy bar."

"Seriously?" Autumn asked in disbelief.

"Yeah, I think Jace wouldn't mind."

"Okay, let's celebrate at your house." Summer sighed in defeat.

"Great, let me text Ryan first," I said, pulling out my phone to message Ryan and Ralph and invite them over.

*       *       *

"Tada!" Summer and Autumn yelled as soon as Jace got out of his study.

Jace looked peeved for a moment, but his scowl immediately faded when he saw me. Without another word, he walked over and gave me a short kiss on the lips.

Summer was making swooning noises, but I ignored her and focused on the feeling of Jace's lips on mine.

"Okay, okay. Stop being so mushy and let's get on with the celebration already!" Summer said.

Jace frowned. "Celebration?"

Worried about Jace's reaction, I immediately grabbed his hand and pulled him to his study, making sure to close the door so the triplets wouldn't overhear me explaining the situation to him.

"*Mon beau*, what's going on?"

"I may or may not have told them that we're kinda official now, and um, Summer insisted that we, um, celebrate?" I slowly explained, anxiously waiting for his reaction.

Jace's eyes narrowed briefly, and the anticipation of his reaction made me nervous. Then his expression softened, and he kissed me again. Lately, he seemed to be doing that a lot—a habit I certainly wasn't complaining about.

"Of course, *mon beau*. You and your friends can have fun," he said, ruffling my hair.

I let him play with my hair for a bit before Ralph's voice came from just outside the door.

"Hey, lovebirds! You better not be doing what I think you're doing in there!"

Jace's calm façade broke cracked, and his expression immediately transformed into that of a furious, ill-tempered businessman.

I took a few steps back and laughed nervously.

*Oh God . . . this will not go well.*

"Why is Ralph here?" he asked in a calm but intimidating voice.

Before I could answer, the door swung open, and Ralph barged in, holding a bottle of wine in one hand. He winked at Jace and nudged him with his elbow.

"*Alors, quand allez-vous adopter des bébés?*"[50]

I frowned, and Jace glared at his brother. I didn't catch everything Ralph said, but judging by the words I did undersand and the way Jace looked ready to yell at him, it was clear it was something inappropriate.

"*T'es en colère?*"[51] Ralph asked. There was a brief pause before he continued, "*Eh bien, maintenant que vous êtes officiellement mariés, il est grand temps que vous ayez des enfants . . . eh, par adoption ou par gestation pour autrui.*"[52]

My jaw dropped when Jace hit Ralph upside the head. Even more surprising was that the older sibling merely snickered before leaving.

I turned to Jace and asked, "What was he talking about?"

Jace surprisingly blushed. "Nothing, *mon beau*. He just said something that—"

"Pissed you off?" I cut him off with a raised eyebrow.

Jace sighed and put an arm around my waist before he said, "Let's just go."

We walked toward the kitchen where the "celebration" was taking place. Autumn and Winter were sitting on the countertops beside the sink, while Summer was perched on one of the stools around the island. Ralph was pouring wine into glasses, and Ryan was leaning against another counter near the fridge, laughing at something Autumn had said.

"Here come the lovebirds!" Ralph yelled.

I grimaced. "Please don't call us that."

"Why not? It suits you," Summer added.

---

[50] So, when are you going to adopt babies?
[51] Are you angry?
[52] Well, now that you are officially married, it's high time you had children . . . whether by adoption or through surrogacy.

"It's just weird."

"No, it's not!"

I groaned in annoyance.

Jace just laughed and kissed my cheek before joining Ralph. The two chatted in their language, appearing semi-serious throughout. Knowing him, it was likely business-related.

I hopped onto the stool next to Summer and helped myself to a glass of wine.

Ryan came over to give me a side hug. "Congratulations, man."

I smiled. "Thanks."

"So are you ready?"

I frowned. "For what?"

Ryan exchanged looks with Summer before he sat down next to me. I narrowed my eyes at the two of them. *What were they planning to do?*

"You know PDA is normal for couples, right?" Summer asked.

I slowly nodded.

"And you know that Jace is a public figure, right? Ryan added.

I nodded again.

"Then the paparazzi are gonna be on your tail once Jace starts something in public."

"What? What are you talking about?"

Ryan sighed. "Look, Kei. We all know that Jace is somewhat performative. He does not shy away from attention, so Summer and I believe that Jace wouldn't hesitate to show public affection from now on and become more openly affectionate. You already know you love each other, so those things are gonna happen eventually. What happens if the paparazzi catch you two being all mushy together in public?"

"The word *mushy* sounds wrong when it comes out of your mouth." I couldn't help but laugh.

199

"Ugh, that's not the point here!"

Summer butted in, "What he's trying to say is that you won't have a peaceful life from now on. Think you can handle that?"

"Then I'll tell Jace not to smother me in public," I said.

"That's not gonna happen. Imagine this: the CEO of a world-famous company with his husband, strolling around the mall"

"I don't think Jace likes malls."

Summer glared at me. "Will you stop interrupting?"

I pretended to zip my mouth, then threw the imaginary key as far away as possible.

"Okay, so imagine this, the CEO of a worldwide famous company is strolling around the mall with his husband, then *poof!* People are gonna follow and take pictures and videos of you two together. Paparazzi, stalkers, and jealous women and men will follow you everywhere you go. You know, crazy shit," Summer said.

"Don't you think you're getting a little too far with the stalker thing?" Ryan asked.

Summer smugly held her chin up. "You gotta be prepared for everything. It's the twenty-first century."

\*　　　\*　　　\*

My last class for the day finally ended, and just as I was about to head outside the building, my phone vibrated in my pocket. I grinned, already knowing who was calling.

"Yellow?"

"Done for the day, *mon beau?*" Jace asked.

"Yup. Just heading out, actually."

"Good! I'm on my way to pick you up. Wait outside the gates."

I smiled. "Okay."

After standing near the gates for at least ten minutes, Jace's black Porsche pulled up right in front of me. It was five in the afternoon, so the college grounds weren't crowded. Not that I was worried about what Summer had warned me about, but still, better safe than sorry.

Jace hopped out of his car, walked around it toward me, and kissed me just as I was about to open the car door. I resisted the urge to scream when he greeted me that way. *Man, being married to him sure has its perks.*

"How was your day?" he asked after I had taken my seat and gotten comfortable.

"It was okay. Yours?"

Jace just chuckled and leaned down to kiss me again. I was about to wrap my arms around him when several flashes just a few feet from the car caught my attention. I frowned as Jace let go of me, closed the car door, walked around to the driver's side, and got in, completely unaware of what I had just seen behind the gates.

As soon as Jace started the car, I let out a loud sigh and forced myself to relax.

*Maybe it was just a trick of the light or my imagination . . .*

"Are you all right?" Jace asked.

I glanced at him and patted his thigh. "Yeah, I'm good."

Jace didn't buy it for a second. He opened his mouth to speak but, deciding it was better to drop it, turned his focus back to the road.

I looked at the college gates shrinking in the rearview mirror. Maybe I was just becoming paranoid for no reason, or perhaps Summer's warning was just complete and utter bullshit. There was no way I had actually seen a man standing behind the gates in black clothes with a camera around his neck.

# CHAPTER THIRTY-FIVE
## Life Sucks If You're Famous

The car finally stopped, and I looked out the window, expecting to see a five-star restaurant. Instead, it was the ice cream shop I had visited with Ryan. I hadn't expected Jace to know a place like this, and the fact that he actually brought me here erased every trace of that earlier memory with the guy and the camera.

We both got out, and after Jace locked his car, he made sure to hold my hand as he led me inside. The shop had a few customers when we arrived—some were seated in booths, while others were with their families or on dates.

We stopped in front of the glass counter, where several ice cream flavors were on display. I grimaced in disgust when my eyes landed on the melon-flavored one. *Eugh!*

"Hello! Welcome to Creme D-Lite! What can I do for you?"

Instead of a girl, a boy about my age stood behind the counter. His name tag read Connor.

I tugged at Jace's sleeve and pointed to the Double Dutch ice cream.

"Jace, I want that one."

Jace nodded and said, "Okay, we'll take that one, and—"

"Wait, are you Jace Langlois?"

My eyes snapped away from staring hungrily at the ice cream to the speaker, Connor, who was now looking at Jace with wide-eyed excitement.

*Oh no.*

"Whoa, I can't believe it! It's really you!" he exclaimed.

"Yes, but could you please keep it quiet? I'm with my husband, and we just came for some ice cream," Jace said, wrapping an arm around my shoulders protectively.

Connor's eyes widened further before he turned to look at me. For a moment, he seemed stunned, but he quickly forced a smile, though I caught the hint of a glare he shot before that.

I frowned. *What the hell was that for?*

"Of course, Mr. Langlois."

Jace smiled in relief.

After we accepted our orders, Jace and I headed to a booth that was well away from the door and the occupied seats. We sat down across each other, before I immediately dug my spoon into my Double Dutch, savoring the first bite. I closed my eyes in bliss before taking another scoop.

Jace chuckled, but I ignored him.

"Do you really love ice cream that much?" he asked after he took a small bite of his Black Forest ice cream on a cone.

I nodded. "Yep, a lot!"

"I hope you love me more though."

I blushed. "Of course I do."

To escape my awkward reaction, I blathered about my day, forgetting my ice cream in the process while Jace finished his. Then he leaned forward over the table as if intending to give me a kiss when two girls approached. One was holding a magazine, while the other was extending her phone.

I froze in my seat and watched them with a raised eyebrow.

"Yes?" Jace said.

"Um, are you Jace Langlois?" asked the girl with the magazine, a brunette, her voice shy.

"Yes."

The two girls looked at each other before they let out a synchronized shriek. I couldn't help but flinch at the high pitch.

"Oh my gosh, you're so handsome! Can we have your autograph?"

Jace was about to respond when the blonde nudged me with her phone. "Can you take a picture of us?"

*What the fuck?*

I was about to protest, but the girls were already on either side of Jace, who had stood up.

I mentally counted to five to calm myself before holding up the phone and taking the picture. Afterward, I handed the phone back to the blonde girl. She snatched it up and examined the photo. Just as Jace was about to sit back down, the blonde handed her phone back to me, pouting.

"I don't like it. Can you take another?"

She pushed the phone back into my hands, then grabbed Jace left arm and hugged it. The brunette giggled and did the same with his other arm.

I grumbled but took the picture anyway, noting the attention we were drawing. While taking group photos was not uncommon, Jace's movie-star looks and stature were unusual in this setting.

When I was finished this time, I held the phone out in front of the girls so they could see the result.

*This better be the last one.*

"Perfect!" the brunette said. "Okay, another pose."

She jutted her denim-clad butt out and leaned her head on Jace's shoulder. The blonde adopted a similar pose, standing on her toes and pressing her lips against Jace's cheek.

*That's it.*

"Listen here, you—"

Jace's actions stopped me from making a potentially rude comment. He slowly freed himself from the girls' hold and faced them with a serious expression.

"That's enough pictures, *oui*? My husband and I still have a date to enjoy," he said as he took the phone from me and handed it to the blonde before circling his arm around my waist.

The two girls went silent at this, but it didn't last long before they erupted into giggles. No, scratch that. Their laughter was more akin to cackling because, upon closer hearing, I couldn't help but think of the screeching hyenas from the *Lion King*.

"Aw, Jace! That was so funny!"

"Yeah! Totally!"

I frowned. "What's so funny?"

They stopped laughing and looked at me with contempt. The brunette one said, "We're not talking to you. Who are you anyway? Jace's errand boy or something?"

I snapped, "What the hell did you just say, you bit—"

Jace took hold of my face and turned it toward him, giving me a warning look. Then, he faced the girls, gave them a nasty grin, and said, "This *errand boy* is my husband."

They gasped, and before they could make any more disdainful comments, Jace added, "And it's about time you two left. You have overstayed your welcome."

I stopped struggling against Jace's hold and watched as the two girls huffed and left. Jace sighed in relief as he let me go and returned to his seat.

I, too, took a seat—this time beside Jace—and grumbled, "Sometimes, I hate how famous you are."

He looked at me with an amused smile. "Is that so?"

"Yeah, can you believe those girls? They were so rude! What did they think I am, a fucking photographer?"

"Well, you are taking photography classes, so . . ."

I pouted. "Those are my minors."

Jace chuckled. "Of course."

"Great, now my ice cream is all melted."

"Do you want me to buy you another?"

205

I shook my head. "Nah. I'm craving for some popcorn though."

Suddenly, a bright idea crossed my mind. With a smile, I grabbed Jace's hand and led him out of the shop to his car. As soon as we buckled in, Jace shifted around in his seat and looked at me with a curious frown.

"Where exactly do you want to eat popcorn?" he asked.

I grinned excitedly and leaned closer to turn the key in the ignition.

"We're going to the movies!"

# CHAPTER THIRTY-SIX
## Movies

We arrived at the movies a few minutes later. Jace had been wary ever since we stepped out of the car and went to the ticket booth. The lady behind the glass looked up with disinterest, but the minute she saw Jace, her face immediately lit up.

I rolled my eyes. *Great. More fans.*

"J-Jace Langlois? Oh my gosh," she stammered, her cheeks flushing more with every second.

I cleared my throat. "Excuse me, but can I have two tickets for *Zootopia?*"

She spared me a brief glance before shifting her focus back to Jace. I gritted my teeth in annoyance, resisting the urge to strangle her as she shamelessly threw a flirtatious smile his way. She batted her eyelashes at him, a gesture I couldn't help but roll my eyes at. Whether Jace didn't notice or was pretending not to, I immediately reached over and gripped his hand tightly.

He flinched and immediately snapped his head in my direction. Ignoring his confused expression, I glared at the stupid girl's face.

"Miss, two tickets for *Zootopia*, pleeease," I said.

She jolted from her daydream and looked at me. "Yes, what can I do for you?"

For the second time that day, my patience snapped.

"Why, you—" I stopped when Jace freed himself from my grip and patted my head to calm me down.

Unfortunately for him and the girl, I was not calming down. I glared at the girl, and if looks could kill, she would be six feet under by now.

Jace sighed, turned to the lady behind the glass, and said, "*Mademoiselle*, my husband and I would like to have those two tickets right away please."

She froze as if she had just been doused with a bucket of ice-cold water. Her eyes, wide with shock, were locked on Jace's face and mine, then slowly moved to his arm wrapped around my waist and my body leaning against his.

She blushed, clearly embarrassed by her behavior, and finally did her fucking job.

After Jace paid for the tickets, we bought a double-sized popcorn and two Cokes before heading to the theater, where movie trailers were already being shown.

"Don't be jealous too much, *mon beau*. I am yours now, remember?"

I pouted. "I'm not jealous."

"Whatever you say."

"I'm not jealous. I'm just pissed because those girls in the shop and that woman in the booth were bit—"

Jace cut me off, "Kei, calm down."

I sighed. "I just hate it when other people look at you the same way I look at you. Does that make sense?"

Jace maintained a serious expression as he said, "Who cares if they're looking at me? What matters is that my eyes are on you alone. No one else."

I nodded and moved ahead of Jace to search for our seats, feeling him follow closely behind. Just as I was about to enter the aisle to our seats, I stopped, remembering something. Jace, not expecting me to halt, bumped into me. The light from the screen illuminated his face, revealing a curious look.

"From now on, Jace, consider us exclusive because I don't plan to share you," I said with a goofy grin.

Jace laughed. "Consider it done."

"Great."

The seats we chose were in the middle of the very last row, and Jace followed me without a word. Even before we could get comfortable in the uncomfortable seats, the movie started. Nothing slowed me down though. I quickly grabbed a handful of popcorn and shoved it into my mouth before chomping down in satisfaction.

*Damn, I didn't realize I was that hungry.*

I felt Jace shifting around in his seat, so I glanced sideways to see what was up. He was frowning at the giant screen, and I took advantage of distraction by leaning my head against his shoulder.

I could feel him relax at the gesture. Without saying a word, he leaned back further into his seat and lifted his left arm to drape it around my shoulders.

"I never pegged you as the type to watch these kinds of movies," he said after finishing the popcorn I silently fed him.

"Who doesn't love Disney movies?"

"Ralph, for one."

"He hates Disney?"

Jace shrugged. "He prefers movies with Nicolas Cage in them."

I laughed. "That's weird."

We stayed like that for the rest of the movie, with me feeding him popcorn and us occasionally discussing characters in the film. I was glad for the almost empty theater, given that it was a school day.

To be honest, I wasn't really focusing on the movie anymore. Instead, I found myself frequently stealing glances at him, blushing whenever out eyes met.

Honestly, I didn't know what to do or how to feel in this moment. I had never had the chance to go out to the movies on a date or even date anyone before Jace and I met.

Then again, I didn't think what Jace and I were doing could be considered "dating," since we had been married for almost a year now. On the other hand, I also didn't know a single thing about dating and relationships.

I smiled to myself as Jace pulled me closer, his lips brushing against my hair. I couldn't help but grin like an idiot. A lovestruck idiot.

In the end, I didn't really mind that I had no experience with dating before Jace and I got married. What mattered was the present, and right now, I loved how our relationship was more than just a contractual obligation. After finally figuring out how our relationship would be, I knew it was going to be permanent, which was what I had been praying.

*    *    *

"So, how did you find the movie?" I asked once we got outside of the movie theater.

"Good, but we should have watched *Fifty Shades* instead of *Zootopia.*"

My jaw dropped. "What the fuck? Jace!"

He laughed. "I was joking, *mon beau*. Though it might be a good idea to tie you up once in a while."

I could almost feel steam coming out of my ears, like a boiling kettle, because I was so mad at the fact that I was blushing at his words.

I smacked his shoulder hard and walked ahead, intending to leave him behind—but not really, of course. I just wanted to have a little fun with him.

"Kei, I was joking!" he yelled as he ran to catch up with me.

I didn't turn around and just kept speed walking to the sidewalk, where many people were already passing by. A few even glanced at Jace and me. I didn't mind them and continued walking. I resisted the urge to grin like a fool when I heard Jace curse not too far behind me. Sneaking a glance back, I saw him almost trip over a street cone.

He looked up and saw me watching him. I stuck my tongue out before continuing to walk ahead, but I was abruptly stopped when Jace finally caught up and pulled my hand toward him.

"That's for mentioning *Fifty Shades of Grey* to me. Like, seriously?" I said as soon as we stopped, and I turned to face him, both of us standing in the middle of the sidewalk.

"It was just a joke, Kei."

"BDSM is not a joke, Ja—"

I was cut off when Jace suddenly covered my mouth with his. As usual, I instantly melted against his warmth and pressed myself closer to him.

The kiss was short, but it felt like we were kissing for an entire lifetime. With my eyes still closed, he caressed the sides of my body as he slowly pulled away. I didn't budge and simply enjoyed the moment. I didn't even care that we were in public, in the middle of the sidewalk with multiple people watching us.

I didn't care anymore.

*I love him. So much.*

"I love you, Jace," I whispered, opening my slowly at the same time.

Jace's eyes brightened, and I smiled as his lips formed a full-blown grin. I raised my hands and gently cupped his cheeks, my gaze locked on his.

"You have no idea how much I love you," I said quietly, afraid that the moment would vanish if I raised my voice above a whisper.

"Yeah? Care to tell me how much?" he replied with a smile.

I looked up and pretended to think about it.

Jace chuckled and said, "I love you, Kei."

I stared back into his eyes.

"I know," I responded cheekily.

Jace stepped away, and I frowned. He simply smiled, took my hand in his, and he led us back to his car. I couldn't help but blush and hide my face with the sleeve of my jacket as more people passed us by, apparently having seen the small spectacle we created a while ago.

Jace and I buckled into our seats and drove off, his right hand still clasping mine.

I sighed.

"What's the matter?" he asked.

I shook my head. "Oh, nothing. I was just thinking about how our marriage started."

His hold tightened, but thankfully, he didn't say a word and just focused on the road.

"At first, I thought being married to you was a burden, like fate hated me and had just thrown a whole baggage of problems on my shoulders," I said, recalling the time when Jace and I met at my school. I took a deep breath, let the air out slowly between my lips, and continued, "I was just a normal person living my life the way I wanted, but then my parents' will came, then I met you. It was . . ."

A brief silence followed before Jace spoke. "At first, I thought that being married to a complete stranger would be an utter disaster and a burden."

"Hey!"

"But then, months later, I realized something."

Unable to wait for him to continue, I asked, "What is it?"

He stopped the car at the red light and looked at me with his hazel eyes. His expression was filled with undeniable sincerity that I felt I could almost drown in it.

"I realized that being married to you wouldn't be a disaster. It isn't a burden, and if anything, it's a privilege."

He leaned closer and sealed his confession with a sweet kiss.

# CHAPTER THIRTY-SEVEN
## Sexual Tension

Over the past few days, as the initial excitement of our confessions settled, Jace and I continued to build on our emotional connection, exploring ways to deepen our intimacy.

One of those days, Ralph practically barged in unannounced, dragged me out of bed, led me to the living room, and started ranting at six in the morning, thereby ruining Jace's chances of serving me breakfast in bed.

Jace and I sat side by side on the couch while Ralph paced in front of us, rambling nonstop about the complications of relationships. He had been at it for about an hour.

Jace hadn't said a word, though I imagined he must have been silently seething. I would have been annoyed with the inconvenience, but I couldn't help but notice that Jace and I were wearing matching maroon robes, which made me internally grin like a teenage girl.

Nevertheless, Ralph wasn't going to stop anytime soon, so I went back to listening since Jace obviously wasn't going to. Judging by his expression, he was still irritated by Ralph's unwelcomed visit and had decided to keep quiet about it.

"So hypothetically . . . how do you know if a relationship between two people is official?" Ralph asked for the hundredth time.

I watched as Jace sighed in frustration, slumping further into the sofa with his right arm resting idly on the back of my shoulders.

Ralph didn't notice his brother's reaction and simply waited for an answer. This was strange since I had been giving Ralph some advice in between his ramblings, which he quickly dismissed with responses like, "I don't believe you." or "Are you sure?"

I decided to go with a different approach and ask a question instead, "Ralph, just tell us the truth. Are you talking about Ryan?"

His lips pursed into a straight line, and his face reddened a bit.

I smirked; my guess was right.

*Huh, it's about time.*

"That's why I'm asking you," Ralph said softly.

I shrugged. "Well, what did you do?"

He hesitated. "I took him out on a few dates, and he let me meet his parents."

My jaw dropped. "Wait, wait. You met Ryan's parents? How come he didn't tell me?"

"He was afraid of how you'd react," he answered sheepishly.

I groaned.

Jace shifted in his seat before finally saying, "I believe you've already slept with Ryan, judging from your convoluted and conflicted questions and ramblings."

I blushed in an instant. *Slept together? As in sexual intercourse?*

"Am I correct?" Jace asked seriously.

Ralph was silent for a few minutes before he muttered, *"Oui, mon frère."*

My jaw dropped at the revelation. My husband's brother, Ralph Faucher, had just confessed that he had gotten intimate with my friend, Ryan Roberts. I didn't know how to react. I honestly didn't know.

Jace stood up, pulled me to him, and then stopped Ralph from pacing around by giving his shoulder a couple of pats.

"You should go and tell Ryan how you feel. If it all goes well, ask him to be your lover."

My eyes widened at this. I never would have pegged Jace as the type of guy who gave solid relationship advice.

Ralph contemplated this for a while before he nodded and went back to his usual self. He thanked both Jace and me and left.

Once he was gone, Jace placed a hand on my lower back and guided me to the kitchen. He ushered me to sit on a stool as he turned on the stove and started to fry some eggs and bacon. Once he was finished, he made some coffee for the both of us and even sliced some bread.

I was surprised when he put Nutella on my bread instead of caviar, and I couldn't help but smile gratefully when he handed me my plate.

He sat next to me and sipped his coffee.

The house was silent except for the distant sound of music from the radio perched on the kitchen counter beside the microwave. All of Jace's house staff had a day off, so we had the house to ourselves.

"I could get used to this," I muttered as I poked at an egg yolk.

"Well, don't. You know how busy I get because of work sometimes. You're just lucky this time," Jace teased.

I smacked him with my spoon, and he just laughed.

I laughed too. His laughter was rare, and every time I heard it, it practically lit up my day. It was one of the things I loved about him.

We continued eating like that, talking and laughing about anything and everything that popped in our minds. Jace's phone rang every now and then, but he ignored all of them, saying he was going to spend the entire day with me instead.

He was such a sap sometimes.

215

"You're sweating. Should I turn the heat off?" he suggested as I grabbed our empty plates and placed them in the sink.

I shook my head. "No, it's fine. I'll just take my robe off."

I untied the robe and draped it over the island counter before washing the plates. Without the robe, my attire was exposed—one of Jace's white shirts, which was too big for me, and a pair of pale blue boxers.

I started to wash the plates, utterly unaware of Jace's reaction.

"Oh," he said, sighing.

When Ariana Grande's "Side to Side" played on the radio, I grinned excitedly, feeling my hips involuntarily sway.

*Ah! Ariana Grande! One of my guilty pleasures.*

I sang along with Ariana's voice, aware that I wasn't a great singer but willing to give it a try. After putting the plates in the rack, I turned around and gasped in shock. Jace was standing directly right in front of me, and I hadn't even notice him move from his chair.

"Oh my God, you scared me, Jace. I thought you had gone to the living room," I said, stepping back.

Jace took a step forward. "No, I didn't."

"Oh, okay. I should probably go have a shower now," I said, sidestepping Jace.

Without warning, he grabbed me by the waist, pressed our bodies together, and kissed me.

I whimpered as his tongue licked my mouth open while his hands started to roam all over my body. Instinctively, my hands reached up and entwined around Jace's neck. I wanted to remove his robe to see his . . . essentials, but decided against it. Instead, I stood on my tiptoes, pressing myself closer to him—to his mouth.

I gasped against his parted lips as his hand gripped my ass, causing me to tug hard on his hair and mess it up. I smirked smugly when he growled.

"Kei," he muttered heatedly.

I didn't respond and just smashed our lips together again. Our tongues clashed until I finally gave in, and he explored every corner of my mouth—licking inside. His knee slid in between my legs, and my eyes widened as I felt a thick, hard bulge grinding against my inner thigh.

I couldn't help but let out a strangled moan as his hand on my ass began rubbing and kneading the fabric-covered skin; his other hand found its way underneath my shirt, making goose bumps rise all over my body.

*Oh my God, it felt so good. I hoped this wasn't a dream, and that I wasn't gonna wake up with wet boxers and an empty space beside me.*

We continued to kiss, each second growing more and more passionate until Jace pulled away and grabbed the back of my thighs.

"Up," he demanded, and goddamnit if that growl didn't turn me on even more.

I obliged and jumped up, holding on tight to his neck as he carried me and placed me on top of the counter. Our mouths connected once more, our breaths mingling. I could taste the bitterness of his morning coffee against his tongue, and I loved it.

Eventually, our fervent kisses made it harder for me to breathe, but every second was worth it. If Jace was the reason I was breathless, then I would die in bliss.

Slowly, his hands moved up to my chest before he began unbuttoning his own shirt that I was wearing.

I groaned in impatience but giggled slightly when he had trouble unfastening the final button that would leave my chest completely bare.

Once he finally unbuttoned the last button, he pulled away from the kiss to admire my chest. I blushed under his intense gaze as a single drop of sweat ran down my chest and settled in my navel.

He licked his lips, hunger evident in his eyes.

"You look beautiful," he murmured.

I blushed. No one had ever called me that before, but I guessed today was my lucky day.

"God, I could taste you forever," he said before leaning closer and pressing his lips against my chest. His tongue brushed against my bare skin, sending a shiver throughout my entire body.

I tilted my head back in pleasure as his tongue trailed down from my neck to my chest.

"Oh my God . . . Jace . . . ," I moaned.

"I want to kiss you all over."

I sighed shakily. "P-please, kiss me. Kiss me."

"Shhh, Kei. I got you."

My breathing quickened when his hands moved to the waistband of my boxers. The anticipation was torture, and as I waited, my hands shook as they held Jace's shoulders tightly.

I closed my eyes and bit my lower lip. I could feel my boxers sliding lower and lower until . . .

"*O mon dieu!*"

My eyes snapped opened, searching for the source of the interruption. When I spotted the figure that disturbed Jace's "adventures," my face instantly turned as red as a cherry. I hastily hopped off the counter and clumsily straightened Jace's shirt, fumbling with the buttons as I tried to cover myself quickly.

Without turning around, Jace demanded in frustration, "Mother, what are you doing here?"

His mother didn't reply, but her expression made it clear she wasn't planning to set foot in the this kitchen again anytime soon.

# CHAPTER THIRTY-EIGHT
## Mother-in-Law

"Mother, what are you doing here?" Jace asked again as we entered the living room, where her mother was now seated demurely on the couch.

I smiled shyly at Jace's mother as I tried to hide my blush. It took Jace and me a few moments to catch our breath and to compose ourselves before we followed her. I was doing my best to hold it together despite the fact that I was mortified that had been caught—and by his own mother of all people.

"*On dirait que tu ne me veux pas ici,*"[53] his mother said with a scowl.

Jace responded with a scowl of his own and crossed his arms like a petulant child.

"*Quel est ce visage? Maintenant, fais un câlin à ta mère,*"[54] she retorted.

"*Maman, Kei est là.*"[55]

Jace's mother waved a hand dismissively before standing and grabbing her son without restraint. I watched, wide-eyed, as she smothered her son with kisses all over his face, leaving lipstick marks everywhere.

---

[53] It seems like you don't want me here.
[54] What is that face? Now, give your mother a hug.
[55] Mama, Kei is here.

I couldn't help but laugh when Jace escaped from her hold and quickly wiped his face with the back of his hand, smearing the lipstick even more.

Jace's mother smiled, clearly proud of her work, before turning to face me, opening her arms wide.

Grinning, I hugged her. Her expensive perfume wafted through my nose which made me hug her tighter.

"*Mon cher*,[56] it's so nice to see you again," she said as she combed my ruffled hair with her fingers.

I smiled wider at her nickname for me. "I missed you, Mrs. Langlois. It's been a long time since we last saw each other."

She nodded. "*Oui*, I agree. Jace here never shares you with me."

"*Maman*," Jace warned.

"Hush, I am not speaking to you. Now, *mon cher*, let us talk. Jace, make some tea for us."

I shot a sympathetic look at Jace while his mother returned to her seat and patted the space next to her. I sat down at once. She didn't speak at first and instead waited for Jace, which surprised me since she did send Jace away so we could talk. Her silenced increased my nervousness.

Jace returned in record time, carrying a tray with a teapot and two cups. He placed the tray on the coffee table, poured tea into the cups, and sat next to me. However, his mother tutted in disapproval, grabbed his hand, and pulled him to sit on her other side. He made a face at this but decided it was best not to complain.

She smiled smugly, clearly pleased that her son didn't protest about her being in the middle, before reaching out for her own cup.

"Now, *mon cher*, tell me how you've been," she started and took a dainty sip of her green tea.

"Um . . ."

---

[56] My dear.

"*Maman*, why didn't you call me before you arrived here?" Jace interrupted.

"Hush, you," his mother sternly said.

Jace huffed, leaned further into his seat, and shifted his focus to the fireplace in front of us. His eyes narrowed, and he once again resembled a petulant child.

"I've been great, Mrs. Langlois," I said politely.

"*Non*, just call me Maria. Remember, you are also my son now."

I nodded sheepishly and subtly made eye contact with Jace, whose expression softened into a comforting smile that made my heart flutter.

Once the awkwardness died down, Maria and I talked for hours, but not before she made Jace and me change into something appropriate for receiving visitors, saying, and I quote, "Even if they are just family visiting." I blushed again when I realized that we were still in our sleepwear. At some point, Jace requested an earlier brunch since we had not finished breakfast. Once again, I blushed at the implication.

Throughout the light conversation, every so often, Jace would interrupt, grumbling like a child. Strange as it may sound, I actually found it adorable. He was like a child who didn't want to share his toys but knew better than to complain. Not that I was his toy or anything—that would be so weird and very disturbing.

Eventually, the topic turned to Bridget.

"Now stop your pouting, Jace. *J'ai entendu dire que Bridget est revenue en Amérique*,"[57] she said in a serious voice.

I perked up curiously, wondering what his mother would say about Bridget.

"*Oui, Maman*. She told me about the company. Her grandfather and I discussed and negotiated things at an online

---

[57] I heard that Bridget has returned to America?

221

conference, and I somehow managed to stall them enough to prevent any rash actions for the moment," Jace replied.

*Thank God Jace is considerate enough to speak in English.*

"I do not like that woman."

Jace laughed at his mother's words, and I did too, inwardly.

"Oh, you'd love to hear this then, *Maman*," Jace said. "Kei called Bridget a jobless woman, because, according to him, she's not married to me."

Maria laughed and playfully patted my thighs. *"Mon cher, je suis fier de toi.*[58] I am proud of you."

I grinned. "Thank you."

Jace then recounted the rest of the "witty banter" between Bridget and me. Maria laughed and even threw a few insults of her own regarding Bridget.

After we had afternoon tea, Maria expressed her desire to leave. I invited her to stay with us, as it was her house as well, but she declined, insisting that she needed be with her husband, who was waiting at their favorite hotel. She had told Jace earlier that he would visit us at a later date since he was busy with some business deals. Now, she was explaining that if she didn't pull him from his work, he would forget to stop.

"I am sorry, *mon cher*. I would love to stay but my husband . . ."

I nodded in understanding and hugged her one last time before Jace took her hand and led her to her car, where her driver was waiting. I watched the car until it passed through the gates and disappeared onto the highway.

Jace came over to me and wrapped an arm around my waist.

"I love your mother. She's so nice," I said softly as we both retreated into the house and headed to the kitchen to make dinner.

I was amazed at how much time had passed and how quickly it had flown by.

---

[58] My dear, I am proud of you.

Jace hummed in agreement and grabbed a pan, but not before he also grabbed some meat and vegetables from the fridge. I was about to go help when I caught a whiff of myself. *Yuck.*

"I'm gonna go and take a shower," I said instead.

He stopped what he was doing and looked up at me, his gaze intense.

I shrugged innocently and turned my back, letting the maroon-colored robe slip from my body as I walked. To top it off, I swayed my hips as I made my way out of the kitchen. I smirked to myself when I heard the clatter of a knife hitting the floor.

*"Merde,"* he groaned.

Just before I climbed up the stairs, I called out, "Don't even try to follow me!"

I laughed to myself when I heard him mutter profanities in French.

# CHAPTER THIRTY-NINE
## She-Devil

I was so high up in the clouds with Jace's presence for the past couple of weeks that I had nearly forgotten about my final exams, which were in five days. I only remembered when Summer called me to ask if she could borrow one of my reference books in art history because hers was with her brothers. I paled so much at the limited time that Jace almost panicked. Almost.

It was Sunday, and I was sitting in the middle of the bed. The space around me was filled with textbooks and notes, while a few of my highlighter pens were scattered across the carpeted floor. It was already dinnertime, and I still hadn't bathed or taken a quick shower.

Jace had gone to work early in the morning. He just sent me a text message to tell me that he was on his way home. I didn't bother to reply and instead went back to cramming. I was in the middle of reading a few summaries from my photography notes when Jace entered our bedroom. He loosened his tie as he approached me with a frown, but I just ignored him and continued to read.

"Have you eaten dinner yet?" he asked.

I shook my head, still not looking up from my notes. I heard him sigh, and before I knew it, he grabbed the notebook that I was reading and tossed it carelessly on the other side of the bed.

"What the hell Jace? I was studying!"

I glared at him in disapproval, but he merely ignored me and continued to undress, as if he hadn't just done something that was incredibly rude.

He changed into a T-shirt and sweatpants, then gave me a quick glance before opening the closet. After finding what he needed, he walked over to me without another word.

"What?" I grumbled, still annoyed at his rude action.

"Take off your clothes."

I gaped at his words. *Oh God! Of all the things he wanted, he wanted to do it now?*

My hesitance must have been evident because he just sighed and went back to the walk-in closet. I watched him rummaged the contents within before he tossed a few clothes over to the space beside me. The pale blue long-sleeve shirt and navy jeans immediately caught my eye.

"Put those on. We're going out."

I blushed when I realized that was what he actually meant. *Oh.*

Jace didn't miss my deep blush and smirked in amusement. "Why? What did you think I meant, *mon beau?*"

"Oh, just shut up," I grumbled as I got dressed.

Once I was finished, we immediately headed to the car and were on our way to God knows where.

"Where exactly are we going?" I asked. His habit of taking me somewhere without explanation still hasn't changed. "And don't lie about it, because if you do Jace, I swear to God, I'll—"

Jace shut me up by increasing the volume on the radio, which was also playing my favorite song. Shania Twain's "From This Moment On" blared to the speakers, and I couldn't resist closing my eyes as I allowed myself to drown in the lyrics.

I could hear Jace chuckle from behind the wheel, but I merely ignored him as I started to sing along. Somehow, I had forgotten the lyrics, but that didn't stop me from humming the rest of the song until a new track by some boy band played next.

I glanced at Jace and said, "That should have been our wedding song."

Jace frowned. "I don't think One Direction is my style."

"I meant Shania's song, you jerkface!"

"Ah." Jace nodded in understanding. "But then we would have to have another wedding for that then."

I blushed upon hearing those words, and instinctively, my mind began to conjure an image of me saying my vows to the man I would love for the rest of our lives. It would be so romantically perfect: Jace and I in matching suits, and instead of a judge or justice of peace, this time it would be a pastor or priest.

I grinned at the thought.

"What are you smiling about?" Jace asked.

"N-nothing!"

He gave me a skeptical look before turning his attention back to the road.

After another twenty minutes, the car finally stopped. Jace and I got out and walked to what looked like a five-star restaurant, prompting me to glance down at my clothes. I didn't want to be underdressed.

"You're fine," Jace assured me in a whisper.

I nodded. He was the one who picked out the clothes after all. I opened my mouth in amazement as soon as we stepped inside. Heavy drapes hung over the large windows, and shiny sage-colored marble floors echoed beneath our shoes. There were tables covered in olive-green tablecloths, and the diners inside were engaged in either deep or pleasant conversation—several of whom were either couples on dates, families, and even a few business associates.

The smell of gourmet food wafted through my nostrils. My stomach grumbled, reminding me that I hadn't eaten properly since I started studying for my exams. Hurriedly, I grabbed Jace's hand when we were escorted by a waiter to one of the secluded tables.

"Please tell me that we're eating full-course meals today because I'm starving," I muttered excitedly as we sat down.

226

Jace smirked. "Sure, whatever you want."

I grinned. "Okay then."

*     *     *

*Burp!*

I felt my face grow warm while Jace laughed at me. I gave him a glare, but it was pointless because he kept laughing until we got our bill, which he unsurprisingly paid. Still, it wasn't my fault that I burped in front of him. I just felt so full after eating a humongous amount of food. I could have sworn I earned another roll of belly fat after this. I pouted at Jace as he helped me got up.

"You're purposely making me fat," I grumbled as we made our way to the car.

Jace stopped laughing a moment ago, but he chuckled when he saw me pout. "What are you so worried about? I'd still love you even if you do get fat."

"Shut up."

Jace was about to open my door for me when a woman's voice stole our attention. We turned around, and my blood instantly boiled when I saw Bridget standing just a few feet away from us.

Despite my total hatred for the she-devil, I couldn't help but eye her from head to toe. As usual, she looked like a Victoria's Secret model, wearing a dark red halter blouse, skintight white jeans, and six-inch red heels that made her look taller than me. Her hair was up in a ponytail, which perfectly showcased her diamond earrings.

*Damn it. I hated to admit it, but she was gorgeous.*

"What are you doing here, Bridget?" Jace asked, which snapped me out of my thoughts.

Bridget smiled sweetly at Jace before looking down at me and giving me the once-over with her gray eyes. I fought the urge to hide behind Jace and instead stood my ground as I looked into her eyes.

She walked over to us and stopped when moved to shield me.

"I just want to have a word with you, Jace. How about we go to your office?" she asked as she gave me a glance.

Jace opened his mouth to answer, but I stepped in front of him and glared at her. "Listen here you, bit—"

I stopped when Jace squeezed my ass, causing me to retreat with a blush.

"I mean . . ." I gathered myself before continuing, "Bridget, I don't want you taking Jace anywhere. If you have something to say to him, then say it here."

She raised a brow. "It's a private matter and doesn't concern you."

"Oh, but it does. You know why? Because Jace is my husband. So go ahead. Talk," I retorted.

Jace sighed behind me, but I ignored it. Frankly, we wouldn't be in this situation if he hadn't almost married this she-devil years ago.

Bridget gritted her teeth.

I ignored her and continued our staring contest. Jace stayed silent behind me, as if he were afraid of what might happen if he ever tried to intervene.

After a few seconds, Bridget sighed and pulled out a few papers from the folder she had tucked under her arm.

"Whatever. But we need to talk somewhere private for this," she said.

I turned my head to look at Jace, who nodded without a word.

I faced Bridget again and nodded. "Fine."

# CHAPTER FORTY
## The Truth Hurts

Jace, Bridget, and I decided to discuss matters inside a pastry shop just a few blocks away from the restaurant. Jace ordered two slices of red velvet cake for the two of us, while Bridget ordered a coffee crumble muffin.

As soon as the waiter walked away, Bridget spread the papers on the table.

"It's about your company," she said, her eyes fixed on Jace with a blank stare.

Jace stiffened beside me. I clasped our hands together under the table and squeezed his hand in reassurance. He didn't look at me, much less say anything, but he did squeeze my hand back in silence, which made me smile. It was a silent reassurance that he was willing to accept my help.

"My grandfather arrived from Paris last night," Bridget started.

"I take it he really wants to buy my father's company?" It wasn't really a question. Jace knew.

"Yes, and—"

I frowned. "Wait a second. Why are you telling us this? Jace, don't you think this is suspicious? She might have a motive for warning you about her grandfather."

"What?" Jace replied, turning to face me with a frown of his own.

Bridget smiled. "I know a way to save your father's company, but of course, I need you to cooperate. If you agree, I can tell my grandfather to cancel everything."

I had a bad feeling about this. Not only did I trust Bridget as much as I would trust a pyramid scheme, but I knew she was an evil, conniving bitch who wouldn't stop until she got what she wanted.

"Thanks, but no thanks. I'm sure Jace can solve it by himself. He doesn't need help from the likes of you. Let's go, Jace."

I was about to stand up when he stopped me by grabbing my wrist.

"Jace, what are you doing? Don't listen to her!" I hissed.

Our orders had just arrived, so I forced myself to sit back down while the waiter arranged our desserts on the table. He probably sensed the thick tension around us, because he hurriedly left as soon as he finished.

*Lucky bastard.*

"What are you proposing exactly?" Jace finally asked, ignoring his food.

Bridget smiled and decided to ignore her food as well, getting down to business. She set aside her muffin and pushed the papers toward us.

Jace took them and scanned the document.

I tried to read a few paragraphs, but I only understood a few words before I stopped. Business terms weren't exactly my forte.

After two minutes of silence, Jace dropped the papers on the table and glared at Bridget, who took it in stride and clasped her manicured hands on the table.

"Jace, what's in the papers?" I asked cautiously.

He tensed. "My father's company can still be saved."

"Really? That's good news, right?"

Instead of nodding, Jace gritted his teeth and avoided my eyes.

I frowned. "What's wrong?"

230

Bridget cleared her throat, causing me to look at her. She had a glint in her eyes, and I was certain the papers she held contained terrible news for Jace and me.

"Let's just cut to the chase, shall we?" Bridget said.

Jace and I didn't speak.

"For your company to be safe, I propose you send me a couple of papers that I want from the two of you," she said.

"What are you talking about?" I asked.

Bridget smiled sweetly and said, "Oh, just divorce papers."

My eyes widened. I turned to Jace to confirm whether Bridget was joking, but all he gave was a grim look.

"What . . . a-are you serious? You must be joking," I stammered.

"If you don't agree to my proposal, then I'm afraid I can't help you. Jace's father's company, including all branches, will be bought by my grandfather. Additionally, all profits, commodities, and licensed assets will be transferred and reassigned under my grandfather's enterprises in Paris the minute that buyout contract is signed," she explained.

Jace clenched his fists.

I just sat there, unmoving and speechless. The food in front of us forgotten.

"And don't bother lying to your lawyers either. I have definite proof that your company profits have been dwindling for the last couple of years. The only reason the media hadn't caught it yet is that your parents managed to cover several expenses out of pocket. You remember the letter, don't you?"

Jace could only manage a nod.

I snapped out of my stupor and looked at Jace when I heard the word "letter."

"Jace, what—"

"It's the letter that stated the terms that I must marry you, so you could get your inheritance," he explained.

I frowned, recalling the last time the letter was mentioned. It was during an argument between Bridget and him back in the house.

*Did that letter have anything to do with Jace's company?*

My gaze shifted between Jace to Bridget to Jace. I looked at the two for the longest time; neither seemed eager to break the silence.

Bridget, who seemed to read the question in my mind, suddenly spoke. "Before your parents died, they left a substantial amount of money for you. You were informed when their last will and testament was read, but you could only access the funds when you turned twenty-five. I'm sure you know all about it already. What you probably didn't know or were unclear about was that the will specified that Jace's parents would manage the money for you because they were business partners and close friends. However, Jace's father mismanaged those funds, which led to losses."

My mind froze at this.

"Mind you, not all of your money, just some. But then their company started losing money as well. So now, there are two financial issues to resolve. Mr. and Mrs. Langlois believed they could address both if you and Jace got married. The marriage would give them time to recover most of your inheritance while using what remained of it to rescue their company from bankruptcy. They convince Jace to marry you you with a fake letter."

"Fake?" I managed to say in a whisper.

Bridget nodded. "Yes, Jace knew it was doctored from the very start. He could tell that it was written by his parents instead of yours. He confronted his parents, of course, and that was when he learned about his father mismanaging your trust fund. Jace decided to proceed with the plan and follow the terms because it was the only way to save the company at the time. He also knew that the amount left in your inheritance was more than enough to get his company in the black again, at least for a few years."

She smirked at me, her contempt barely hidden, and continued, "In the black means that the company is profitable and operating with positive financial performance. It indicates that the company's revenues exceed its expenses, resulting in a net profit."

I glared at her, then at Jace, who remained stoic. Everything she had said made me want to run, but it also made me want to know the truth.

"Jace knew that marrying you wouldn't prevent his father from going to prison if the mismanagement was discovered, but it would give him time to recover your money, thus saving his father while also rescuing his company."

She seemed to be mulling over her next words. Jace, on the other hand, grew paler but he didn't stop nor interrupt Bridget as she continued, "If you had paid attention, the fake will stated that you would receive additional inheritance if you married Jace. They banked on your overall naivety and ignorance of finance to avoid any a fuss. And you didn't. You just married him, lived in his house in complete bliss of ignorance, and never questioned anything. And if you must know, that was also the reason why Jace canceled our engagement." She frowned at this. "Of course, I was mad—furious even—but he assured me he would find another way out soon. I, of course, expected Jace to get everything back to normal, and he did. Your parents' money was able to save his father's company, and he managed to recover the majority of what his father had lost of your money. Given time, he would be able to recover everything and return it to your trust fund."

I could feel myself growing paler at this. I had a sinking feeling that things were about to get worse, but I couldn't stop it now. I had to know the truth. I *needed* to know the truth.

"Oh, his parents were *relieved* when Jace finally proposed. So relieved, in fact, that they knew Jace had to marry you quickly to secure themselves. They were positively beaming when you both officially tied the knot." She leaned back in her seat and picked her nails delicately, as if bored with recounting everything.

233

"Oh, and before I forget," she said as if just remembering, "those letters that you thought your parents sent you? They're all fake. Jace's parents wrote them too."

She didn't say anything after that, and neither did Jace or me. Her words replayed over and over again in my mind, and even though I wanted them to stop, I couldn't. It was all too much to bear, and a swirl of conflicting emotions swept through my entire being until I felt numb.

I looked down at the table. Amidst the turbulent thoughts and emotions, a few things stood out clearly:

*Jace lied to me.*

*Everything we had was a lie.*

*I was just an escape route to keep his company from failure and his parents from prison.*

*My parents never left anything but a lump sum—no words, no hope, and no reassuring words. All those letters I believed were from them were fabrications. But they were very clever with the penmanship—they looked authentic.*

"Kei, where are you going?"

I could barely hear Jace's voice yelling at me when I stood up and ran toward the door. I could barely hear the sound of his footsteps pounding behind me. I could barely feel the cold chill of the evening wind against my skin as I continued to run. I could barely hear the panicked screams from people on the sidewalk as I broke free from the crowd and into the street. I could barely hear the loud honk of a truck as it sped toward me.

And then, I stopped moving altogether.

234

# CHAPTER FORTY-ONE
## Numb

I wasn't dead.

The only reason I knew that was because I didn't experience the tunnel with a very bright light at the end—a common occurrence reported by people who said they were on the verge of death. Instead, all I could see was darkness, and all I could hear was a deafening silence until . . .

*Beep. Beep. Beep.*

The sound of electronic beeps as well as faint hiss of a machine drifted through my ears. I tried to open my eyes, but it was no use. It was as if they were sewn shut.

I clenched my fists, and as I slowly woke up from the darkness, I could feel myself lying on an unfamiliar bed. The sheets were rough and uncomfortable, and as I sniffed, I could detect a faint smell of rubbing alcohol.

I tried to open my eyes again, and after a few struggles, finally managed to do so. I was immediately met with bright lights, causing me to shut them again. I waited for a couple of seconds and slowly blinked them open. The first thing I could make out was a white ceiling.

I frowned. *Where am I?* And then it hit me—I was in a hospital room.

I moved my head, which was difficult to do, until I faced a huge window on the left side of the room. Loud honks from several cars could be heard from the outside, and I could also hear the sound of the ventilation system nearby as air drifted in and out of the room. The latter sound was calming, peaceful . . . and I welcomed it.

It didn't take long for me to realize that I couldn't control my body except for my head and neck, but instead of panicking, I felt . . . numb about it. For once, I was glad that I couldn't move.

*"Oh, and before I forget, those letters that you thought your parents sent you? They're all fake."*

Bridget's words echoed through my mind, and I sucked in a breath. My chest tightened at the memory, and I clenched my fists while my lips parted every so often for air.

*Beep-beep-beep. Beep-beep.*

The beeping sound from the machine on the left side of the bed got louder and faster. It was getting difficult for me to breathe, and I struggled to move my limbs even for just a bit.

Panic rose within me and my eyes darted from one direction to another until I heard the door slam and footsteps coming closer. My vision started to blur, and I could faintly make out four or five people in blue and white scrubs as they placed their hands on me. I felt a sharp, quick sting prick my right arm, and within a minute, my mind fogged up, and my vision slowly faded into nothingness.

Jace's face was the last thing on my mind before darkness consumed me once more, and I fell into a deep sleep.

*       *       *

"Up! Wake up . . . Kei."

It was a female voice.

"Kei, please . . ."

The voice was familiar, but I couldn't quite place it.

*Where have I heard that voice before?*

"For weeks now."

*Huh?*

After a couple of minutes of mindlessly listening to the voices around me, I slowly managed to crack my eyes open. I groaned out loud as bright light flooded my vision for a few seconds before it all began to clear.

The first thing that greeted me was Summer's face. Her hair was in a messy bun, and her eyes were bloodshot, like she had been crying for a long time. Her face lit up when she saw me, then she hurriedly stood up from her chair before she ran out of the room in haste.

As I lay there alone, I realized that this was the second time I woke up in the same hospital room. As I slowly started to gain the logical part of my brain, I remembered the last time it happened. It was when I felt a slight panic attack, and a group of medical professionals barged into my room and gave me something that helped me fall back asleep.

It wasn't the only thing I remembered though, and I immediately recalled Jace, Bridget, and the fake letter.

"Ugh . . ." I groaned as a wave of dizziness hit me at the thought.

"Kei!"

I jolted from my thoughts as Ryan, Summer, Autumn, and Winter burst into the room, all looking exhausted yet relieved.

Summer rushed to hug me but stopped. I glanced down, seeing nothing wrong.

"W-what happened?" I asked shakily.

Summer sat on one side of the bed, Ryan at the foot, while the two brothers took seats on the small couch to my right.

"You got into an accident, Kei. Don't you remember?" Summer asked as she smoothed out the wrinkles on my blanket.

I frowned, tyring to piece together the fragmented memories. The room was silent as I tried to recall what happened. When the memories resurfaced, they came back with vengeance, replaying over and over again in my mind.

*Bridget approaching Jace and me after a romantic dinner to discuss a few things . . .*

*Bridget revealing the bombshell that Jace's parents lied to me . . .*

*Me running away from the pastry shop and into the street before it all went black . . .*

I let out a breath I didn't realize I was holding, causing Summer and the others to look at me with concern. I nodded slowly and said, "Yeah, I remember . . ."

They all sighed in relief.

"What? Did you think I'd get amnesia or something?" I retorted.

"Like that would happen." Autumn scoffed.

I forced a smile, which Ryan noticed as he placed a hand on my sheet-covered foot.

"How are you feeling?" he asked.

I shrugged. "Numb. How long was I out?"

I frowned when they all exchanged worried looks before turning their gazes back to me. Autumn cleared his throat awkwardly, Winter stayed quiet, Summer played with a loose strand of her hair, and Ryan's eyes darted around, avoiding mine.

"Guys . . . ," I said, catching their attention.

Summer spoke first. "You . . . you've been out for about six months. You were in a coma."

Before I could react, Ryan tightened his hold on my foot. "You actually woke up a couple of nights ago, and a few times since then, but we weren't here. It seems that you don't remember. The doctor told us you were only awake for about five minutes each time before you went back to sleep."

"B-but I remember waking up . . . I remember being held down by the nurses . . ."

Summer winced. "That happened about a month into your coma. You don't remember?"

Six months! I had been in a coma for six fucking months. My mouth opened and closed, unsure of what to say. I didn't know how to react to that. It felt like I was in the darkest place in the world, all alone and cold. I didn't know what to do.

"Oh." That was all I managed to say without breaking down. "Where's Jace?" I asked.

All of them grimaced, as if the mere mention of Jace's name was a bad idea. Ryan let go of my foot and stood up from the bed, taking a few steps back.

I frowned. "Guys, where is Jace? Did he visit me while I was here?" I asked impatiently.

"I don't think—"

Autumn cut her off. "Summer, don't."

"But he deserves to know."

"What is it?" I demanded.

Summer and Autumn exchanged glances before sighing in defeat. I watched Ryan move toward where the triplets were, then glanced back at me. His expression was a mixture of hesitation and sadness.

The air was thick with tension, and I felt suffocated, dreading the potential impact of Ryan's words—they might crush my heart.

"I believe it's best if Jace tells you himself. That's all I'm going to say."

# CHAPTER FORTY-TWO
## It Hurts

"This is Jace Langlois. I'm not available at the moment, so just leave a message."

I groaned out loud and angrily smacked the phone screen first onto the hospital bed. Summer and Ryan looked at me warily, neither saying a word.

I glared at the phone as if it were to blame for all of my problems. I had been trying to contact Jace, but it was futile. All my calls just went to voicemail, and my text messages were left unanswered. I even sent him an email, but there was still no reply. Every second spent trying to reach Jace made me furious, and I could tell that my friends were starting to worry.

Autumn and Winter decided to leave, citing something about their parents, which was obviously a made-up excuse since Summer didn't go with them. Ryan stayed as well. Frankly, it seemed useless for them to do so. I mean, they wouldn't even tell me where Jace was. They just let me do whatever I felt necessary, which only made me look stupid and desperate.

Deep inside, I had a feeling Jace was probably with Bridget now. I knew what Bridget told me was meant to hurt and keep me away from Jace, but it was hard when you loved someone so much. I was still angry at all the things I finally knew, like Jace and his parents lying to me, but right now, I just wanted see him even for just a while.

To tell the truth, I was aching inside. Not physically, but mentally. I had been in a fucking coma for about six months, not knowing whether Jace had ever visited me. My friends wouldn't even give me a hint that he had visited me at all during those months that I was out like a dead person. But I knew for sure that he hadn't come to see me since I finally woke up a week ago. Jace wasn't here.

My chest felt like it was being punched a thousand times, and I knew it wasn't because of the broken ribs from the accident. The doctor said they had healed well, including the bruises all over my body. Thankfully, I only had minimal scars on my chest, and the scar from the wound on my head was covered by my hair. And ever more thankfully, my brain did not sustain any damage.

Ryan and the triplets were relieved to hear the doctor's news, but they didn't know I was devastated inside. Sure, I had healed, but what about the state of my emotions? No one would tell me where Jace had gone, and it fucking hurt not to know.

I sucked in a deep breath and let it out before I grabbed the phone and dialed Jace's number for what felt like the millionth time. It kept ringing and ringing until his voicemail started.

"This is Jace Langlois. I'm not available at the moment, so just leave a message."

*That's it!*

I snapped. "Where the fuck are you, asshole? Answer my fucking calls, or else I'm gonna fucking kill you! You hear me, asshole? You're a jerk, and I fucking hate that! Where are you? Do you even fucking know that I was in a coma for six months? Six months, you son of a—"

My voice cracked at the last sentence, and I wasn't even slightly shocked when tears blurred my vision.

"I h-hate you . . . you know that? I fucking hate you. I don't even know why I f-fell for you, you stupid idiot. I just . . . hate you."

Tears finally fell just as a long beep sounded through the phone.

241

Ryan took the phone from my hands, and Summer approached me, pulling me into a hug. I cried like a baby in her arms, but I didn't really care.

"Shhh, it's okay. We're here," Summer said soothingly.

I couldn't help but let out a loud but short sob.

*It fucking hurts. My heart feels like it's being stabbed repeatedly. Everything hurts.*

"I hate him. I hate him. I hate him," I said over and over again, clutching Summer's shirt.

*It hurts.*

*     \*     \**

*One month later*

Christmas was two weeks away, and honestly, I wasn't feeling it. People around me were excited and happy about the cheery winter season, but personally, I just wanted to lock myself in my house and sleep. Once I finally discharged from the hospital, I went back to my house. Lucy was beside herself with worry.

Of course, I didn't dare step foot into his home. I had Ryan, Autumn, and Winter get my things, and unsurprisingly, Jace wasn't there.

At first, they suggested I move in with either the triplets or Ryan, but I refused. I told them I had Lucy to consider, so I insisted on staying at my own house, explaining that I just needed some time alone. They reluctantly agreed, which was kind of them. Having good friends like them made it a little easier to cope with my problems. I was glad I had Summer, Autumn, Winter, and Ryan with me. They were the best friends that I could ever ask for. And of course, I had Lucy—she took care of my physical needs while giving me the space I needed to heal my heart.

I was currently snuggling against the couch in my house, watching cartoons on TV. My eyes were on the screen, but my mind was elsewhere, much to my chagrin. Despite my mental vow on the day I got out of the hospital to stop calling and messaging Jace, I couldn't help but think about him. I kept my phone turned off, not wanting to receive any calls or texts from anyone.

As for my friends, instead of contacting me by phone, they would come over and keep me company. On the days that I was really alone, my mind would wander, and everything would just come rushing back, including the final exams I had missed and now needed to take as special exams. I had also missed an entire damned semester.

My mood and my emotions had been going up and down, making me feel nauseated. One moment, I had been in a state of calm, and the next, a sudden ache would hit me from within. That was the kind of emotional turbulence I had been feeling for the past couple of days.

*Bark!*

I looked down and watched Frenzy try to climb onto the couch, his tail wagging in excitement. I smiled, picked him up, and patted his furry head a few times before kissing his nose. He looked at me with a cute scrunch of his nose, making me laugh a little.

"Thanks for being here with me, buddy," I said to him.

He barked in response, which was good enough for me.

I pulled the fluffy blanket toward me and shifted to get into a more comfortable position with Frenzy in my arms. After a while, he was finally asleep. I kissed the top of his head and closed my eyes.

Despite the calming silence that surrounded the house, I still couldn't help but let a few tears fall from my eyes.

It still fucking hurts.

# CHAPTER FORTY-THREE
## Nothing

I grimaced when I heard another Christmas song play inside the café. This was probably the hundredth Christmas song I had heard ever since I decided to go out of the house. Honestly, if I heard another yuletide tune, I was going to pull my hair out. It was annoying to hear multiple cheery tunes when all I wanted to do was mope around in misery.

It was four days before Christmas, but it felt like any other day to me. There was no excitement in the air at all.

"Kei, your coffee is getting cold."

I looked up and saw Ryan's concerned face.

I gave him a forced smile, took the cup of café au lait, and sipped loudly just to annoy my friend. I smirked triumphantly when he made a face.

"Ugh, I hate it when you do that," he stated.

"Mind your own business," I playfully retorted.

He rolled his eyes and then looked at me with an expression that clearly say, "Are you okay?" which was annoying.

*Why do people always want to know if someone is okay or not? It's none of their damn business.*

I understood that they were worried and wanted to help, but sometimes, I just needed some time to myself without anyone looking at me like I was about to break down or something.

Watching Ryan act all concerned irritated me to no end. Worse, he still looked at me with those pity-filled eyes. And to top it off, "White Christmas" was still playing.

Fortunately for him, I managed to calm myself down and reel back the pent-up emotions to myself rather than venting them all out like a fool.

"I'm still mad at you, y'know," I mumbled.

Ryan frowned. "For what? What did I do?"

"You won't tell me about Jace."

The air around us thickened with tension when I mentioned Jace's name. Ryan avoided my eyes and shifted in his seat, choosing instead to watch the falling snow outside the café.

I followed his gaze. People in winter clothes entered the stores, gathering as many Christmas presents as they could before all the good ones were sold out.

*Lucky them*, I thought bitterly.

My thoughts turned tb Jace as I watched the people passing outside the café. I wondered what he was doing right now. He was probably back in France, drinking coffee with Bridget.

I sighed and closed my eyes for a second before I opened them again. I was so stupid. Nothing good ever came out from thinking about the man who left me with a broken heart. It wasn't helping me at all.

Ryan and I looked away from the glass window at the same time. He picked up the empty packet of sugar from the table and fiddled with it, while I stayed silent, waiting for him to say something. A few minutes passed without us moving or saying a word until my phone rang.

Ryan jolted at the loud sound.

I took my phone out of my pocket and saw that Summer was calling.

"Hey, what's up?" I answered.

"Kei, where are you? Is Ryan with you?" she asked in a rush.

I frowned and glanced at Ryan, who mouthed, "What's wrong?"

"Yeah, we're at the café a couple of blocks from my house. Why? What's wrong?"

Summer sighed in relief, but hesitation tinged her voice. "Uh, I think you should come here, and please bring Ryan with you."

"W-what? Summer, what do you—"

The phone beeped loudly, cutting me off.

"What did she say?" Ryan asked, his voice filled with worry.

"She, uh, told us to go to their apartment," I replied, curiosity gnawing at my guts.

"Why?"

"I don't know."

Ryan frowned, clearly thinking, before he said, "We should go."

After paying for the coffee, we ran out of the café and hailed a cab. Once we arrived at the triplets' building, we raced to their apartment and knocked on their door.

Autumn opened it with a grim face. "Come in."

Once Ryan and I got inside, Autumn locked the door.

"What's going on? You looked like you saw a ghost," I joked.

Autumn simply looked at me without a word and led Ryan and me down the narrow hallway to their living room, where Summer and Winter stood near the television—both of them looking just as grim as Autumn.

"Guys, what's going on?" I asked cautiously, waiting for one of them to answer.

Autumn and Winter avoided my gaze, looking anywhere but at me. I looked at Summer, who pursed her lips and kept glancing at the kitchen doorway.

"Summer?" I asked, following her gaze.

246

There was a full three seconds of silence until it was broken by my gasp when someone came out of the kitchen and stood just a few feet from me.

"J-Jace?"

Jace stood there, his body tense and his face stoic, but his intense eyes were on mine. His expression was filled with heavy emotions.

I felt like a fish out of the water right then, and my mouth opened then closed. I expected to lash out at him, but nothing came. I felt nothing.

"What is he doing here?" Ryan suddenly broke the tension-filled silence in the room, his question directed toward the triplets.

Summer flinched at Ryan's tone, and Autumn noticed it. He stepped in front of his sister as if to protect her from Ryan's anger. Winter stood not too far away, his face contorted into a deep frown.

As for me, I felt like it was just Jace and me in the room, both of us staring at each other, waiting for the other to speak first.

My chest constricted as if a cold hand reached in, wrapping its callous fingers around my heart and squeezing it tightly. For a moment, I could have sworn I forgot to breathe. I had to steady myself to keep from falling. My knees were shaking, making it difficult to stand properly.

Jace hovered in the kitchen doorway, and each passing second made it harder and harder to breathe.

I wanted to scream.

I wanted to scream at him for lying to me.

I wanted to scream at him for leaving.

I wanted to scream at him for betraying me.

I wanted answers. I wanted an explanation. I wanted to know everything.

*But at the same time . . .*

I desperately wanted to touch him. I craved for him, and he stood so close yet so far away.

I wanted to reach out and hug him, holding him tight.

I wanted to tell him that I missed him so much.

I wanted to throw myself into his arms and kiss him.

But I couldn't move. I seemed to have forgotten how it was done. All I could manage was to stand there and look at him.

He appeared to be contemplating what to do next, as if he was afraid of what I might say or do that could make him run for the hills.

The triplets' and Ryan's voices were muffled. All I could focus on were my own breathing and the faint sound of my beating heart. It felt like I was having an out-of-body experience, quietly watching everything unfold before me. And I hated it.

Finally, after what felt like an eternity, Jace spoke.

# CHAPTER FORTY-FOUR
## Breakdown

"We need to talk."

I briefly glanced at my friends after Jace said those words. The triplets seemed to get it. They nodded and walked out of the room, leaving me alone with Jace and Ryan.

I looked at Ryan, praying that he would understand and leave us alone for a bit. He didn't react at first, but then he sighed in resignation and nodded.

I sighed in relief when Ryan walked out and shut the door behind him. I looked at Jace and gasped as he rushed toward me and engulfed me in his strong arms. He pressed his lips against mine, and my eyes widened in shock.

His embrace was tight, but I didn't reciprocate. My arms hung limply at my sides. He noticed my lack of response and reluctantly loosened his hold, though his arms remained around me.

I swallowed nervously as his eyes bore intensely into mine. His gaze seemed to last forever as he slowly exhaled and pressed his forehead against mine.

Neither of us spoke. The atmosphere in the room was thick and heavy, and I involuntarily shivered at the tension.

Slowly, his hands reached up and cupped my face, his thumbs gently stroking my cheeks. I couldn't help but close my eyes at his touch. It had been so long, and I missed him more than words could express.

"I missed you, *mon beau*," he whispered in my ear.

I resisted the urge to whimper. God, his deep voice was something I would never forget. I truly missed everything about him, and now that he was finally here in front of me, it took every ounce of strength I had not to cry.

He lied to you! My mind screamed.

As if doused in ice-cold water, I snapped back to my senses as reality sets in. I shoved Jace away, making him stumble backward. Before he could react, my palm connected with his left cheek in a brutal slap.

The sound of the slap made me gasp, but fortunately, he didn't seem to notice.

Jace touched his left cheek in shock. He opened and closed his mouth as if to respond, but no words came out. He stretched his jaw and licked the inside of each of his cheeks, checking their integrity.

Luckily for him, the slap wasn't hard enough for his mouth to bleed.

"You fucking deserved it, you asshole," I hissed.

He looked at me again, his eyes filled with hurt and guilt. His entire spirit and hope seemed to crumble as he took a few unsteady steps backward.

A pang of guilt tugged at my heart, but I coldly pushed it away. What was the point of feeling guilty over what I just did? After all, I could never hurt him the same way he hurt me. Whatever he felt at this moment was nothing compared to what he made me feel.

*Everything we had were just lies . . .*

Everything didn't matter now. No matter how pained or utterly guilty he looked and seemed, it meant nothing to me.

In fact, I had half a mind to walk away and leave him here alone so he can wallow in the pain and guilt he felt.

*If I leave right now, it would save me from even more pain.*

The idea lingered in my mind but quickly faded when the thought that I might never see Jace again came up. That same thought brought with it an ache I could never ignore.

*I can't.*

I couldn't leave him. No, I didn't want to. I couldn't explain it, but I knew that if I walked away right now, I would never forgive myself for it.

The more I tried to figure out that thought, the more confused I felt . . .

*Why does the idea of leaving him feel so awful? Why is it so hard for me to walk away? Why couldn't I just be a heartless snake and leave him to suffer? Didn't I have every right to react the way I did?*

*Why didn't everything go the way I wanted it to?*

And the final question came to mind:

*Why is it pure torture to see him about to break down?*

"I hate you . . . so much," I whispered as tears ran down my cheeks.

In the end, I knew I didn't have the guts to leave, so I just stood there and cried silently as Jace slowly stepped forward once more.

He hesitated for a moment but then wrapped me in his embrace again. He buried his face in my hair while he soothingly rubbed my back with a hand.

As the walls around my mind and heart slowly came down, I broke into a sob. The pain of everything that happened came back in full force, and it was futile to stop it.

*I'm pathetic.*

It didn't matter how hard I tried to fight this, I knew I couldn't push him away anymore, not after I was finally in his arms.

"Shhh, don't cry. I'm here, Kei."

"I hate you."

"I know."

"You lied to me."

"I know."

251

"You left me behind."

"Shhh, I know."

I sniffed and felt his lips brush against my head.

"I am sorry for everything, *mon beau*. I know I made so many mistakes, but please, give me a chance to explain everything to you. I love you so much that it pains me. *Je t'aime, mon beau. Je t'aime.* I don't know what I would do without you," he said desperately, making no move to let me go.

Tears continue to stream down my face as my sobs turned quieter. It was getting harder for me to breathe, and I tried to calm my shuddering breaths by mentally counting from one to four. After two minutes or so, I was finally able to calm myself down.

I sniffed and wiped my tears away with my jacket sleeve.

Jace didn't say a word and just waited.

I let out a deep sigh and slowly pulled myself away from his hold, all while I tried my best not to look into his eyes. I took a couple of steps backward and kept my distance from his reach.

He inhaled sharply.

I shut my eyes tight, then opened them again. My eyes were still fixated on the floor as conflicting thoughts slowly emerged in my mind once more. There were so many questions I wanted to ask him, but my mouth was unwilling to cooperate.

*Should I give him another chance to explain himself?*

*What will happen next if I forgive him?*

*Would everything go back to normal again?*

*How could I even trust him anymore?*

Honestly, I didn't know what to feel anymore. My emotions were all over the place and spiraling out of control. I didn't know if I should stay angry at Jace for lying and leaving me behind, or get rid of my pride and be utterly ecstatic that he finally came back.

*I am weak . . . so damn weak . . . pathetic . . . pitiful. And so fucking confused.*

I didn't even know what to think anymore. Maybe being alone with Jace wasn't such a good idea. Maybe I was foolish for letting him embrace and comfort me. Maybe I should just leave and never look back.

*Maybe . . . maybe . . . maybe . . .*

There were hundreds of *maybes* and *what ifs* that seemed to bounce endlessly inside my head.

"Kei, please look at me. I understand if you'll never forgive me, but please, just give me one chance to explain myself even . . . even if this will be the last time I'll ever see or talk to you again," he pleaded, his voice breaking as he said the last part, which made me look at him.

"W-what do you—"

"I am sorry," he cut me off as a lone tear slipped from his eye and ran down his cheek—the same cheek that received my slap. His face was still and stoic, but his eyes were not.

I couldn't believe it. The strong, confident, and intimidating Jace Langlois was crying in front of me. It was the first time I had ever seen him like this and another thought crossed my mind.

*Why now?*

He never cried in front of me. He never showed vulnerability throughout our marriage, and even when things were great, he kept most of his thoughts and worries to himself.

*"Je suis sincèrement désolé."*[59]

I bit my lip at his apology, trying to keep myself from crying again. Breaking down wouldn't solve anything, and I knew that now.

"Jace, I don't know what to say."

He just nodded in understanding.

I took a deep breath before I started, "You—you have to understand it from my point of view. It wasn't just you who lied. All this time, your parents lied to me as well. They used my dead parents' will against me, they forged letters to get me to marry you, and you went along with it. How am I supposed to know what was real between us and what wasn't? I—I just can't let that go. Even

---

[59] I am sincerely sorry.

worse, you left me for months . . . *again*. Did you even know that I was in a fucking coma?"

My voice cracked at the last part, but I held my resolve. I refused to let any tears fall. A part of me expected Jace to nod and apologize profusely like a broken record, but he didn't. Instead, his eyes widened at what I had just said. His shoulders tensed and his hands clenched into fists.

"Jace?" I asked, unsure why he was reacting this way.

He looked up at me and shook his head.

I frowned. "What?"

He didn't answer. He just shook his head once more.

That momentary confusion passed as the truth slowly sank in. After finally realizing what Jace meant, a wave of fury washed over me. I kicked the coffee table in anger. It toppled over, but it wasn't enough. My blood felt like it was reaching its boiling point, and as I looked around to find something break, Jace rushed toward me and gripped my shoulders to bring me back to reality.

I shifted my focus to him, burning with rage, but this time, it wasn't directed at him.

"She didn't tell you, did she?" I asked, my tone eerily calm while I felt the urge to punch a certain model straight in the face.

"No . . . ," he said softly. "I'm sorry, she—"

I cut him off, "Tell me everything." The urge to find her and strangle her was strong, but vengeance would just have to wait.

# CHAPTER FORTY-FIVE
## Clear Things Up

"Tell me everything, or else that woman will regret the day she decided to mess with me."

Jace hesitated, torn between whether or not he should reveal the truth. However, when he looked into my eyes and saw my grave expression, he let out a sigh and nodded.

I decided to sit down on the couch, and he followed suit. I had a feeling this conversation was anything but brief, so we might as well be comfortable.

"After you got run over by a truck, I rushed you to the hospital myself. I didn't have time to call the ambulance, and it would be faster if I took you there by car . . ." He paused.

I wanted to tell him that what he did was more dangerous than waiting for EMTs, especially since I ended up with broken ribs, but on second thought, it wasn't the time and place for that. I was already safe. I gestured for him to continue.

He sighed. "Bridget was with me in the car, and we rushed you to the ER where the doctors immediately brought you in for emergency surgery. Y-you lost a lost of blood, *mon beau*. I was terrified. It's all my fault, and I'll never forgive myself for what happened."

I listened as Jace spoke. He propped his elbows on his knees, leaned forward, and ran his fingers through his disheveled hair. His face was laden with stress, guilt, and exhaustion, which nearly made me want to scoot over and hold him in my arms.

I resisted the urge and just waited for him to continue.

"I waited for hours until a doctor approached me and told me you were . . ." He stopped, as if the memory pained him to continue.

"What did the doctor tell you?" I asked.

He glanced at me briefly before returning his gaze to the floor. "He told me you were in critical condition, and that there was a fifty percent chance of you surviving."

I sucked in a breath. *Oh God.*

"I couldn't take it. The pain was too much, and I blamed myself, so—"

"So you left? Just like that?" I cut him off.

My voice cracked, and I could feel tears pricking my eyes once more.

He shook his head. "No, I was only going to stay away for a while to clear my mind and then come back later, but then my parents called. Apparently, while I was pacing the hospital waiting for news about your surgery, Bridget left. I didn't notice at the time because I was panicking and didn't really care what she did. She went to see my parents and then informed them about what had happened, and just as they were about to join me at the hospital themselves . . ." He swallowed a lump in his throat. "She threatened to get the media involved."

His tone shifted from pain to anger. My eyes widened at this. I didn't bother to interrupt him as he continued.

"She said she would release reports about the company nearing bankruptcy—a fact my parents had worked so hard to keep hidden—and start a gossip about the loss of your trust fund. Her threats, of course, prevented my parents from coming to see you." He closed his eyes. "Fortunately, my mother managed to call and told me what happened. Bridget also gave an ultimatum: If I didn't fly back to Paris with her and her grandfather, she would make it a point to destroy the company along with everything my father ever worked for."

I gritted my teeth at the realization. Before I knew it, another wave of rage coursed through my veins. My hands shook, and the temptation to confront her and give her a piece of my mind increased tenfold.

"You know how devastating malicious gossip can be. There would be no need to bring legal action against my parents for losing your money. Just spreading rumors and eroding trust would suffice to gradually dismantle my father's company."

*The fucking nerve of that bitch! How dare she?*

"Kei . . ." His voice was gentle and full of regret. "Please understand, I never wanted any of this to happen. If I could go back in time, I wouldn't have gone back to Paris with her . . ."

He turned to me, reaching out to take both my hands, but I pulled away with a grimace. *I can't . . . not yet.*

Jace sighed but didn't push further. "I hope you understand that I can never stop loving you, *mon beau*. But you also need to know that, at the time, I was conflicted and in a state of panic. I had to make choices that wouldn't jeopardize everything, especially when it involved my family—the people I loved."

I kept quiet. I didn't want to interrupt him.

"You are my husband, and I will always love you despite how things turned out. But I am also a son, and I had to do what I necessary to save my father's company. I could never forgive myself for leaving you behind in the hospital."

He swallowed another lump in his throat, and I had to restrain myself from reaching out to comfort him.

"If I had known what had happened to you back in the hospital while I was in France, I would've come back to you at once, but Bridget had my phone at the time, and I just . . ."

That last part completely caught me of guard. *Bridget had his phone?*

I frowned. So she was the reason why Jace disappeared without a word and why he hadn't responded to any of my calls and messages. Not only had she deliberately kept me in the dark, but she had also threatened Jace's parents.

*His parents.* Despite the fact that Mr. and Mrs. Langlois had lied to me, I couldn't ignore Jace's earlier confession that they had tried to see me.

*Maybe they did care after all.* A glimmer of hope tugged at my heart as I remembered the times they treated me like their own son. When my parents died, they welcomed me with open arms, and it didn't take long for me to treat them like my surrogate parents. Even though I rarely saw them, they ensured I was fed, clothed, and stayed in school. Despite the money being my parents', I still felt a deep sense of gratitude.

*I guess I'll have to figure that part out later.* Whether or not they actually did like me was an issue for another day.

"So why are you here, then?" I asked with a frown. "And where's Bridget?"

"She's here."

My eyes widened. "What?"

"I arrived in America yesterday with Bridget. She came back to look for potential investors and stockholders as instructed by her grandfather. She doesn't trust me yet, so she wanted me to be with her," he explained.

I frowned. "Does she know you're here with me right now?"

He contemplated this for a moment. "I'm not sure. I sneaked out of the hotel while she went down to the lobby to meet some people. I went to the mansion first, but Harry told you had left and moved out for a while now. They couldn't even contact me. Everything went through my lawyer, and I could only communicate with him while Bridget was present."

I avoided his gaze at this. *Wasn't what Bridget did criminal?*

*"Mon beau."*

258

I jolted slightly as his hands clasped mine tightly. I lowered my eyes to our intertwined hands and nearly teared up again when I saw that he still wore his wedding band on his left ring finger.

"Will you give me one last chance and forgive me?" he whispered, caressing the back of my hand with his thumbs.

I slowly looked up and met his intense yet warm eyes—the same eyes that had taken my breath away the moment I first saw them. I opened my mouth to respond when—

"Um, guys? Sorry to interrupt, but we have a problem." Summer suddenly barged into the living room with her brothers.

Jace stood up, but he didn't let go of my hand. I followed suit, my face heating up as I tried to avoid the curious looks from the Winston triplets and Ryan, who had just entered.

"What's the matter?" Jace asked calmly.

Autumn cleared his throat. "Ralph is in the lobby downstairs."

I gave him, confused. "So? Why didn't you bring him here?"

Which led me to question, where was Ralph all these time? What sort of help he extended to his parents, his brother, to me?

Ryan gave me a grave look. "Bridget is with him."

# CHAPTER FORTY-SIX
## Blood and Forgiveness

Right now, I felt the urge to hurt someone without caring about the consequences. The elevator ride down to the lobby was quiet. The triplets and Ryan insisted on joining, just in case Bridget tried something. Frankly, I didn't really care because I was trying my best not to unbridle my rage.

It didn't take long for the doors to open, and my eyes immediately spotted the she-devil herself, standing proudly some distance from the receptionist. Behind her was Ralph, who gave a sheepish wave at his brother as we all stepped out of the elevator.

"I tried," he said.

Jace ignored him and focused on Bridget, who looked tensed.

"How did you know that I was here, Bridget?" Jace asked calmly.

"You have clearly underestimated me, *mon amour*," she responded coolly, not bothering to hide her displeasure. "You shouldn't have taken me as a fool—I have my ways," she finished as she eyed both Jace and me with scorn.

I returned her look with a deadly glare. "You should keep your damn mouth shut," I started, my voice laced with venom. "You have a lot of nerve coming here and acting like you own the place. You think that just because you threatened my in-laws, you can take my husband away from me?" My voice shook with rage as I stepped forward.

Bridget's eyes widened, but luckily for her, Jace grabbed my arm and pulled me back.

She smirked triumphantly at this. The expression in her eyes taunting. "You know, I do feel sorry for you," she said.

Jace let go of my arm after he made sure I wasn't going to maul her, then turned to face her again.

"Bridget, don't . . ."

She scowled. "Don't tell me what to do, Jace. You, of all people, should know what I'd do to anyone who dares to step in my way."

"Bridget, stop." His voice firm. "You're only going to make things worse. I already made up my mind. You can do anything you want with the company. In fact, I don't care anymore." He reached down and held my hand, though he kept his eyes on her. "After realizing what I would lose if I chose you, I've made my decision."

I held in a deep breath as Jace continued, "I'd rather be without a job, have no money to my name, and live happily ever after with the one I love than save a company and live the rest of my life in suffering. You can do whatever you want, just please don't drag my parents and Kei into your schemes. You know you can't threaten my parents with Kei's trust fund anymore. They are the trustees, and it was stipulated that they could invest a certain percentage of the funds. They did just that and have since recouped the losses and are turning a profit."

Bridget looked at if she had just been slapped. Judging by her expression, it was obvious that she had never expected Jace to say that, much less give up his father's company. Her face contorted into rage, and she gritted her teeth.

The opposite was happening to me. Jace's words cooled some of my anger. Although I cared very little about how much of my inheritance was gone, I did care about feeling scammed—about the fact that Jace's parents only cared about me only because of my money. But now, it seemed they did have a legitimate reason for using my money. I only wished they talked to me about it instead of forging letters . . .

"I can't believe you," she started. "After everything that I had done, you still chose *him*?"

Anger coursed through my veins once more, and I couldn't stop myself. "Everything you've done for us?" I let out a bitter laugh at her delusion. "What have you done exactly? Aside from making threats, spreading lies, keeping your supposed *amour's* phone away from him, aaand having him under false imprisonment?"

Sure, I couldn't get closer to her thanks to Jace, but she can still hear me from where I stood.

"You've done absolutely nothing for anyone else but yourself," I continued. "You don't care who you hurt. You're a selfish, spoiled, and entitled bitch who can't accept reality, and to tell you the truth, I feel sorry for you," I finished, echoing the same words she used.

Jace gripped my hand tightly, but I pushed him away. I knew he was trying to protect me, but this had gone too far.

"Don't try to stop me, Jace." I glared at him as I pulled my hand away. "If you want me to forgive you, then shut up and stay out of my way."

He looked at me with a determined expression. "No, I can't do that. I won't step aside and let you deal with her when I'm the one to blame here. It's my fault, and I'm sorry I didn't try harder to come back to you, *mon beau.*"

The anger I felt slowly evaporated as Jace held both my hands in his. His eyes were on mine and mine alone.

"I won't make any promises, but if you give me another chance, I vow to never leave you alone again. I won't go anywhere without telling you because if I lose everything, I know I'll be alright as long as I'm with you."

Tears pricked my eyes, and Jace wasn't finished.

He continued, "No matter where life takes me . . . *us*, just know that I'll work each and every day to make sure that nothing will ever take me away from you again."

I couldn't hold back any longer as the tears I had fought so hard to suppress fell down my cheeks.

"I'll make you breakfast, but there won't be any caviar," he said with a little smile. "I don't think we can afford that after I file for bankruptcy. I'm sure I have some assets left that will allow us to start over and get by. We'll live in a simple home, Frenzy will grow into a strong dog, you'll finish school and get your degree, and I'll find a way to make sure we'll always be happy."

I bowed my head and sniffed, pulling one hand away from his hold to wipe my tears with a sleeve.

*"Mon beau."*

I couldn't bring myself to look up at him. I couldn't. Every word he said was everything I needed to hear because I knew he meant them. Suddenly, it didn't matter what Bridget did with the company anymore. Jace was right. As long as we had each other, we'll be okay. Sure, his parents will would need time to adjust, but things will get better.

"Whatever you choose to do, just know that from now on, I wouldn't trade you for anything. I'm happy to be your husband."

His words sent a ray of hope through my heart. *We'll be alright.*

I looked up. His eyes darted to the side where I saw Bridget's furious expression. Her eyes were ablaze, and she was gritting her teeth, which meant that she probably heard Jace's confession.

Her eyes met mine as she reached into her bag, and in a flash, the atmosphere between our group shifted as she pulled out a pistol.

"Jace!" I screamed.

"Oh my God! Kei!" Summer called out.

"She's got a gun!" Autumn screamed, alerting everyone in the lobby.

People immediately stopped what they were doing and panicked. There were screams, running, and ducking behind objects and furniture, like the receptionist who disappeared behind the counter. Amid the chaos, the security guard and what was probably the concierge or doorman rushed over to quell the panic.

I stood frozen on the spot as fear gripped me.

"Kei, move!" Ryan shouted.

"Bridget! *Arrête*,[60] Bridget, *arrête!*" Ralph cried out as he rushed toward her, only for her to point the gun she was holding with both hands at him.

Jace seized the moment and immediately pushed me behind him.

"Nobody move," Bridget demanded, her voice and eyes manic.

Her lips trembled as she murmured something under her breath, her eyes roaming around the area as if she were conversing with someone unseen.

I glanced over to my shoulder and saw the triplets standing close by, their stances cautious and alert.

Ryan, on the other side, was shifting his gaze between Ralph and Bridget, his eyes filled with worry for Ralph, who remained at the other end of her gun.

As the chaos among the other residents subsided, the male staff kept their eyes on Bridget like hawks from a considerable distance. I knew they were hesitant to act rashly, fearing that any sudden movement might provoke her to shoot.

"Bridget . . ." This time it was Jace who spoke. "Drop the gun. You don't know what you're doing." His voice was gentle, desperately trying to placate her.

---

[60] Stop.

"Shut up!" she roared, her hands shaking as her eyes darted from Jace to me, then to the male staff, and everywhere else.

"You're crazy!" Ryan exclaimed.

"Oh am I?" Bridget snarled, shifting the gun to point at him instead.

My eyes widened. I moved past Jace, about to yell and distract Bridget, when he grabbed my hand in a tight grip.

Ralph, still the closest to her, quickly realized what she was about to do. He rushed toward her, but she beat him by a second, swinging her gun to point at me.

"Too late," she said to Ralph, though her eyes were on me. The barrel of her pistol was aimed directly at my heart. One squeeze of the trigger, and it would all be over.

Time seemed to stop. Her lips curled into a Cheshire cat-like grin.

"Say *au revoir*, bitch," she said.

In what felt like slow motion, Bridget's finger curled as she squeezed the trigger.

*Bang!*

Time sped forward after the deafening shot rang out. Ralph tackled Bridget from behind and wrestled the gun away. Summer let out a scream of fear while her brothers shouted her name, and Ryan cursed vehemently. Sirens wailed, growing louder by the second.

The fear that had paralyzed me slowly began to fade as I saw a pool of blood. Tears welled up as I was overwhelmed by the sight of crimson. An incredible pain surged through my chest as I realized what had just happened.

*Jace, I love you, and I forgive you.*

# CHAPTER FORTY-SEVEN
## Safe and Sound

"Say au revoir, bitch," Bridget said.

Her right index finger slowly curled around the trigger, squeezing it unhurriedly. The bullet traveled through the air, seeming to move in slow motion, before it finally pierced into flesh.

Hazy shadows and earsplitting screeches of fear echoed throughout the place, making me cover my ears. Then came a loud, pain-filled gasp, and I immediately looked down on the floor.

My eyes widened at the sight and my jaw dropped. Blood. There was blood everywhere. The immaculate white walls and floor of the room were now stained with scarlet, casting a frightening yet strangely beautiful glow over the scene.

I jstood frozen in the middle of the room as blood continued to pool around my feet.

"Kei? Kei," a voice whispered behind me, rough and hoarse, as if struggling to breathe and speak at the same time.

Who was that?

Before I could discern the owner, another voice interrupted, "It's your fault he's dead, you imbecile!" someone yelled, and suddenly Bridget appeared, advancing toward me menacingly.

I stepped back. "What are you talking about?"

She glared. "You! You're the reason for all of this! It's because of you that Jace died!"

I paled. "What?"

*"Jace died because of you! This is all your fault! You are nothing but a piece of trash in this godforsaken world!"* Her screams were growing more hysterical by the second. *"Jace was mine! Mine! You hear me? I loved him with all my heart! He loved me first! We were supposed to get married until . . . until you came along! You stupid son of a bitch!"*

Her words felt like sharp daggers, each one piercing through my chest. I couldn't breathe as I stumbled backward. Tears pricked at the corners of my eyes as she moved closer, waving the gun in her right hand.

*"I d-didn't do anything to y-you,"* I stammered.

She stopped in her tracks and shot me a look of disgust.

Suddenly, and without any warning, a pair of ice-cold arms wrapped me from behind. I screamed in fear and fought to push the cold arms away. As soon as they let go, I turned around and was confronted by Jace's eyes.

Tears streamed down my face as I let out a cry of disbelief. Jace's handsome face was now covered in blood, dripping from his head. My eyes were drawn to the single bullet hole in his forehead.

*"No!"* I gasped.

A sadistic smirk crossed Bridget's features before she face slowly disappeared into thin air. The scene changed once more, and I screamed when I saw Jace standing there. The blood continued to stream from his head, and it seemed like he was slowly fading away.

*"Kei . . ."* His voice was barely a whisper as he continued, *"You killed me."*

I shook my head and slowly backed away. This wasn't Jace. It couldn't be. Jace would never blame anyone but himself. This wasn't him at all.

*"You killed me,"* the figure repeated, reaching out a hand toward me.

*"No!"* I screamed as I covered my ears and shut my eyes. *"You're not Jace! Stop it!"*

*"You killed me . . . ,"* he repeated in a groan.

Silence followed. My eyes remained shut, and the cold seemed to dissipate somewhat. Slowly, I opened my eyes and saw an undead corpse manifesting in front of me. The figure, whose skin used to be intact, now decayed in several places. Its eyeballs bulged from their sockets as it looked at me with *hunger. Dried flood stained its lips, and as it opened its mouth wide, sharp fangs filled its rotting mouth.*

*"No!" I screamed as it pushed its rotting arm forward and gripped my throat with ease. Its sharp nails dug into my skin as it came closer . . .*

\*　　　\*　　　\*

My eyes shot open, and I gasped for air. Cold sweat clung to my skin, and a wave of relief washed over me, knowing it was just a dream. However, that relief was short-lived as the memories of Bridget pointing a gun at me and the loud gunshot in the lobby came rushing back.

I started to hyperventilate, an oncoming wave of panic threatening to overwhelm me. I gripped the sheets that lay beneath me.

"Kei!" a voice screamed, and I immediately sat up.

I looked around and was met with the familiar setup of the bedroom Jace and I shared. To my right, Summer look at me with concern, while Autumn and Winter were on the plush burgundy couch positioned in the furthest corner of the room. Winter was sound asleep with his head resting on Autumn's lap, while Autumn looked at me with worry. Ralph and Ryan were nowhere to be seen.

"Kei?"

I looked at Summer, who, aside from her concern, also seemed hesitant, as if on high alert. She appeared worried that one wrong move might make me panic and run out of the room.

*Jace.*

"Where's Jace?" I asked.

"Um . . ."

I didn't wait for her answer. Instead, I stood up groggily, ignoring the dizzy sensation in my head. I paused as my vision was somewhat blurry, but it eventually focused. Heading to the door, I pushed it open, disregarding both Summer and Autumn's pleas. I couldn't understand why I was suddenly so weak, but it was probably related to the nightmare.

Just I was about to step out, Summer and Autumn pulled me back into the room. I shoved them away and stumbled a little. Winter, now awake, leaned against the door.

"Guys, just tell me where Jace is? Is he all right? What happened to Bridget? Where is she?" I asked, firing off questions one after another, not bothering to calm down as I became fully alert.

"Whoa, woah, woah, calm down. Everything is fine," Autumn reassured.

Winter grimaced. "For now, anyway."

I frowned. "Why? What happened? Did I pass out? How long have I been out?"

Summer gently placed a hand on my arm. I averted my gaze to her and saw her bite her lip.

"You've been out for four hours," she said with a sigh.

Somehow that didn't bother me as much as it should have. Right now, I didn't care about myself.

"And Jace?"

The triplets exchanged worried looks, and my heart drop. *No, please. God no.*

My eyes stung, and suddenly, it became harder to breathe. I clamped a hand over my mouth, struggling to keep the loud sobs from escaping. After everything I had been through, I had never known pain like this. It was like a part of me was slowly being taken away, and all I can do was watch.

Slowly, I dropped my hand and let the sobs come.

*    *    *

It had been three days since that night. Since then, I had spent most of my time at the hospital, visiting Jace, and waiting for him to recover from his gunshot wound. Often, my friends would come with me so I wouldn't be alone. Ryan, who also visited Jace regularly, kept me updated on Jace's vitals when I wasn't there.

So far, there hadn't been any dramatic changes. Jace was still unconscious, and unlike in my nightmare, he hadn't get shot in the head. The bullet had hit his leg. Nevertheless, he lost a lot of blood, and my hopes for a speedy recovery were slowly dwindling by the day.

Jace looked peaceful as he lay on the hospital bed. His eyes were still closed, and his breathing was even. The room was quiet except for the constant beeping of the machines that monitored his condition.

I checked the time and realized that I had been sitting there for three hours now. The next nursing round wouldn't be for another hour or so, so I decided to get lunch. When I got back, he remains the same

*    *    *

I operated on autopilot for the next two days. I would drop by the hospital, spend time with Jace, talk to the nurses, and sometimes, find distraction to keep my worried thoughts from taking over.

At the moment, I was seated on one of the plush couches in the lavish waiting room. I was told I had to wait there because a team of doctors were currently keeping a close watch on Jace.

The apprehension was killing me. I didn't know what they were going to do, but it sounded urgent. Normally, I would use this time to find any distraction on my phone, but after hearing that they needed a team of professionals, I couldn't help but worry.

I propped my elbows on my knees and ran my fingers over my hair.

*Was this it?* My heart sank at the thought. *What if it is over? What if Jace doesn't wake up? What if Jace died?*

Before the tears could fall, a familiar deep voice sounded behind me. I turned around and saw Ralph smiling.

"Surprised?" he asked playfully.

Tears fell down my cheeks. He wasn't alone. Ralph was pushing a wheelchair—with Jace in it.

I covered my mouth with a hand as sobs of shock, relief, and overall joy overcame me. Jace stayed seated, a silly grin adorning his handsome features. Ralph made sure Jace was right in front of me before stepping back a few paces to give us space.

"Hi, *mon beau*," he said, his deep voice tired but very much alive.

I didn't waste a single second. I didn't even think about the possibility of hitting Jace's bandaged thigh. The joy and relief of him finally waking up made me lose all sense of caution, and I immediately hugged him like my life depended on it.

Jace grunted at the sudden action, which made hard contact with his injury, and I immediately pulled away.

"I'm sorry. I just . . . are you alright?" I asked in concern.

Jace shrugged. "It's still a bit painful, but I can manage."

I let out a sigh of relief. "Good."

Then, without a second thought, I smacked his arm.

Ralph, who had been watching us from a distance, spluttered profanities in French at my gesture. In a flash, he stepped forward and pulled me away from Jace, who groaned in pain.

"You, asshole! Don't scare me like that! You have no right to do that to me! You hear me? Don't ever do that again, you jerk!" I hissed.

"Kei! Stop. You're hurting Jace!" Ralph exclaimed.

I glared at him. "I don't care! It's less than what he deserved for—"

Jace grabbed my arm and pulled me down, nearly making me topple over. Before I knew it, I was pressed against his chest as he wrapped his arms around me in a tight embrace.

271

I broke down into sobs. I probably looked disgusting, but I didn't care . . . All the fear I felt was now gone with his touch.

Jace was back.

# CHAPTER FORTY-EIGHT
## Love and Trust

"Here, drink this."

I smiled at Ralph as he handed me a steaming mug of coffee. Jace lay on the bed while I sat beside him.

The triplets had stepped out briefly and were talking about getting some Chinese takeout to celebrate.

Ryan arrived a few minutes ago in Jace's room, which was one of the hospital's best private suites. It didn't take long for me to realize that this hospital was owned by Ralph. In addition to the hospitals he owned in France, he also had three other divisions in the United States.

"So, how are you feeling?" Ryan asked as he sat on the lilac couch on the right side of the room.

Ralph sat beside Ryan, his arm resting behind him as his fingers played with Ryan's hair. If it weren't for all the events that happened, I would have teased them about it.

"I'm well. Jace here, though, not so much." I shrugged and then sipped on my coffee.

"Hey! I'm as healthy as a horse," Jace asserted. "Can we go home now?"

I glared at him. He was so stubborn. "Oh no, you don't. Stop being a spoiled brat for once and just listen to whatever the doctor tells you—or better yet, listen to me. Understand?"

Jace kept his mouth shut and averted his eyes from mine.

Ralph couldn't help but laugh at his reaction. "You better do what your husband says from now on, *mon frere*," he teased with a sly smirk, which earned him a jab to the gut from Ryan.

I felt Jace tense beside me. I don't blame him. It was difficult for either of us to talk about our relationship right now. After everything that happened with Bridget, it seemed that we both had a silent agreement not to discuss our marriage yet and just see how things would unfold.

Unfortunately, Ralph was oblivious to this and never seemed to miss a chance to tease us about our relationship problems.

I shut my eyes and let out a sigh. The warm coffee mug calmed me down, and it felt good to finally breathe.

*     *     *

*The aftermath*

Bridget finally got what she deserved. Not long after Jace got shot in the leg, the cops arrived, and immediately arrested her. I never saw her again after she was taken away.

Jace getting shot made me burst into sobs that didn't stop even after we got him to the hospital, leaving me a complete mess. Fortunately, Ralph was there and was able to provide updates on Jace's condition as well as what had happened with Bridget.

Once Jace was awake, it didn't take long for him to contact his lawyers, and the team immediately acted on his wishes with very few issues. The verdict was clear: Bridget was convicted of attempted murder and was sentenced to jail. Her sentence was reduced with the condition that she would seek psychiatric help in France after serving her time. This condition gave me a sinking suspicion that her family might have had some influence. However, the fact that another condition of her reduced sentence was that she could not enter the United States for ten years made me believe it was Jace's family's influence at play.

To top it all off, only very little information was leaked to the public. It seemed that even though the company was clearly struggling, the Langlois name still had enough influence to shut out any unwanted attention including nosy paparazzi. It wasn't too long ago that one "photographer" was apprehended for trying to stalk me while I was visiting Jace in the hospital.

It seemed Bridget's family felt the same. They managed to keep the surveillance footage of Bridget's attack at Silverline Apartments hidden, along with a few more skeletons in their closet. During the trial, it was revealed that Bridget had been suffering from mental health issues, and her condition had deteriorated over the years. It seemed to have worsened around the time when Jace and I got married.

She had suffered from delusions of grandeur, paranoia, auditory hallucinations, bouts of rage, an inability to recognize boundaries, and other symptoms . . .

I guessed it all seemed too much for her. Unfortunately, her parents didn't take her mental health issue seriously and immediately cut off her medication. Her grandfather, who seemed to be the only one who truly cared for her, wasn't always there to ground her back to reality.

Speaking of her grandfather . . .

After the trial ended and the sentence was clear, it didn't take long for the lawyers to inform him about what had happened. While Bridget's parents were clearly shocked by the outcome, her grandfather seemed unfazed.

As an act of goodwill, he contacted Jace and informed him that he would back out of his plan to buy out the company. Jace, still the savvy businessman, saw this as an opportunity and offered him the option to become partners instead.

The ink had dried and the two were now partners, with Bridget's grandfather holding a stake in any future ventures the merged companies undertake.

Still, I couldn't bring myself to trust the man. He was a conniving shark, and it didn't take a genius to figure out where Bridget got her traits from.

So we had a little private "chat," and let's just say, he won't be messing with Kei Langlois-Forest the way his granddaughter did.

He wasn't the only one on the receiving end of my ire.

Yesterday, Jace's parents flew in for a visit. I, of course, was with Jace in his private room. The minute I saw them, it took every ounce of self-restraint I had not to lash out at them for their lies. Nevertheless, I didn't hold back as I told them off for everything they had done. Jace didn't interfere either—after all, he was a part of their scheme.

They apologized profusely. Jace's mother even bowed her head in shame and remorse. After the tension died down, both of them assured me that they had never touched a single dime of what my parents left me, not for personal use anyway. The investments they made were all aboveboard and in line with their responsibilities as trust fund trustees. They handled the wealth just as my parents would have done had they still been alive. Unfortunately for them, they invested in riskier ventures, but fortunately for all of us, they managed to recoup the losses.

They left soon after. Whether they truly cared for me as a son-in-law remained up in the air. It was hard to trust them again.

*     *     *

"Kei, *mon beau* . . ."

I snapped out of my thoughts and saw Jace's face filled with concern. I looked up and noticed that Ralph and Ryan weren't in the room anymore. They must have left a while ago.

276

"What is it, Jace?" I asked, running a finger though his hair. The strands felt rough—he really needed a shower.

"You were quiet for a long time. What were you thinking about?"

I shrugged. "Nothing. Besides, it's all in the past now."

"Are you sure?"

"Positive."

He seemed unconvinced but decided against pressing further.

I mentally thanked him for that and shifted closer to him. "I hope everything goes back to normal," I muttered to myself.

\*     \*     \*

*One month later*

"Jace, I swear to God, if I stub my toe against a table or accidentally step on Frenzy, you're so going to taste my wrath," I grumbled as Jace led me to God knows where.

Right after I came home from college, Jace took it upon himself to wrap a blindfold around my eyes, explaining that he had a surprise waiting for me. After I consented, he led me around the house for a few minutes, although it honestly felt like an eternity.

"I'll take my chances. Besides, Frenzy is playing in the backyard." Jace laughed.

I huffed and kept quiet after that. Since I couldn't see, I had to rely on my hearing and hope that Jace won't steer me wrong. The house was eerily silent, which meant we were the only ones there. Every so often, I would hear Frenzy's happy yips, which sounded closer than I expected. I quickly deduced that we were in the kitchen, since there were French sliding doors leading to the backyard.

"Okay, I'll have to let go of you for a second."

"Jace, don't you dare—"

"Do you trust me?"

I paused. *Well, I love Jace, and isn't trust an important part of love?*

I was about to answer when Jace sighed from behind. My heart ached at that. It was hard to let go of the past. The pain from his and his parents' betrayal would always linger at the back of my mind. I knew I had already forgiven Jace, and to some extent, his parents as well, but letting go was difficult. It was one of the lessons my parents taught me before they passed away.

*You can't force forgiveness.*

Still, I wasn't bitter anymore. There were no more grudges between us. Jace, in particular, worked hard to keep his promise. Throughout the weeks of our "reunion," he did everything to ensure I would never feel unloved. From me waking up and seeing his handsome face, to him making me laugh at every opportunity, from his constant affection to his reminders that he would never leave me again . . .

*I knew I trusted him.*

"I love you, Jace, and yes, I trust you with all my heart," I whispered, worried that if I spoke too loud I would ruin the atmosphere between us.

A wave of silence followed. Worry gripped my chest. *Did Jace leave?* I reached up and was about to remove the blindfold when I felt his warm lips pressed against mine. My face heated up as Jace caressed my jaw with his thumb.

"I'm glad," he whispered.

I grinned.

"Okay, now I have to leave you here for a sec. Let me just open the door," he said.

"Okay."

I heard the door slide open, and a breeze carrying the winter cold entered the kitchen. I shivered slightly. Winter was still at its height, and its harsh chill could still be felt.

I didn't move an inch and waited for Jace. I could hear a few hushed voices not too far outside and even made out someone shushing Frenzy. I couldn't help but smile at that. There was no way anyone could boss that cute husky around.

A few seconds passed, and Jace's footsteps were drawing closer. I chuckled as he struggled to remove the blindfold from behind. When I finally blinked my eyes open, what I saw before me was so breathtaking that it made me grin.

The backyard was blanketed in pure white snow, with not a patch of earth visible. Frenzy, sporting a customized red sweater, was running and rolling around in the snow—the perfect environment for his breed.

He wasn't alone. The triplets, Ryan, and Ralph, were all dressed in matching red winter clothing, each holding a white cardboard with different words written on them:

*WILL*

*YOU*

*MARRY*

*ME*

*AGAIN?*

I didn't think twice. I turned around, grabbed Jace by the neck, and gave him the longest and most loving kiss anyone could ever imagine.

# EPILOGUE

"Shit, shit, shit, shit, shit," I muttered to myself, adjusting and readjusting my bow tie. It felt like it was trying to choke me.

"Kei, are you ready?" Summer asked from the slightly open door of the room.

I turned away from my reflection in the mirror and faced Summer.

She frowned when she noticed my face.

*I bet I look like a zombie.*

"You look constipated."

I rolled my eyes. "Thanks."

"I was just kidding. You look cute, seriously." She giggled.

I couldn't help but smile in relief. Summer was one heck of a friend, and I was fortunate to have her here with me, especially as I was still trying my best not to collapse in a panicked mess.

It was the thirtieth of December, and it was eight-thirty in the morning. We were in Saint-Jean-Cap-Ferrat, in the southeastern region of France, at a private villa owned by Jace's mother, Maria. All of my friends, Jace's family, a few of his own friends, and business partners were gathered here to witness and celebrate one of the most memorable and meaningful moments of my life.

Jace and I were getting married today.

Despite it being our second time, I knew this one was different. The first wedding we had was a civil ceremony that involved the expected formalities, like signing papers and going over mutual agreements with no emotions involved. Today would be different; it would be the one special day where we finally did it right.

*I'll be walking down the aisle with my beloved waiting for me at the other end. Jace and I will finally become real husbands in every sense of the word, and I can't wait for it all to happen.*

At least, that was what I thought I would feel. Right now, though, I was a bundle of nerves. The anxiety and panic I felt made me want to throw up, and it was getting harder for me to breathe.

It was like being dropped in the middle of the ocean, struggling to breathe as the waves engulfed me. No, it was more like being in the middle of the desert, struggling to find water and shelter.

It didn't matter what comparison I used. I just wanted to get rid of these confusing feelings once and for all. Yet, strangely enough, there was something comforting about them.

Because deep down, beyond all the fears and worries, I knew it just felt right.

"Will you stop pacing? You're going to make a dent on the floor if you keep that up, and you know Mama Langlois won't like that one bit. Do you know how expensive everything is in this palace?" Summer ranted, her thin arms flailing about to make her point.

"You mean villa."

"Villa, palace. Same thing. What's the difference, really?" She snorted just as the rest of my friends came barging in the room.

I smiled at their outfits.

Autumn and Winter wore almost identical black suits, except Autumn had a red tie while Winter sported a crisp red shirt sans tie. Ryan also wore a black suit with a matching red bow tie and vest underneath the suit jacket. Summer, of course, looked stunning in her strapless scarlet dress.

Honestly, they all looked like a bunch of models in their clothes. The theme of the wedding was red and white.

I had a white suit on with a red bow tie around my neck. I didn't know what Jace was going to wear, as I hadn't seen him since yesterday. His mother and Summer, of course, wouldn't allow us to see each other the day before the wedding.

"Bad luck," they said.

Well, whatever floats their boat, I guess.

"How are you feeling, Kei?" Ryan asked, draping an arm around my shoulders.

I anxiously shook my head. "I'm so nervous. I wanna die."

"Hey now, don't say that. Do you really wanna leave your hubby at the altar?" Autumn joked.

"Well, I guess that's still fine. It just means I'll finally have a chance with a hot and rich French guy," Summer said with a wink.

I glared at her.

"I'm kidding! Geez. Calm your tits, Kei," she said.

"Ugh! I can't stand it anymore! I need a drink. Like a shot of tequila or something." I groaned and pushed myself away from Ryan's grip to search for any alcoholic drink I could find.

Before I could head over to the mini bar, one of the wedding organizers peeked into the room and announced, "It's time."

My stomach dropped. My throat closed up, and my hands shook so badly it felt like I was having a seizure.

The triplets hurriedly gathered around me to calm me down, while Ryan ushered the wedding organizer outside and asked for an extra ten minutes. He then he closed the door and approached me.

"Kei, calm down. You're going to be fine," he said, gently rubbing my back.

I covered my face with shaking hands. "I can't! I don't know what to do!"

"Kei Forest-Langlois! Will you stop being a drama queen and put on those big boy panties of yours? Man up! It's your wedding day, for God's sake!" Summer snapped.

I wearily raised my head to face her. "Huh?"

282

Autumn sighed. "Listen, dude. We get that you're freaking out. Believe me, it's perfectly normal for brides to panic like crazy on their wedding day."

I glared at him at the word "bride," but he ignored me and continued, "But it's also a once-in-a-lifetime—wait, scratch that—in your case, twice-in- a-lifetime moment. You can't waste it away acting like a coward. Just calm down, take a deep breath, and knock Jace's socks off with your smile."

We all stared at him quietly, making him avert his eyes and clear his throat.

"So yeah, that's all. Stop looking at me like that! Winter, aren't you supposed to back me up?"

Summer grinned and gave her brother a kiss on his cheek, leaving a red kiss mark. "That was very nice of you, Autumn. Am I right, Winny?" she said, glancing over at Winter, whose eyes were glued to his brother.

Unsurprisingly, he didn't say anything but gave his brother a proud smile while adjusting his suit.

Ryan nodded. "Autumn is right, Kei. Just calm down, okay?"

It took a minute before I finally answered, "Okay."

Summer grinned and clapped her hands. "Then let's get your wedding started!"

I gulped as I stood behind the huge double-oak doors that would open in a few minutes. I kept tugging at my bow tie while the wedding organizer and her staff paced around, speaking into their little headphones to keep everything in order.

"It will be fine, Kei. Trust me," Ryan said, standing beside me.

I looked at him. "I know. It's just that . . ."

Ryan smiled at me and nodded in understanding. I smiled back and waited for the organizer's signal.

The Winston triplets were already on the other side of the closed doors, along with Ralph and the rest of the people who would be witnessing our wedding day.

As we waited, I couldn't help but think about my parents. They would have been so proud of me. I would have loved to see my mother's warm smile and my dad's comforting eyes.

Ryan had decided that he would be the one who would walk with me down the aisle. Of course, I was deeply grateful for that. He had been there for me when my parents died, and now he was still here. He was my best friend and my best man.

The sentimental thoughts were abruptly interrupted when one of the staff approached us and said, "It's time, Mr. Langlois."

Suddenly, all my fearful and worrisome thought about the wedding vanished into thin air. I held my head up and breathed out.

"Okay, I'm ready."

The doors slowly opened to reveal the villa's back garden. The scenery was wonderful. A white carpet lay on the ground with red rose petals on either side, leading to a small pavilion where Jace and I would stand side by side.

The pavilion itself was spectacular, its dome-shaped roof perfectly complimenting the scenery with green vines and red roses on the interior. Around the garden were flowers and décor in shades of red, white, and gold.

It was perfect.

"From this Moment On" began playing across the garden.

Ryan and I started to walk down the aisle. He kept a warm grip on my elbow as I carried a tiny bouquet of red roses in my left hand. At first, I didn't want to carry the flowers, as it seemed a little too much for me, but the wedding organizer insisted, so I did.

I was now halfway to the altar when the song reached its chorus.

All eyes were on me, but I focused solely on one pair of eyes.

Jace stood at the other end, looking as handsome as ever. Ralph was beside him, grinning excitedly like the playful man he was.

I couldn't help but glance at Ryan and smile when he grinned back at his lover, as if they were the ones getting married.

When we reached the front, Ryan let go of my elbow and said, "Take care of him."

Jace nodded. "I will."

The wedding song reached its second verse, and the timing couldn't have been better.

Ryan nodded and stepped aside with Ralph so that Jace could hold my hand.

My heart skipped a thousand beats when his warm hand touched mine. I looked into his eyes as a thought crossed my mind: *Is this real?*

We stared at each other for what felt like an eternity, and my eyes burned from trying my best not to cry. Jace looked so handsome in his red and black suit. He truly was the one for me.

"I love you," Jace whispered as the officiating reverend began the ceremony.

I smiled widely, and tears finally fell down my face.

They say a person needs only three things to be truly happy in this world: something to do, someone to love, and something to hope for.

Today, I felt that I finally had all three. Part of the thrill of achieving these things was taking chances and risking everything.

I wanted to stop crying, but the wedding song wasn't helping—its bridge was too good.

Life was never meant to be easy. It takes a lot of courage to navigate it from beginning to end.

I had learned that no matter how difficult life could get, there is always hope. Hope will remain in every person's life as long as they allow it.

We just have to be patient and to never give up trying. We may struggle, but you know what they say—every cloud has a silver lining.

As if to confirm my beliefs, the chorus of the song played once more, and my heart melted at the words.

"In sickness and in health, as long as you both shall live?"

Jace and I stared lovingly at each other.

"I do."

"With the power vested in me, I officially pronounce you husbands. You may now—"

Jace didn't wait for the reverend to finish. He immediately grabbed my waist and sealed our love with a scorching kiss.

My heart exploded with pure happiness as our lips danced together. I could vaguely hear the loud cheers, claps, and whistles from everyone, but Jace and I didn't stop kissing. We kissed as if our lives depended on it, and I cherished every second of it.

It was sweet and passionate. It was also the most important kiss we had ever shared. It symbolized all the rights and wrongs we had faced together. Every memory came rushing back as our lips moved in sync.

I sighed peacefully into the kiss, and Jace did the same.

This moment proved that Jace and I were stronger together. My life with Jace might have started out poorly, but it ended so beautifully.

This wedding showed that we had one last shot at being together. Now, all we needed to do was ensure this shot would last forever and a lifetime.

I guess I could finally say that life doesn't suck when you're married to a billionaire.

Do you like lgbt romance stories?
Here are samples of other stories
you might enjoy!

DANTE CULLEN

THE

FORBIDDEN

# CHAPTER ONE

ZAC

"I'm sorry Zac, it's just...it's no longer working out between us."

He'd said those words—finally. I should have been happy, but I wasn't. I should have been angry, but I couldn't even muster that. They say anger is easier than happiness, and that people are more inclined to show anger than happiness.

But not me.

At that moment, I surprisingly didn't feel anything. I didn't do anything either. I just stood there, looking at the guy whom I'd given my heart to.

"Zac, say something," he said, almost pleading.

What did he want me to say? *"Well, we can start working out. I can register us for a gym membership. That should be enough, yeah?"*

I couldn't say that out loud. There was no point anyway. I couldn't pretend I didn't understand him. It would only make the situation more awkward and tense than it already was.

"Bruce?" I whispered.

Just saying that name suddenly filled my eyes with tears. It was as if it was only then that his words sank in. The ice was melting, and my cheeks were getting wetter by the second. I hated it. I hated this feeling. I wanted nothing but to be numb again, but there was no going back. He was breaking up with me.

I wish I could say I hadn't expected it, but I had. I just wished that knowledge could have helped soothe the pain.

I watched the shocked look on his face at what I said. He was going to say I was delusional. He was going to say I was lying. The least he could do after breaking my heart was not lie to me.

"What?" He had the audacity to ask.

"Are you—are you leaving me for Bruce?" I asked, my voice breaking as the tears trailed down my cheeks.

He shifted uncomfortably, and his eyes darted to and from. He couldn't decide whether to flee or to stay and answer my questions.

I wasn't waiting for the answer, because I already knew. I knew the things that went on behind my back. He'd been cheating on me with Bruce Carlisle for the past two months. My heart broke when I found out, but I stayed, hoping we'd fix whatever was wrong with us—with *me*. I tried to become the best boyfriend I could ever be. I made time for him, and he had his way with everything.

He would cancel dinner plans at the last minute just because he didn't "feel" like it; he'd stand me up countless times because he "ran late at gym", and, when it came to making plans, his input was barely there.

I didn't argue with him about the missed calls that he never returned, or the incoherent explanations he offered to excuse his behavior. I did my best to understand him. Clearly, my passive approach hadn't worked the way I thought it would.

"What? No, Zac. I don't know where you got that," he said.

I felt a thud in my heart. Even after breaking it to me, he wasn't willing to be honest. I'd been faithful to him, and this was how he was repaying me?

He thrust his hands in his sweater pockets.

"I'm sorry, Zac," he said, turning to leave.

"I know, Chase. I know about you and him. I've known for a long time," I said, a strangled sob escaped my lips as tears started to fall on my face.

Chase turned, and his face fell. "How'd you find out?" he asked, finally admitting.

"I saw the messages. I saw you together in his room," I said.

"Zac, I never meant to hurt you. Things happened, and it…it got out of control and—"

"What is wrong with me?" I asked firmly.

"That's unfair," he said.

"Is it? You cheated on me for two months and still pretended we were okay. You lied to my face whenever I ask where you've been. You lied to my face about me being the *only* one. How is it unfair to ask you what's wrong with me? I want to know what is it with me that made you not only cheat on me but *lie to me over and over again!*" I demanded, my voice rising a few decibels.

"Zac, I'm not doing this!" he spat back, his voice rising to match mine.

I knew I shouldn't have pushed to find out, but I just needed to find out something—anything. Because truth be told, I'd been nothing but a good boyfriend. I didn't deserve to be dumped. I didn't deserve to be cheated on. I tried everything I could to make him happy.

But it wasn't just that. I *loved* him. Dating Chase was a dream come true.

I had a crush on him for a long time before I gathered the courage to ask him out. We met during our first year in college, and I spent the whole school year crushing on him. We saw each other a lot because we stayed in the same building on the same floor and started hanging out towards the end. I asked him out at the beginning of our second year, and we became a couple. We'd been dating for about a year, but all along, he'd been spending the last two months cheating on me, if not more.

"I just want to know, Chase," I said softly.

"Zac, I…," he said, a bit hesitant, before heaving a sigh. "I never loved you."

My heart stopped. Everything came crashing down yet again. I shook my head, refusing to believe what he was saying to me.

He let out a breath loudly. "I knew you liked me, and I felt sorry for you. Bruce and I, we started out way before us. I mean, I liked him, but he was unwilling to come out. I said yes to you just to spite him, but I couldn't stay away from him."

I had opened up a can of worms. Each word he said was like a knife to my heart, stabbing me over and over and over again. I couldn't believe what I was hearing. *Could someone really be that cruel?*

"I didn't mean to hurt you," he said.

"You used me!"

"This is why I didn't want to tell you," he said, starting to walk away.

"And you think that makes it all better?!"

He shook his head and walked away from me. I watched him leave as memories of our time together filled my brain. Watching him leave was all I could do. There was no hope of saving our relationship anymore.

Chase didn't love me.

He had only been pretending. He lied about everything.

Our whole relationship was a lie.

The door closed. Fresh tears made their way onto my face. I closed my eyes, as if that could stop the tears. It couldn't. Neither could it stop the pain that seared through my heart, eliminating everything in its path.

I fell to the floor as Chase's words swam around.

*"I never loved you."*

So, what did those *I love yous* he had uttered mean? What did our lovemaking mean to him? Had he wished it was Bruce instead of me? Was Bruce the only person he saw when he was with me?

They say real men don't cry. I guess I'm not a real man then, because I was crying to my heart's content.

I heard some vibration and a beeping sound in the room. Judging from the sound, it came from the bed. It wasn't my phone because mine was in my pocket.

Chase had left his phone in the room, which wasn't unusual as we shared the room. It was my suggestion when we returned for the second year, and it had been convenient. Now, it was just going to be awkward and unpleasant.

I ignored his phone for a few seconds, wondering how it was going to be like staying together in one place but not together. It was going to be torture for me. He would bring Bruce over, for sure. He would try to be considerate and ask to have the room for himself to study or something, but my mind was only going to wonder if he was with Bruce.

His phone vibrated again.

I got up from the floor and followed the vibration to the bed—my bed. My mind temporarily went back to the moment he'd put the phone there. We were kissing then before he decided he was ready to break my heart.

His phone lit up. The line "Two New Messages" splashed on the screen.

An insane thought came into my head, and before I knew it, Chase's phone was in my hand. I chastised myself. I couldn't open his messages; they were private.

Even though my mind protested, I found myself clicking "Open."

Both of the messages were from Bruce. My heart sank as I read each one.

*Have you told him yet? You've been in there forever.*

*Come to my room afterwards. I have something for you. Jackson is out. Hurry up.*

I felt fresh tears graze my cheeks. Every time I calmed down, my wound would open again. It felt worse than finding out Chase was cheating on me. Back then I had hoped one day he would stop, that one day he would see that I was enough for him. I realized now, with a burning ache in my heart, that was something he was never going to see; the pain gripped me with its rawness, scorching me.

I put Chase's phone on the bed and realized something, which comforted me. If Bruce sent Chase a message that meant Chase wasn't with him at that moment. It was silly of me to think that, but I just wanted anything to lessen the pain.

I sat on my bed, wondering what on earth I was going to do. I felt lost.

My phone rang. I took it out of my pocket and looked at the Caller ID. It was my mom. I didn't feel like answering, but I didn't want to make her worry either.

I cleared my throat, erasing any trace of me crying, and answered.

"Hello?"

"Hello, honey. How are you?" she asked, her voice filled with excitement.

"I'm fine. How are you?"

"You don't sound fine," she said, her excited voice now immediately replaced with concern.

"I just have a cold," I lied.

"My poor baby, do you have medication?"

"Uh, Mom, it's just a cold. I'll be fine."

She sighed. "All right. Are you excited about spring break?"

I shrugged. "Uh…I guess."

"I know this is short notice, but I really hope you don't have any plans. I want you to meet someone," she said.

Chase and I had planned to spend spring break at his family vacation house with some of his relatives. I guess that's no longer going to happen. I hadn't yet decided on what I was going to do—

we just literally broke up minutes ago!—but maybe going home wasn't a bad idea.

"Uh, I guess it's serious between you and Mark?" I asked.

She giggled. "I think so. He wants to meet you, Jessica, and Noah."

"I'll be home, Mom," I said.

"Thank you, Zachary. You don't know how much this means to me," she said.

"How does Jess feel?"

"You know your sister. She's throwing a tantrum. I don't think I'll survive it this time," she replied.

"Don't worry, I'll talk to her. She'll be fine."

The way I replied confidently when, really, I felt like breaking apart, was amazing, even to me.

"Thanks, honey. I love you, Zac," she said. She seemed a lot more at ease now.

"I love you too, Mom," I said, and she hung up.

My life was a mess, and I was assuring someone else I'd fix theirs. It was laughable how I thought I could do that, when I couldn't do it to myself. But I needed a distraction, and meeting Mark couldn't have come at a better time.

If you enjoyed this sample, look for
**The Forbidden**
on Amazon.

# all
## it took
## was one
## look

T. LANAY

# CHAPTER 1

AIDEN

Senior year, the last year of high school, but to me, it's almost the end of my four-year long prison stay. No, it was not because I didn't like school work. Actually, I was a straight-A student. It's just a constant reminder of my problem.

I knew the school like the back of my hand. That meant I knew the people. The thought of being picked on and thrown in dumpsters every day terrified me.

Why, you may ask, was I scared of my fellow classmates?

Well . . . I wasn't scared of them. I was wary of what they might do to me when they would fnd out that I'm the big G A Y.

Yeah, now you knew my problem. You could say I was ashamed of my sexuality. My parents always told me I should be proud. Yeah. Could you believe that? I was shocked, too.

Okay, okay. I was not totally ashamed. Maybe I shouldn't use that word. Here's a better one: scared. I was scared of it.

So here I was, incognito, playing the straight guy in my anatomy class and writing notes, being the awesome student that I was. The teacher was ranting on and on about medical studies and whatnot. This class was my favorite. I planned on going into the medical field. Jeanine, who I called J and my all-time best friend, was tapping her pen against the desk next to me which made me want to snatch it and throw it across the room. I gave her a narrow-eyed glare while she frowned at me.

I eyed the pen suggestively, hoping she would get the hint. I even raised my eyebrows at it. Apparently not, since she mouthed 'what' to me.

Rolling my eyes, I picked my pencil up and waved it at her.

"Oh," she mouthed and set her pen down.

"Finally," I said, heaving a heavy sigh.

"Mr. Walker, is there something you would like to share with the class?" Mr. Simons asked, giving me a stern look.

I shook my head and said a sheepish no. Jeanine giggled at me along with the rest of the class.

Glaring at her, I turned back to my notes grumpily. Why is it that I was always the one who gets in trouble when Jeanine and I talk in class? Slowly, I laid my head on my desk and ignored the rest of what Mr. Simons said because basically, I knew it already.

I suddenly found myself dozing off, and Mr. Simon's voice was starting to become a low mumble when a huge banging sound erupted. I looked up to see what was happening. Two well-built men burst through the door, practically breaking it down and tumbling to the floor. There was a collective gasp from the class along with a few screams from the girls.

Everyone quickly stood from their desks to see what was happening.

And of course, I would be caught up in the fight since I was the one right next to the door. They rolled too close to my desk, making it tip over with me on it.

I hit the floor with a hard thump and the pain came screaming in my wrist and head as the fight progressed next to me.

"Mr. Parker! Mr. Moore, stop this now!" Mr. Simons yelled at them while I was still struggling to untangle my legs from the desk.

"Aiden!" I heard Jeanine exclaim. I never had the chance to look at her before something hard hit my stomach, knocking the wind out of me and causing my head to hit the floor again.

*I really needed to get up now!* I screamed in my head.

Again, the person was slammed back into me, ruining my motivation to even move. I was waiting for it to happen again, but it didn't. Everything was quiet now, or maybe it was because I was trying to sort out my head. All I know was that I was having trouble seeing straight.

*     *     *

The nurse's office smelled funny when I woke up. I tried sitting up, but my head was swimming and pounding so badly. I decided that staying still was my best option.

I looked around.

'Why am I here again? And seriously, why does it smell so weird in here?'

"Aiden? Are you up?" Jeanine's voice sounded from behind the curtain.

"Yeah."

She pulled it back with a small smile on her face. "Hey, how are you feeling?" she asked taking a seat on the bed.

"Like hell. What happened?" I asked and watched as her face changed drastically to some sort of dark expression.

*Uh-oh*, I thought.

"You don't remember?"

I shook my head. "No."

"Well, those stupid jerks came barging in the room in a huge fight, making you fall from your desk. You hit your head pretty hard. Are you sure you're not feeling woozy or anything?"

Ignoring her concern, I asked who was fighting.

"It was Kyle and Liam."

I stared at her wide eyed. "You're saying that our school's star football players were fighting in our class, and I got dragged into it?"

She nodded.

"I'm lucky to even be alive right now!" I exclaimed.

"Yeah, Mr. Simons had to break them up because he feared for your poor pathetic little life," she said with an evil smirk.

"Haha, very funny. It makes me feel so good inside that you care." I rolled my eyes.

"I know, you should feel honored. No, but seriously, I'm going to get the nurse to make sure you don't need some serious medical attention." With that, I watched her disappear behind the curtain.

It didn't take long for the nurse to examine me and see if I was okay. When she released me, she told me she called someone so I didn't have to walk home. She gave me instructions on how to take care of my wrist and head since I had a sprain and might also have a mild concussion.

Jeanine walked me out and down the hallway. School let out ten minutes ago, and I was glad because I couldn't survive class with this major headache. As we made our way outside, J told me everything that went down in class since I missed most of it.

When we were passing the principal's office, I suddenly heard raised voices. I had this odd sensation that was begging me to look through the room's window, so I gave in and saw the principal, of course, giving a very expressive lecture to none other than the hooligans that squished me.

Maybe it was just because he had this look-at-me type of persona going on, but my eyes specifically trained themselves on Liam—well, his back. And might I say what a nice broad back it was? His hair looked ruffled and crazy from his earlier fight, but I had to say it was pretty sexy from the back. I was sure it was more so in the front. I had never really seen Liam up close, and the only reason I knew him was because he's the famous star quarterback. But from what I heard, he's a total heartthrob or whatever girls said about him. Personally, I never looked because I didn't want anyone to see me checking out dudes.

The abrupt tugging on my arm caught my attention.

"Aiden, what's up? What's wrong?" Jeanine asked, watching me with concern.

I shook my head. When did I stop walking? I was drawn to look into the window again and noticed Liam staring at me. He had a confused, shocked, and an almost angry expression. With a yelp, I moved for the front doors at hyper speed.

He saw me staring at him!

Oh god! Now he would think I was a freak or worse, he discovered I was gay! He's going to tell, and I was going to be best friends with the dumpster for the rest of my senior year. I was such an idiot!

Jeanine was staring at me weirdly. Her dark brown eyebrow was raised at me.

"What?" I asked innocently. "You know, that top really compliments your skin tone," I said, distracting her with the best extreme gay fashion designer impression I had seen on TV which always made her smile. But really, she was wearing a yellow blouse that went well with her light brown skin. It really did look good on her even though I know nothing about fashion. I might be gay, but fashion went over my head. If I could, I would still let my mom picked my clothes in the morning.

"Uh-huh, whatever. Your dad's here by the way," she said, pointing to the Mercedes waiting in the front.

"Crap. Thanks." I gave her a quick hug. "I'll call you later?" I said, slowly walking backwards towards the car.

She shook her head. "I have dance practice, so I'm going to be dead tired later."

"Oh, alright. I guess I'll see you tomorrow then." I opened the car door, ready to slide in.

"Yep, feel better," she said.

"I will." It was the last thing I told her before closing the door. Buckling up, I rested my head against the head rest.

"What is this fight I heard about?" my dad said as he started to drive. "Are you hurt badly? I know because the nurse called me and said you were knocked out. No need to go to the hospital?" he said, giving me a concerned sideways glance.

"No, Dad. I'm fine. I just have a headache, and I sprained my wrist." He nodded.

"Okay. We'll go to the store and get you a wrist brace and aspirin, alright?"

"Okay."

*     *     *

At dinner, I got a whole bunch of questions about what happened to me and answered them to the best of my abilities. My mom, like always, thought that a gay basher was constantly terrorizing me. Dad stayed quiet and just agreed with everything she said. It was really annoying. My fourteen-year-old sister, Connie, was sneaking text messages under the table since phones weren't allowed at dinner. My parents thought our generation was ruled by technology.

*I know. Crazy, right?*

My brother, Nash, was out with his girlfriend as usual. Since he went to the community college, he was still living with us. He hadn't heard what happened to me yet, and I was hoping it stayed that way. Ever since I came out to my family, my brother had been the most protective one.

Like this one time, the family and I were over at my great grandparent's house for a family reunion. Connie, Nash, and I were hanging out with our cousins. And you could imagine how everyone had a douchebag cousin, right? That one guy who always put you down whenever you're feeling vulnerable or a straight-up bully. Well, mine happened to be Brent. So anywho, Connie accidentally slip out that I was gay at dinner. She was only eleven and probably didn't even know what that meant yet or thought it wasn't a big deal.

So, like the douchebag Brent was, he made a huge scene, saying it was disgusting and wrong. He then did something I least expected. He called me a fag. No one had ever called me that before, and to be truthful, it was kind of traumatizing. I mean, if my own family didn't like who I was, how would everyone else take it? Bad, that's how. Nash's face had gone bright red as we all sat at the table, shocked. My brother had shot to his feet so fast no one had time to stop him as he socked Brent square in the face. Brent went crashing to the floor with his chair.

"Never say that to my brother again, you piece of shit!" Nash exclaimed, snatching Brent from the floor, and that was when a full-scale war broke out. My dad and his brother, Brent's dad, were struggling to separate them.

I remembered how afterwards everyone was arguing and pointing accusing fingers at me like I was the bad guy.

It took so much in me to keep myself from crying.

They told my parents to never come back with me. So my dad told them if I couldn't be a part of the family, then none of us would ever come back. He took my arm and walked out of the house with his dignity intact while mine crumbled and got blown away by the particularly strong wind that day.

The second we arrived home, my father instructed everyone to go inside while he kept me out with him. I could still remember how hard it was to look him in the eyes at that moment.

"Look at me, Aiden."

I shook my head, too ashamed at what I was. There's no way he didn't feel the same. I was a disgrace. No matter how much he tried to put on this facade to make me feel better, I knew I was a screwup.

"You don't have to pretend," I whispered. "You don't have to pretend that you love me." The sob tore through my throat as I said those words. Before I knew it, I was suddenly drawn into a bone crushing hug. Too shocked to say anything, I just let the tears come, sobbing in his chest as his arms tightened.

"I will never stop loving you! You are my son, Aiden. Nothing is going to stop this family from loving you unconditionally!" He pulled me at arm's length, and for the first time ever, I saw tears in my father's eyes. And just like the stubborn man that he was, he refused to let them fall. "They were in the wrong, not you. And I swear that I will never let them hurt you again. Do you hear me?"

I stared at him, unable to move nor speak.

"Aiden, I need you to understand. Tell me you do."

I then nodded, wrapping my arms around him tightly.

"I love you, Aiden. More than you'll ever know," he said, kissing my hair.

"I love you too, Dad."

That was the last time I had seen my dad's side of the family. My mom's side was more accepting, so now we had been going there for reunions.

*     *     *

I put my dish in the sink and headed upstairs to my room. I didn't realize how tired I was till my head hit the pillow. I was out.

If you enjoyed this sample, look for
**All It Took Was One Look**
on Amazon.

# ATHENA SIMONE

# KISSING OLIVIA WINCHESTER

# CHAPTER 1
## The Kissing Booth

I wasn't here because I wanted to be. I was here because I was forced to be—forced by my monster of a mother, Melody Montgomery.

My mother was a part of the high-class country golf club. The men —who included my father, Hal—played golf in the club, boasting about the success of their businesses and their large sums of money while their wives drank tea, planned parties, and bragged about their oh-so-well put together sons and daughters.

The women raised money by holding a plethora of charity events to be able to fund the club without having to get a single penny from their pockets. It also gave them purpose.

Usually, my mother doesn't involve me in her schemes to show off to the other women. That's my sister Gwendolyn's job. I am not what you could call very social. I'm barely able to speak when it comes to people I am not very familiar with, so that leaves my sister to be the socialite of the family.

Since I turn into a stuttering idiot when people are around me, my mother brags about how amazing my sister is and takes her to the fancy get-together the club holds and leaves me at home.

Not that I'm complaining or anything. I'd rather read a book and be left alone anyways.

But this time, my mother just refused to leave me alone. She claimed it was life or death.

My mother's grand plan for fundraising this week was a carnival – with all the Ferris wheels, cheap roller coasters, greasy corn dogs, and creepy clowns that came with them. Every job was to be done by the children of the country club members, so they didn't have to pay for employees.

There was one job that wasn't taken by someone, most likely because it was the most unappealing position, even next to the person who cleans the leftover garbage. Since I was the only offspring left of every member of the country club, I was stuck working at the kissing booth.

I know, I know. It sounds like I'm over exaggerating, but I'm not. Not only is it embarrassing as hell, but it's also disgusting. Sure, you get to kiss a couple of cute guys here and there, but then come along the old geezers that probably haven't been kissed by anyone in years or the people that just don't know how to keep their saliva to themselves.

Oh, and if you're pretty, you're lucky enough to get a whole line of people just waiting to put their grimy lips against yours.

I'm fortunate because I was born with my mother's long flowing blonde locks and my dad's sea green eyes. Where I live as a natural blonde is like God's gift or something. I wasn't ugly or anything, quite the opposite. But my bright sea green eyes were usually hidden behind the lens of my glasses, the curves of my body covered by my baggy clothes, my hair was unkempt when I don't feel like brushing it through. I wasn't the type to get all dolled up.

And the worst part about the whole kissing booth ordeals was that I was forced out of the clothes I was comfortable in and stuffed into a square neckline knee-length white summer dress that flared out at the waist. The dress wasn't hideous, it just wasn't my thing. It made me feel incredibly awkward. And to put the cherry on top, I was obliged to wear pale yellow heels to go along with it. The curves of my body could be seen from a mile away.

To make sure my mother came out on top of making more money than the other women, she even tried to curl my hair.

Luckily, my sister was having a hair crisis herself, so my mother just ran a comb through my hair to make it look presentable.

So here I was, sitting on an uncomfortable stool, with the hot sun beating down my neck in this tight ass dress. Nothing could make this better, and the carnival hadn't even started yet.

I sat there with nothing to do but rub my dry eyes due to the contacts my mother forced me to wear and stare back at the people who stared at me as they walked by. Apparently, no one recognized me, since I was in such an unusual attire. Well, for me that is.

"Josephine! Is that you?" I jumped in my seat at the loud shriek coming from behind me.

I turned to see Mrs. Ramsey, with a broad smile on her face and her son standing behind her. She had her arms open, waiting for a hug. I stood up and gave her a tight squeeze.

Susan Ramsey was the most down to earth, sweet as homemade cherry pie, mother in this whole entire country club. Others were at best stuck up and rude, but not Mrs. Ramsey. She was kind no matter what the circumstances were. Her exuberant personality and bright red hair attracted lots of attention like moths to a flame.

For some odd reason, a kind woman like her decided to latch on to my dysfunctional family when we first moved to Cranbrook when I was at the tender age of seven. She was always around to babysit me when my parents had more important things to do than take care of their own child.

I latched on to her just as much as she did to my family. She was my self-proclaimed godmother. Her husband was kind too—until Mrs. Ramsey found out that he was cheating with a co-worker of his.

Their divorce was a mess, but only because it was filled with false sympathy thrown at Mrs. Ramsey. The sympathizers themselves were only thinking about sleeping with newly-divorced Mr. Ramsey. Her son, Neal, handled the divorce surprisingly well.

Neal had become my best friend, since his mother was around most of the time. She was obligated to bring him along.

Neal wasn't so much of a pariah as I was in our little world; he was only an outsider to the children of the country club members. He was the smartest kid I had ever known, which made him pretty badass in my book. But to everyone else, not so much. Although Neal wasn't like any other nerds, he was very outspoken and at times, immature. He was still the guy that the lacrosse players pushed into lockers when they felt like it. He was the guy that the cheerleaders felt the need to ridicule just because he got good grades.

But to the parents, he was the guy they wanted their children to be, which only made kids hate him even more in return.

Since we were both outcasts in some way, we decided to stick together rather than to fend off the vicious high society alone. Now, at the age of seventeen, we only always had each other.

Mrs. Ramsey and Neal were the only two other people outside my family I felt remotely comfortable around.

"My, my. You look gorgeous, honey. Your mother did one heck of a job cleaning you up, hardly even recognized you!" Mrs. Ramsey exclaimed, giving me a once-over.

"I'll say." Neal snickered from behind his mother, clearly making fun of me. I knew he was fooling around because we were practically siblings. We didn't look at each other that way.

And if it weren't for the dress I was wearing, he would be screaming in pain right now. I just settled on glaring at him.

"Neal, be polite." Mrs. Ramsey chided her son.

He huffed before folding his arms across his chest, wrinkling his nicely-pressed pale blue button-up polo shirt.

"You look very pretty, Joey."

"Thank you, asshole," I retorted with an awkward grin, not used to the attention.

"Language. You look more than pretty, you look absolutely stunning. How about a twirl?" Mrs. Ramsey suggested, pointing with a circular motion.

I groaned, staying still. Mrs. Ramsey again twirled her finger. I knew my resistance was futile.

I turned very slowly, trying hard not to fall on my ass in these heels since we were standing on the grass. Mrs. Ramsey clapped excitedly.

"Wonderful. God knows your mother has been trying to put you in a dress for years. Speaking of your mother, let me go and find her to congratulate her on accomplishing such a feat."

She tapped me lightly on the shoulder and pointedly looked at Neal as if to say, *Stay out of trouble*, and then she walked off in the fray of people milling about trying to set up the carnival.

"You do look ever so lovely, darling," Neal said with a heavy country drawl.

Now that his mother was gone, I didn't have to be so polite. I punched him square in the shoulder.

"Ow!" Neal shouted, rubbing his shoulder. "That wasn't very ladylike now, was it?"

"I don't care if it was ladylike or not. I'll kick your scrawny ass if you don't shut it." I smirked, knowing it was true. Neal was almost darn near a pacifist.

"Fine, fine," Neal said, holding his hands up in mock surrender, then he bashfully put his hands in his khaki shorts. "How much did your father give you this time?"

My face hardened at his question. Usually, when my mother has some scheme to make me look presentable like my sister and the other daughters in the club, and I resist, my father pulls me to the side and bribes me to make my mother happy. But what about making me happy? Nope, it's all about making sure my mother doesn't throw a hissy fit.

Don't get me wrong, I love my father. He was always there when he can be; he at least tried to understand who I was, unlike my mother who only wanted to make me into what she wanted.

"He gave me a fifty," I said, solemnly sitting back on the stool. I didn't like it when my father thought he had to bribe me to keep the peace, and fifty dollars weren't enough compensation for what I was about to endure.

"I'm sorry, I know how much you don't like when he does that," Neal said awkwardly, his right hand scratching his rusty orange hair.

"I'm over it." I'm really not, but I said it to appease him. "What are you still doing here? Don't you have a job of your own?"

"This is my job. Bodyguard at your service, ma'am!" Neal shouts straightening his body and saluting.

"What do I need a bodyguard for?"

"In case anyone tries to get handsy…if you know what I mean. No telling what those scoundrels will try to with you being all swanky and whatnot."

"What can you do, strangle them with your spaghetti arms?" I stated quizzically. Neal had yet to fill out like the other guys his age who had been through puberty. He had wide shoulders but was very scrawny. Neal was about 5'8", which was short for a guy, especially compared to the guys that went to our school. His arms had little to no muscle on them, which made him protect me laughable.

"I'll kick their asses. That's what!" He flexed his arms. I laughed at his antics, knowing he will probably get pummeled if he tried to start a fight with someone.

Sadly, my mother walked toward us as Neal cursed rather loudly. I clamped my mouth shut, sitting up straight knowing my mother will criticize my posture.

"Neal, you really need to improve your language. That is no way for a young man to speak," she said, putting her white Prada sunglasses through her sun-kissed blonde hair. She wore a floor-length robin's egg blue summer dress paired with white pumps. She looked elegant even though we were at a carnival. It was so nauseating.

"Sorry, Mrs. Montgomery," Neal said, hanging his head in shame. She turned her nose up at him as an acceptance of his apology.

"Now, I had Mrs. Ramsey put you two together because I know how Josephine feels about other people, but don't take my kindness for granted," she said with a disapproving glare.

"For Heaven's sakes!" My mother then exclaimed. "Josephine, would it kill you to sit up straighter? Ladies don't slouch. Have I not taught you anything?"

I tried to look like I was sitting up straight if it was possible.

"Good, now the carnival is starting. People should be lining up any minute now since you look…" she paused before giving me a once-over. "Somewhat…decent." Even after she dressed me, she still didn't approve of how I looked. I lowered my head in response, not wanting to make eye contact.

"I'll leave you two to your work." She flipped her hair over her shoulder, then turned to leave, but turned back to point at me "Don't embarrass me."

I nodded, not knowing what to say to her. I rarely had anything to say to my mother.

After she left, Neal looked at me with an apologetic smile. I smiled back, already forgetting about my mother.

"Oh! I forgot to give you something," Neal said before frantically digging in his pocket. He found what he was looking for and stuck it out toward me.

"What is it?" I asked before taking it, apprehensive. There was no telling what he was trying to give me.

A wicked grin broke out on Neal's face. "It's a ChapStick! I think you will need it." He was clutching his stomach now, shaking with laughter. My face heated up, embarrassed at the thought of how many people might line up to kiss me.

It is going to be a long day.

If you enjoyed this sample, look for
**Kissing Olivia Winchester**
on Amazon.

# ACKNOWLEDGEMENTS

I am forever grateful to my college instructors Marvin Pableo, Alexis Ramirez, and Antonieta Minyamin. You all believed in me and kept on encouraging me to write more. To my precious and beautiful dogs Hudson and Chuchay, thank you for being my living angels. To my family and friends, know that I love you. Finally, a massive thank you to my readers for taking a chance on this book. I hope you enjoyed reading it as much as I enjoyed writing it.

# AUTHOR'S NOTE

Thank you so much for reading *Life Sucks If You're Married To A Billionaire*! I can't express how grateful I am for reading something that was once just a thought inside my head.

I'd love to hear your thoughts on the book. Please leave a review on Amazon or Goodreads because I just love reading your comments and getting to know you!

Can't wait to hear from you!

*Krystel Grace*

# ABOUT THE AUTHOR

I'm the type of girl who loves to listen to songs that can make me sleep. I love junkfood and soda, and I cannot sing or dance. I'm a lazy couch potato but can really be determined to do something when necessary.